Once Upon a Mouse

Once Upon a Mouse

The Greatest Story Ever Told

CLINTON EDGEBANK

 iUniverse®

ONCE UPON A MOUSE
THE GREATEST STORY EVER TOLD

iUniverse books may be ordered through booksellers or by contacting:

iUniverse
1663 Liberty Drive
Bloomington, IN 47403
www.iuniverse.com
1-800-Authors (1-800-288-4677)

ISBN: 978-1-5320-5286-6 (sc)
ISBN: 978-1-5320-5287-3 (e)

Print information available on the last page.

iUniverse rev. date: 08/03/2018

CHAPTER 1.0

THE GREATEST STORY EVER TOLD

In the end, a great battle was to ensue. Mankind had learned that they could master the heavens and knew they could colonize space. While many hoped to participate, only a few were selected in a battle that could have ended history as we know it. Yougodid stood behind solid steal doors that were going to open at any second. A single tear began to form and fell from his eye. He had been training for this moment for many years and in that sense most of his life. A glimmer of light shone through the doors and with a hostile brow he could see his opponent for the first time.

But wait, I'm getting ahead of myself. Some might call me a liar but even liars are known to speak the truth. There is no worse fate than accepting a fate that is not your own. For one you give up a fate that was destined for oneself and steal a fate destined for someone else, much like a story with two beginnings.

It had been said that there were three little miracles that happened on how we exist today. One the slightest imbalance of hydrogen gas that formed the stars we know today. Two, the explosion of some these stars releasing relative matter into the universe and three the existence of a tiny planet called Earth, a place we all call home.

However, the occurrence of life on Earth to this day remains somewhat of a mystery. Some scientists turn to religion because the idea of a complex organism such as humans evolving from a single bacterium seems ludicrous. Then again some religious folk turn to science because the idea of something greater than ourselves and this planet, well, may have created life as we know it. In either case the real mystery is how to move forward.

Not many people believe in destiny. It is a very difficult concept to except. For example take a small group of people say a class picture. The only real destiny is that the picture had been taken, from there all ways parted. And this is where this particular story begins – the greatest story ever told.

CHAPTER 2.0

THE ELUSIVE MOUSE

It was a normal day just like any other. I had meticulously placed my butter knife in the dishwasher after using it to spread peanut butter over a nicely toasted piece of bread. *'No big deal'* I thought to myself as I placed the butter knife inside the appliance - *'Today will be the day'*. Then for no particular reason at all I closed the door to this appliance and starred at the window sill, *'still dirty'*. I paced the kitchen floor with my hands behind my back thinking just how easy this should be.

For the last few weeks I'd been trying to catch a mouse, a little tiny mouse with not much purpose, or so it would seem. They eat and poop and make homes where people don't want them, however, this time would be different. In the past I'd been setting mouse traps to catch the little buggers, yet today I would be more humane. *'It's just a mouse'* I thought, *'How difficult can it be to catch'*. I'd been using peanut butter to bait the little guy, just some regular old peanut butter; *'how irresistible to a mouse'* I thought again. However, somehow, this particular mouse was proving to be much more trouble than I'd originally anticipated.

Metaphorically, this mouse resembled my problems that had been occurring in my life. If it were possible I'd catch this mouse and my problems would go away. Somehow and someway if I could just catch this tiny little creature, without killing it, it would expiate the bad things that had been happening to me. So that's what I will do, I'll catch him and release him into the wild, into a place far from humans where it could and can live a normal life.

The first trap was simple, a paper tube with peanut butter on its end and garbage pail underneath, with half the tube hanging off the side of the counter. How delectably irresistible to a mouse, just climb the ramp to eat the peanut butter then 'yes', fall into the garbage pail and once and for all out of my house. As it turned out the peanut butter was gone and no mouse could be found. 'Darn it' I thought. It was time for a much smarter mouse trap.

I'll place a paper roll on a long slender stick with a book as a ramp up to the paper tube. When the mouse climbs the ramp, by stepping from the ramp to the paper tuber with peanut butter on it it'll fall under its own weight. I'll use peanut butter to coerce the mouse onto the ramp and with peanut butter on the tube, 'how genius,' even a mouse cannot resist peanut butter, at least not the smooth creamy butter I would be using. It even has a squirrel on the picture, probably its cousin of some sort, but nonetheless ever delectably enticing even to a squirrel and therefore no match for a mouse.

But even my second trap had failed. The mouse had outsmarted me again. It had eaten the peanut butter from the ramp and left the peanut butter on the trap. Perhaps he'd thought the trap was a trap and decided not to get caught.

So there I was, for weeks I'd being trying to catch this mouse, this tiny rodent that was no match for my intelligence. I'd been cleaning the area it was using to poop, somewhere close to the garbage can, yet there was mouse scat all over the garage, the perfect home for a mouse. It was using the cover of darkness to scavenge through the garage, had found a bag of grass seed and was hiding the seed all over the place. A mouthful here and then hiding this grass seed somewhere else.

Like I said, it was a normal day just like any other; I'd decided to cut off its food supply by moving the grass seed from one of the upper shelves to a small plastic bin that even a mouse could not penetrate. I paced the kitchen looking for things that could keep me from thinking about this improbable predicament. What difference does it make it's just a mouse, maybe I could just use a standard spring loaded trap to catch him. 'But no' I thought if the mouse represented my problems, even metaphorically, there was no way I could kill it. I truly needed to be humane, just catch this mouse than release it using my delectable treat, the peanut butter.

I ran some warm water over my face. Using a towel to dry my face, I wondered if my reflection was going through the same frustrations as I was. *'Naturally it must be'*.

I had stubbed my toe on the stairway back into the house. In doing so I unexpectedly dropped some boxes that had been irresponsibly placed inside the garage. This made opening the door to the house rather difficult, as a stubbed toe can linger longer then a cut or even a sprain, especially, since it always happens at the most unexpected of times and occurs in the most careless of environments; situations that could have been avoided. The boxes were of no particular importance but the pots and pans inside the boxes made a loud racket as they hit the floor. After healing from the most irresponsible of stubbed toes, I picked up the pots and pans and placed them back in the box.

Now if a mouse were a mouse, this commotion might have set him off just enough to keep away from any peanut butter available to a mouse especially since peanut butter had been placed meticulously throughout the garage. So now, it wasn't one just one trap that I'd be setting but two. Two mouse traps are better than one. With peanut butter to entice the little guy, and a shortage of grass seed, it was only a matter of time before this mouse fell into my trap and out of my house.

I decided to water the plants inside my house which had somehow given birth to a number of small flying bugs. Now, normally, I would swat these small winged creatures but because they have wings and I don't, I decide to gently persuade them towards the nearest exit, and kindly out of my house.

So with that in mind I walked over to the kitchen counter to make myself a piece of toast. *'Peanut butter toast'* I thought. I don't particularly remember why I wanted that toast so bad. It must have had something to do with a bunch of boxes crashing down on me as I was searching for the little rodent. I'd moved the bag of grass seed only to find that the seed itself had been mischievously and meticulously placed throughout the garage. As I was particularly examining the trail of seed I'd managed to carelessly tug a small item out from under another item that sent boxes flying from top to bottom. *'Mmm,'* delicious peanut butter toast.

My head was aching, but only a tiny bit because a number of pots and pans had fallen on me while scouting the seed trail. The pots made a cling and clang sound as they fell to the cement floor, but not before leaving a tiny bump upon my head. Although I winced in pain I imagined this mouse quietly and conveniently going for the peanut butter bait falling into my harmless trap, before stubbing my toe in the entrance into the house.

That's when I noticed another small winged creature that had been trying to escape through a window, a small fruit fly. As far as I know bugs don't live that long especially when they're in your house. Over time a small number of winged bugs had met their fate while battling this window only to at some point give up to the most unlikely of opponents, the window. I caught this small winged creature and released it into the wild where no window could do it any harm.

To make matters worse, I have a small dog very special to me, and every night it would sniff out this mouse to a tiny corner inside the garage at approximately the same time in the evening. If you can imagine animals talking they might say something like "Hello" or in this particular case "He won't hurt you". Quite true little dog, however this mouse has been pooping all over the garage, found a bag of grass seed that has been scattered, also all over the garage, and refuses to find itself inside one of my most ingenious of humane mouse traps. So little dog please go back inside the house and do what good dogs do, eat and bark at other dogs and maybe you'll get a treat at supper time, some cheese or something. Now some may ask "why cheese?" Well, it's an enticing alternative for my vegetarian dog.

'*Mmmm*' peanut butter - for a split second all the problems that had been occurring over the last weeks didn't matter; not the seed, the pots, the mouse, the vegetarian dog, the winged bugs. Not the stubbed toe or even the bump on the head.

Now I don't know about you, but when pots and pans are stored in a garage they usually go together with other kitchen necessities such as glassware, cutlery, plates and bowls and such. Well in this case, that is exactly what happened. As I moved the box full of these items it came crashing down on me then shattered all over the garage floor. The only thing left to do was move the vehicle out from the garage and then into the driveway, whereby, I could clean the broken kitchenware. So, I jumped into the car after opening the garage door, removed it from the garage, and began to clean the broken glassware and kitchenware with the slightest of bumps upon my noggin – all to the almost silent sound of 'Sssss'. Now this was no snake nor was it the whistling of the wind, no tree, and no bug not even a toy of some sort. It just so happened, that it was a tire punctured by the sharpest of glassware that had fallen under the car. With a grimaced face I thought to myself *'How wonderful'*. Cleaned the broken glass matter and made my way into the house.

'Three mouse traps' I thought, *'surely three is better than two'*. And in the cover of darkness I rigged the best of mouse traps. The most excellent of mouse traps to outsmart any tiny rodent, who dares to build a home from the wreckage and debris inside a garage, that a mouse believed would belong to them. A milk container was then tied to a string and rigged to an overhanging lever system with peanut butter on the end. If the mouse went for the peanut butter, it would find that the entrance had swung around and no longer would be able exit from the pendulum like trap. Surely with a third trap rigged and the delectable treat peanut butter, no mouse, squirrel or even rodent could resist this humane trap.

With that in mind I sipped from a beer, a beer that had been long overdue. While it should have been used a reward for catching this troublesome rodent, instead began to ease my nerves. You see, the flat tire on the vehicle cause me in my frustration to kick an item that had no business being kicked. In fact it left an eerie pain in my foot, a pain entirely my fault yet subsided with the hopping on one foot as I had stubbed the opposite toe. Apparently, hopping on one foot eases the suborn nature of inflicting damage upon an item, that cannot be damaged, somewhat like punching a brick wall then biting your opposite hand.

Now this particular beer was long overdue, for months it sat in a fridge a fridge that kept it chilled to a particular temperature that made the beer irresistible to the drinker. I pondered the nature of my unfortunate circumstances. How one mouse could cause so many problems, especially since I intended on being so humane in first place. But with the grass seed moved, the food supply being cut off and the only source of food available, peanut butter, surely this mouse would be caught. So I grabbed a stick, a stick that might allow me to scare the mouse enough into being detected under the cover of darkness. I'd rap it upon an object just long enough to cause a troublesome commotion to a small mouse. A tap hear, followed by the rapping of another tap further down the length of the garage. I even opened the garage door just enough to allow any particular mouse enough time to make a daring escape back into the wilderness that is outside the house. After all was said and done, there was no mouse that made an escape, no shadow out of the corner of my eye, no silhouette of a tailed creature, not even the slightest commotion of a mouse escaping for its life.

Perhaps if I'd owned a cat, the cat could have caught this mouse much quicker with its keen hunting skills. Rather this mouse had jumped the order of survival of the fittest by befriending my dog who'd much rather chase rabbits or birds and realistically would fight a common house cat just to maintain an obedient dominance over a cat; unaware of larger felines throughout the animal kingdom. In fact this dog would make an appetizing meal to a larger predator such as a crocodile, cougar or bear but was in the comfort of living a worry free existence of being consumed by a larger mammal or reptile.

Now for some particular reason word had spread that this mouse was in relative danger, perhaps in its mind of being eaten. From there on in a large brigade of birds decided it was their best interests to assist this rodent and bring the fight literally to my front doorstep. Several of these winged creatures began squawking through open windows in an attempt to liberate the mouse. Some even took it upon themselves to fly through or rather into windows at the least expected of times. Somehow this mouse was saying 'take that' in animal terms, all to the enjoyable and delightful amusement of a crow whose only words were 'ha'.

So, this beer was well deserved and appreciated, the mouse had not fled from the stick nor had it fallen into the traps set by a would-be mouse hunter. In fact every attempt made me more frustrated than I was when I'd originally started. Especially since my drunken stupor caused me to fall, sideways, on another bunch of boxes. Now this particular bunch of boxes had caught me off guard. While gently perusing the area, for a house belonging to a mouse, a slight stumble, followed by the none-existence of object that appeared to be able to hold the body weight of a fully grown man, I fell into a box of books. Now normally a box of books is completely harmless, however, a 90 degree piece of hardened cardboard can cause quite a bit of damage to the lower torso or skin when applied with force. With a cut on my ribs and bruise on my lower abdomen, I picked up the beer that had now fallen to floor, and began to reorient myself. The broken mirror was of no particular importance, especially since the pain in my abdomen was much more prominent from the books. I grabbed a broom and began to sweep up the glass from the broken mirror. The second time glass would fall and break within the confines' of this garage.

Sometime back I'd heard that a broken mirror makes for seven years bad luck. Now to me bad luck is forgetting your keys in the apartment after locking the door, forgetting about a dentist appointment, missing an important phone call; nonetheless a string of unfortunate events that causes one to evaluate the unfortunate things that happen. "Ha ha" said the crow.

Now let me assure you, this story does get more interesting;

It was an envelope that had caught my attention, when I opened it up I found a letter inside. It said "Congratulations for participating in the toughest contest known to man." Immediately it reminded me of a story I had heard of a while back that for the time being, gave me solace from my problems.

CHAPTER 3.0

THE TOUGHEST CONTEST KNOWN TO MAN

A round the same time, a contest was started, and not just any contest the greatest contest heard of on the face of the Earth.

A bunch of aristocrats somewhere, somehow had conceived of it. It wasn't simple but couldn't just be talked about publically. They'd managed to send the word out through a few simple phone calls and word of this contest started to spread fast. In a matter of days it had reached oil tycoons, steel manufacturers, monarchy and even self made millionaires just about anyone who would listen.

Some of you may have heard the story of around the world in 80 days; well, this was very similar only with a twist. The truth, it wasn't for the faint of heart. In fact, it would test the human spirit and even technology to the max. The prize was an overwhelming 50 million dollars and was only fifty thousand dollars to buy into the contest. Now to most, the winnings meant luxurious houses, giant companies or corporations even sending kids through college generation after generation. It was tax free and technically could be used for anything.

The contest was based on the premise of circling the globe vertically. It meant passing through both poles before crossing the finish line from the starting point. As I mentioned not for the faint of heart, the only condition, no cheating. Before long brilliant minds were being snatched up from colleges and universities to help build and design high speed boats, submarines even hovercrafts. Phone calls were being made to giant cruise liners; boat manufactures used boat lots and so on. Countries who had heard of the race started to become patriotic about the whole thing and were more so doing it for their countries. To some it wasn't about the money but more an issue of national pride with a very large incentive. It was only the American Navy that had declined participating but left the contest open to citizen who wanted to participate, while other armies denied any participation at all.

Here's how it worked, at some point a GPS tracker had to pass both Poles, southern and northern, and needed to reach a ten meter radius of both. The captain also needed to be present while within the ten meter radius, meaning a drone or robot would not qualify if in fact there was no human present as well. Truly, it wasn't going to easy.

People who were serious about participating needed to send a $5,000.00 deposit to a particular address, one that couldn't be reached through normal communications. This meant they only wanted serious contenders for the event. They immediately got the contract outlining the rules of the event and the criteria or contract to participation. It also clearly outlined the rules and premises for disqualification. Many thought it was a scam and refused to pay or participate, however those who did quickly got a telegram with a contract in the mail. Inside the telegram was a contract of pristine quality assuring the victor of the winnings along with a bank account number to transfer the entry fees.

Mrs. Frontinac had lived in her small town all her life. She had had two sons. Her husband had died when the boys were young. It was a car crash that took one of her sons and her daughter in law. She'd lived a solitary existence since then, with only her dog Ralph to keep her company. Although she had one living son, she felt as though she'd lost them both.

Her son Peter lived just down the street from her. He was a scholar, a mechanic and great with technology, but had lost his lust for life since his brother and wife's death. Now he'd sit in the garage and drink himself stupid on a nightly basis. This was ongoing for several years, at least since the funerals.

One day, Mrs. Frontinac came across a leaflet that had been posted on a lamp post while walking Ralph.

"I. – No cheating." "J. – To the winner the sum of fifty million dollars." Now normally, even this sort of leaflet would not be taken seriously, however, it was the stylish and elegant border that made it worthwhile.

"*How much was the entry fee.*" She ran over to the counter and got a pencil and paper. "*$5,000*", She had saved some money throughout the years just in case of this sort of emergency.

"Let's enter him into the contest." She said to Ralph.

She sent the letter and three days later received an envelope in the mail. She opened it in a hurry but tore off the last few sentences. She walked with Ralph over to Peter's house. He was asleep so she left the letter someplace he could easily find it.

It was a Friday, Peter knew this because his mom had shown up three days earlier. Although his sleeping patterns were irregular, he'd still manage to wake up early every morning with enough time to make breakfast, eggs and toast, and prepare the only lunch he could afford, spam in a can with lettuce and bread. Then he'd walk back to his workplace and sip from the whiskey he'd come to love so much. He was months behind on the mortgage and had sold the family automobile just to make ends with the bank. He wasn't greedy but hated asking for help. The previous loans he'd taken were only accumulating debt rather than brining him out of debt. He figured it was only a matter of weeks before he'd lose the house to foreclosure.

He got out of his recliner that for months had doubled as his bed, reattached the undone suspender to his overall and went into the kitchen to make the usual breakfast and lunch. He had hardly been eating, mostly because the sandwich he was eating he could barely stomach. He checked his watch it was 4:15 a.m. He stumbled back into his recliner and pulled the lever to lift his legs. He was almost asleep before peering with one eye at the letter left to him three days earlier. He breathed out callously, and then strenuously, pulled the lever yet again to get him back to his feet. Took a sip from the whiskey flask then walked over to the letter.

It read: "Congratulations in participating in the most difficult contest ever known to man. Because this letter has found you, your name has been entered into the preliminary contest prerequisites."

His interest increased "The rules are simple and are as follows:

a. No planes, helicopters or drones.

b. You must get within ten meters of both poles – North and South. A GPS beacon will be provided to you three days before the race. The captain of the vessel must be present with the beacon.

c. You will start and finish from the same point.

d. There is no time limit, the first to cross the finish line while getting within ten meters of both poles wins.

e. You may bring the needed supplies to win - food, sleds, dogs, snowshoes etc.

f. You may use more than one mode of transportation.

g. You may use a team, as many individuals as necessary.

h. You will need to document your adventure with a camera issued three days before the race starts.

i. No cheating – cheating will forfeit any chance of winning and the entry fee.

j. To the winner, the sum of fifty million dollars.

The competition will start exactly 1 year, 3months and 27 days from now. The race will start on the 2013 year in the month of March during the day of the spring equinox. We hope that you are of strong body and soul to participate. To the winner the all the glory and the Please send the entry fee of...

The page was ripped off. *'Fifty million dollars?' is this real?' 'No planes or helicopters?'* He walked over to a map pinned to a wall in his workplace. *'It's possible'* He looked around the room, *'What a dump.'* He began to wonder how long he'd been living like this. He knew things were tough at the moment, his wife had died and he was living off a 400$ a month budget. He immediately began to reorganize what had been his shanty workplace and living space.

He walked over to his mother's house.

"Hi mom." he said and gently gave her a kiss on the forehead. "Listen, thank you so much for entering my name into this contest. I've spent all afternoon drawing a design for this competition and the funny thing is I don't think anyone else has thought of this. I drew a simple design at first and then a better design and finally came up with something that could actually win this thing and..." Peter was interrupted.

"Peter" his mother said, "I don't know if you'll be able to enter this contest." "What, why, I thought you'd already entered my name and I swear this..." He was interrupted again. "Peter" she handed him the missing part of the contract. His heart nearly broke.

"Please send the entry fee of fifty thousand dollars to the listed bank account. Please be assured that provided your team can win without bending or breaking any of the clauses in the contract you will be awarded the full sum given in clause j. – fifty million dollars. Payment of this fee assures your participation in the event. Thank you for your interest in this competition."

He dropped the contract to the floor. All of a sudden the years of drinking seamed to creep back to him, he knew it was impossible to participate.

"I'm sorry Peter," said his mother as a tear fell from her eye.

"It's going to be too expensive to participate in the competition." Peter exclaimed. He turned to walk towards the door knocking a rolled up paper from his pocket onto the floor. Peter's mother walked over to the piece of paper unrolled it to look at the drawing.

He'd been trying to maintain given the issues that surrounded him. He'd done his best to be a provider for his family. However, his wife and brother passing away a few years earlier truly made him feel alone and overwhelmed. His mother followed him out onto the porch.

"Peter, did you draw this?" she asked. He didn't answer. "Peter," she said "I've been keeping something from you for years, but I need to know if you drew this."

"Yes mom." he exclaimed. "That's my idea."

"Peter, I've been keeping this from you for years because every dime and nickel of your father's money went into this. When he died he left this all to me and this is something I want you to have" His eyebrow raised, intrigued.

"Peter everything your father worked for went to me and I've been protecting it to make sure we didn't lose any of it."

"Mom what are you talking about?" asked Peter.

"You're father started a savings account when you were born its grown to almost seven times what it was that day we walked into the bank; Peter its almost enough to get you into this contest. It's just that if you lose we lose it all."

"How much is it mom?" that spark was back.

"If I take a loan on this house along with the money saved we'd just need to borrow a small amount from the bank, but Peter can you build this?" She held up the drawing.

"Mom, I can build this, probably from scraps in the yard but I have that feeling. The same feeling when I met my wife. I can win this, it's just I'd hate to lose. It means we're putting everything on the line. We have to be all in on this one."

His mother smiled. Fighting to hold back the tears was no longer working, even if Peter wasn't afraid she was. Her entire life went into that money, if they lost, they'd lose it all. But right then and there they made a pact not to tell a soul about their idea. She phoned the bank the following day and within a matter of minutes enough money was wired to the account. The lien on his mother's house meant she needed to move in with her son. A few days after submitting the entry fee another contract appeared in the mail. This one stated:

"Congratulations in participating in the greatest contest known to man. You have hereby met the financial obligations to participate." It was full of maps and documents, a survival booklet, a medal and everything that would be needed to compete in this event. Included was another paper that read:

"You are the 65th applicant to enter this competition, please be at this location for the start of the race." It was somewhere in Alaska. "You need to have your mode of transportation ready to race three days before the start day, March 20th 2013 at noon."

CHAPTER 3.1

Peter began to work on his mode of transportation. Between the three of them nobody talked about the drawing Peter had drawn, especially not Ralph the dog. Day and night he toiled and built. All in all, it became a happy household again. Peter's mother would bring him lunch and dinner as he kept working around the clock rarely finding time to sleep.

Peter was just barely in his forties but wasn't afraid of hard work. In his younger years he was quite accomplished; top marks in high school, a football scholarship to a state college, working for a high paying engineering firm where he met his future wife. He gave all that up to work on an invention, with his wife. Instead he lost his wife and brother in a car crash and gave up on the invention. Peter was the only survivor. He spent weeks in the hospital his mother crying every day at his bedside. Since then, fixing cars had become his only source of income.

Peter had been hard at work as usual when he heard a car pull into the drive. He got off his creeper he was using to get under his contraption. He could see a shadow moving under the garage door. He quickly got to his feet then through an old blanket over all his designs and drawings. The figure came to the door then began to rap on the door.

"Hello" the figure said, "Hello is anybody home?" he began to open the door when Peter opened it from the other side.

"Hey Peter" he said. "Hello Dylan - What brings you here?"

"Oh nothing really, I just wanted to see what you've been up to, you still working on that invention of yours?"

"Nope, been fixing cars at the moment, how's your car running?" Asked Peter.

"Not too bad, you mind if I check out the garage." Peter held the door firm.

"Actually, yes I do, what do you want Dylan." Asked Peter.

"Nothing, nothing at all." Dylan tried to peer inside the workspace. "You happen to hear about that contest, a big prize amount involved."

"What contest?" Peter asked.

"There is some big event to take place, a race around the world."

"Nah, I haven't heard anything about it." Said Peter.

Dylan wanted to investigate further; trying to peer inside the garage instead Peter placed his hand against the door.

"Well." Said Dylan, "Maybe you should read up about it" then he left with a smile and a wave.

It was summertime and Peter's work load was becoming overwhelming. Day and night he toiled with his contraption, grinding, cutting even sewing and stitching. He'd been working 20 hour days, working longer then he'd been sleeping, but still he toiled in his workplace.

As the summer months drew to a close Peter began to fall behind on the project. He began to wonder if he needed help working on his contraption. The start of the race was still months away, but the project seemed to be falling behind. He walked over to his work bench and picked up a little black book that had some phone numbers of friends, most of whom he hadn't talked to in ages. It took a few days just to work up the courage to pick up the phone.

He'd had a friend from his school years, but he hadn't talked to her in years, many years. In fact after flipping through the pages he realized he hadn't really talked to anyone in years. He wasn't even sure if any of the numbers from his book were still recent. He picked up the phone, but rather than dialling a number he hung the phone back up. He walked back into the main garage space. He felt lucky that he still had the large work space. It was a big garage that brought back a few memories, memories of his goals and ambitions, once upon a time. It was funny to think that all that could have changed so suddenly, one fleeting moment that changed his life forever. Instead he tried not think about it.

He walked over to the phone again, this time dialled in the digits. The phone rang three times then a forth, he hung it up no one was going to answer. He walked back towards the contraption then paused; the ringing of his phone startled him. He walked slowly back to the phone and picked it up.

"H-Hello" he said, in a muffled voice.

"Hi" A perky female voice said, "I just got a missed call from this number was anyone there trying to reach Melanie?"

"Melanie, ah this is Peter, Peter Frontinac, we went to University of Michigan together."

"Ah no," she said "I don't remember anyone named Peter,"

"Well than, sorry to bother..." then was interrupted

"I'm joking, Peter you don't remember you used to play jokes on me all the time," He tried to laugh. "What have you been doing? Are you still working on your invention?"

"Well, no, not exactly." He said "I sort of..." He was interrupted again,

"Peter I'm sorry to hear about Patricia and Herman, you three were really close in University, I wanted to call but I figured you'd just need some space."

"Thanks," he said, "It's been a long few years."

"Peter, we should get together for a coffee sometime you can tell me what you've been up to over the last few years."

"Sure." He cleared his throat, "I'd love to."

"Great!" she said, "Is tomorrow okay?"

"Yah tomorrow works fine for me." replied Peter.

"Okay then, the place we used to frequent?" asked Melanie "Yah, ah, how does 2:00 o'clock sound?" replied Peter

"Great," she said

"See you tomorrow." he hung up the phone and smiled.

He walked from the garage back over to the house and opened the screen door, "Mom, I need to borrow the car tomorrow?" His mother smiled, "Going somewhere?" she asked. He smiled back, "Yah, I am meeting up with old friend."

The next day seemed to fly in like a rollercoaster. For the first time in years Peter put on fancy clothing and groomed his bearded face. He hopped into the car and drove to a small coffee shop 26 miles from his house.

She had been waiting for him for at least twenty minutes or so, a bit flustered. She'd had a crush on him during the university years but never really took the time tell him. They worked closely together during school projects, but she never told him how she felt. He was running a bit late, rather than rush into the coffee shop he decided to sit in the car for a bit. It had been the first date he'd been on in years. He threw a tic-tac in his mouth and went in to talk to her.

The conversations went great, they reminisced about the past, caught up on current events in each other's lives. After a while he decided to ask her for help with his building project. He decided not to tell about the details of the contest until it got closer to the race deadline. She had always been great with computers and he was going to need help with the navigation systems, plus, she liked to build things with her hands, after all they were both mechanical engineers. To her, it sort of seemed like an old university assignment and she agreed to help him.

That weekend she came over to the house met his mother and all three of them sat and talked. They talked about school, his departed wife, finances, just about anything they could think of all the while sipping from lemonade that Peter's mother had made. It took a while but eventually Peter brought Melanie to the workshop. She glanced at the blueprints then pointed out a few flaws in the design.

Melanie, herself was going through a divorce as well, in fact she'd married her boss, a combination that didn't work out too well. Her divorce had left her a fair amount of money in her pocket, while the working forefront was a whole other issue. At this point in her life she couldn't work, her boss was also her former husband. She looked over the documents, maps and the invention.

"The greatest contest known to man, and woman." She said jokingly. She put her hand on his shoulder while Peter was explaining some of the ideas. His grandmother chuckled. "I guess I'll leave you two to your work." She smirked, and then went back to the house.

Together they worked all summer, cracking ratchets, running cables, stitching, sewing, welding, hammering, piping, reading, drawing all to the company of old radio from the seventies, that still got great reception.

Summer turned to fall. Peter's mother still brought food and lemonade at lunchtime. Even though Peter was an early riser Melanie was usually at Frontinac household before sunrise and stayed there well after sunset. Once in a while, she'd fall asleep on a cot to the sound of ratchets, grinders and other power tools.

In no time at all, it was Christmas time. Christmas Eve and Christmas day were really the only two days took off throughout the building phase. Melanie found a whole bunch of presents that had her name on them, quite different from the Christmas' past. Even Peter found a gift or two under the tree. Christmas dinner was the biggest banquet anyone had seen in while. There were mounds of food, turkey, veggies, stuffing, potatoes, salads, Jell-O, corn on the cob even several desserts. All in all everyone was glad they'd entered the contest, but nobody said a word about it.

With only weeks to go the apparatus was completed and ready to be tested. Under the cover of darkness they brought the contraption to an open field and tested it for the first time. *'It's going to work.'* They thought.

In the weeks that followed Peter began to get really nervous. He'd devoted his entire fortune, a fortune he didn't know existed. He'd worked constantly; day and night, on a contraption the he wasn't sure would win. Although he'd made a friend along the way, or rather rekindled an old friendship, he was nervous; nonetheless determined and strong spirited. He wanted to bring everyone in his family along for the voyage, unfortunately it was only built for one; just one single soul the entire journey.

His brained raced over every detail, every possible fault in the design, every nut that had been fastened, every, and anything that could go wrong. Instead he sipped from the whiskey flask that he'd been living without over the last few months. *'I'm still going to need this'* he thought to himself.

CHAPTER 3.2

Before long it was March and the race would be underway. It wasn't going to be easy getting the vessel to the starting point. They needed to ship it in two different trucks. The idea was Peter would drive one truck and Melanie the other, and Peter's mother and Ralph the dog going along for the ride. It was going to take several days and the journey needed to be underway soon.

The drive took them to many truck stops, refuelling the trucks as needed. They kept in radio contact the entire way, one truck in front of the other.

They arrived in Anchorage, Alaska in just under 80 hours, eighty long hours. Although Anchorage was not the competition start point the city was bustling with people. They found a small shack on the ocean where they decided to set up their headquarters, in an old ship yard.

The plan was, Peter would pilot the vessel and the ladies would have to look on from the small dockyard they'd rented. Peter's mother and Melanie would tend to the radio, GPS and other technologies they'd invested in before leaving home.

The ladies rented a small house, just blocks from the boatyard. It wasn't pretty but they could walk to the boatyard at any given time. Peter began to assemble his vessel – a hovercraft, but even that wasn't pretty. It looked big enough to fit a whole family but was designed just for one.

That evening under the cover of darkness a figure showed up smoking a single cigarette.

"I don't usually smoke." he said.

"What do you want kid, get out of here you're bothering me." said Peter.

"I know you're not from Alaska". Peter didn't respond instead he grabbed a wrench and walked towards the figure.

"You don't want to hit me." said the figure.

"Well who are you and what do want." Asked Peter.

"I know about this invention. I know that you've got something they'll all want."

"Go on." said Peter.

"I'm a lawyer; I followed you from your hometown. I've been spying on you for the last few months and trust me you're going to need my help." Again Peter didn't respond.

"What else do you know?"

Tim took a puff from his cigarette. "I know you won't be able to spend all that money without my help." He grinned.

"What's your name?" he asked harshly.

"Tim, Tim Piper, at your service." He extended his hand, but without an answer.

Tim waited and waited for Peter to do or say something. Peter was thinking and thinking he was. Until finally he said. "Be here tomorrow, you can help me assemble this piece of junk." Tim smiled and walked away.

The next day came quickly; the four of them were introduced to each other and worked on the vessel. In a matter of days he needed to be on the water and at the starting point, a small town called Wales where the state of Alaska and Russia almost touch. That would be the starting point and finishing point for the greatest challenge ever conceived by mankind.

Then with a wink and a smile the vessel was on the water and it didn't sink. Whether it would win was still a question. In no time they loaded up all the necessities, clothing, fuel, food. Peter took a sip from his flask then waved goodbye and set off towards the start point.

Melanie and Tim spent the next few days setting up all the electronic equipment. They kept in constant contact with Peter who was not very sea worthy. "I feel sick already." He said into the radio. Instead all he heard was laughter.

In the days that followed Melanie and Blanche – Peter's mother, boarded a plane destined for the Alaskan town of Wales. The place was bustling. The few reporters that knew about the competition were covering it, although it was mostly just local news broadcasts. It had turned into somewhat of celebration town. Although Melanie never said anything she figured some of the world's most important people were lurking somewhere within the town. Even the harbour, yes the harbour, was busy. Some big, giant and important ships were there, this was the first time they got to gauge the competition and the competition was going to be tough.

Peter needed to hurry because he was running late, still 1600 kilometers from the starting point with only a few days until he needed to be there. There were no roads that lead to the town of whales so he was going to have to pilot the vessel around the peninsula. He was sure he was going to miss the entrance deadline. He was a three day travel from the start point, with only three days until the start of the race. All in all he was nervous, sick to his stomach only having travelled a stone's throw compared to the rest of the journey. For the time being he wasn't going to be able to sleep. His mode of transportation although it floated, it was difficult to manoeuvre.

He lit his pipe and tried to imagine himself an important captain from books he'd read, captain Nemo or Ahab, maybe even Columbus or Drake and pressed on towards the start.

The start drew nearer and nearer. Eventually friends and family of those participating were put onto a ferry and ferried to St. Lawrence Island. There were tons of people but no media aloud. The organizers set up cameras at the start which could be watched from big screens on the island.

It was about 3 hours till the start. Blanche looked around and saw people of all kinds. There were Russians, Arabs, Europeans, Asian and many people of great wealth, some big, some small. It looked like at there were at least two Monarchies one from the Middle East and another from Europe. In fact Blanche and Melanie really felt out of place and sat near a fence that had a smaller screen to watch from. The meals were all catered and many watched in great anticipation.

As the start time drew near a voice came over a loud speaker. In many different languages it said. "This race is about to begin the entrants have all made their way to the starting point, may the best contestant win." People began to count down until a large whistle blew and racers were on their way. People clapped and cheered as their contestant entrants began to make their way around the globe.

About five minutes into the race Peter got on his radio.

"Has it started yet?" He asked.

"Peter, you're not at the starting point yet?"

"Not yet, I just passed Kuskokwim Bay, I decided to stay along the peninsula rather than crossing Bristol Bay, and I'm exhausted and I need to rest. Can you talk to the organizers and let them know I've fallen behind. I still need to pick up the GPS locator and the camera to document my journey, but I need to rest. I also don't know how to contact the organizers to pick up those things. I'm going to get some sleep while I can. Can you find out what I need to do to get those things?"

"Okay." Answered Melanie. "I'll get right on that."

She put down the radio and went and talked with one of the few people who had radios and earpieces. She was hoping she'd be able to get some answers from them.

"My friend missed the check-in for the start. Is there any way he can get the GPS locator and the camera?"

The man immediately got on the radio and within a few minutes had an answer for Melanie."

"He needs to check in at Whales. That's where all contestants were supposed to check in. Lucky for you one of the check in clerks are here on this island."

He put his hand to the earpiece. "How far is Peter from the starting point?"

"He's about half a day from here." said Melanie

He put his hand to his earpiece again. "If you go meet with the commissions' clerks, they said he can stop by this Island to pick up the GSP beacon and the camera, although there are a few more papers needed to be signed."

"I'll sign those right away." Said Melanie.

After signing those papers she radioed Peter again.

"Peter..." She waited. "Peter..." There was a brief pause. "Peter..?"

"Yah, I'm here." He answered.

"Peter are you sure you can do this by yourself?" she asked.

"Yah I think so. I have my watch set so I can nap once in a while, 20 minutes here 20 minutes there. Sort of like a dolphin I guess."

"Well you're covered by insurance; I signed some papers that ensure you're covered for this race. If something goes wrong you double your money. Also you can stop by the St. Lawrence Island to pick up the GPS locator and the camera. Lastly, there are 163 contestants. There is a website dedicated to letting everyone know who's winning, but remember you can always talk to us if you have any problems. But, Peter you'd better let them know what you're driving."

"It's a hovercraft; I'll let them know before I cross the start." He exclaimed into the radio. "I should be there in a few hours."

***

Within a few hours Peter made it to the Island. He picked up the GPS locator, the camera and made his way to the start.

In less than an a couple hours he was within kilometers of the start, and that's when he decided he'd shock the world. He cut the power to the engine and went into the weather resistant cabin of the hovercraft and pulled the lever. Gases hissed and flaps exploded and slowly his contraption filled with helium. He came out onto the deck of the hovercraft and watched as his contraption took shape. It was a series of balloons designed to take the hovercraft air born. At first it looked like it was nothing more than an airbag or a parachute opening or a sailboat with all sails laying on the deck. Within a few minutes the first balloon was filling, then the second, the third and forth, all inflating inside a giant canopy. He laughed, *'They're going to hate me for this'* thought Peter. He ran to the side of the deck and peered over the side just in time to see it lift ever so gently from the water. A few moments after that the constant pounding from the waves subsided as the entire craft went air born. He chuckled again, this time to the amazement of his own achievement.

The hovercraft had a balloon that was reinforced with some metal meshing, the blade and engine made of materials that would not freeze in the cold. It could withstand low temperatures and high ones. It had a railing around the entire craft, fins to help steer it, was 97% aerodynamic and had recycled water system. Most of the hovercraft was made from a type of carbon fibre Kevlar.

CHAPTER 3.3

He went back inside the cabin and turned on the fan for forward propulsion and the craft began to inch forward ever so slightly. He wanted to make sure everything was working properly; he and Melanie had put everything they'd ever learned into this machine. It ran off a computer guided program so he didn't need to steer it. Cameras were positioned throughout the craft to monitor key points of the vessel at any given time. The cabin wasn't much bigger than a large bathroom with a wood burning fireplace. He could keep warm in there even if the temperature dropped significantly. Supplies were positioned throughout the craft and could be gathered as needed.

He went to his radio. "This is captain Frontinac, nearing the start line, sorry I'm late. Do I have permission to proceed in the race in my flying hovercraft?" An answer, he needed an answer.

"Roger that captain Frontinac, you are six hours behind the rest of the pack. We were informed of your late arrival only hours ago. As soon as you cross the starting point your GPS beacon will activate and transmit your data."

Someone else got on the radio "Did you say flying hovercraft?"

He pictured there funny faces looking at each other in shock.

"That's right." said Peter.

"But the rules outlined no flying machines." the voice repeated.

"Well a hovercraft can't fly..." he paused. "My lawyer is on his way to meet with the organizers lawyers as we speak; but I haven't slept since I left port in Anchorage. It's nice to meet you all." He figured all the contestants had heard that one. Again he pictured their faces and turned off his radio. This was the crucial pivoting point in his mind. He'd always imagined they'd allow him to continue because of a tiny clause that wasn't addressed properly. If, they'd allow him to continue when he woke, he had a great chance at winning. He closed his eyes and went to sleep.

When he woke he'd travelled almost 250 miles from the start point. The craft was able guide itself even though he wasn't piloting it. He stepped out onto the deck. He could see ships and there wakes. He figured he was roughly 10,000 ft above the ocean. He turned on his satellite radio and switched to channel 33. It was the channel they'd decided use to communicate with the base.

"Peter to base..."

Melanie heard this and picked up at her end. "Hi Peter, we were worried about you." She said. "I kept listening to the broadcasts while you were sleeping. I can't believe how many contestants were talking bad about you for your mode of transportation. It seems like everyone was pissed off about your flying hovercraft." She paused "But like I said I'm glad you're okay."

"Melanie," he said. "I can't believe how beautiful everything is up here, it sure beats sailing."

"That's all great Peter, but need to run a diagnostics check of the hovercraft, to make sure everything is running properly. I was worried you were going to crash in your sleep. I also kept a close watch over the designated contestants' channel."

"Where is Tim?" he asked.

"He is on his way to Detroit to meet with the lawyers of the organizers. What are you going to do if they disqualify you, like I said, it seems everyone is pissed that you're in a something that can fly."

"We'll just have to get our money back, there is a good chance of that, or crash, something I'd rather not do"

"Well," said Melanie. "Let's run the diagnostics check anyway your heading into treacherous weather." And over the next few hours they collaborated to ensure the vessel could make it.

Tim on the other hand had his work cut out for him. He'd flown from Anchorage to Toronto then rented a car to drive to Detroit. He was a good lawyer, top marks in all his classes although lately, he was having problems finding work.

He'd come across a leaflet posted in a coffee shop. Then night after night he noticed the lights on in Frontinac house, a few hundred meters from the coffee shop. It took him a while to put two and two together but eventually was convinced the Frontinac's had entered the race. It wasn't until he saw them inflate the craft that he knew it was for sure.

He passed the border then began thinking how the hell he was going to convince the lawyers of the organizers that a hovercraft could be used when it clearly outlined no planes, helicopters or drones. '*But a hovercraft doesn't fly*'.

In just under a few hours he was out front of one of the most prestigious law firms in the country. He'd been practicing his speech for hours and was ready to present his case to the organizers, well the lawyers of the organizers. It was only a few minutes later that he was in front of four different lawyers and began to outline his case.

He finished with "And that is why my client should be allowed to participate."

The lawyers looked at each other then one of them spoke up

"We like it." He said.

"You're telling me that this Peter guy is going to pilot this craft around the globe; from one extreme of the globe to another and still win, by himself, not to mention in a vessel that he built from scratch." They stated. "We like it, it's entertaining."

"The problem is the outcry from other contestants, we had people calling in saying they wanted to use helicopters and planes which the contest guidelines clearly prohibits. Here is the deal," He said. "We can't honour the insurance claim if he crashes along the way; however we will publically state to all contestants that his craft will be allowed to continue in the race."

Tim didn't like it. The contest was dangerous and now it sounded like that danger value was doubled. If Peter crashed along the way they were done for, fifty thousand bucks down the drain.

He changed the subject "Why are you doing this in the first place?"

Another lawyer spoke up "We are trying to turn this into a marketing sensation." "In case you haven't noticed none of the TV stations are covering this event yet. When they do it'll increase the marketing during the coverage. Plus the organizers thought it would be an interesting way to create interaction around the globe; different nations and peoples coming together under the same cause, not to mention this event is downright dangerous."

"Give him half." Tim said. The other lawyers looked at each other, "Give him half." He said again. "If you're doing this for the entertainment value, give him half the insurance claim in case he does crash. At least that way his family can get the money back. Plus, the other participants are going to want to use his idea if they can, and frankly the Frontinac's put every last dollar into this thing, so at least give him half."

The lawyers agreed. Tim walked out of the office then, called in the results to Melanie from cell phone. He returned the car to the airport then booked a flight back to his hometown for the time being.

Melanie then radioed in the results to Peter. It had been some of the longest hours of his life. If he were to be disqualified he'd lose the entry fee, something Tim was always sure he could get back for them, but being allowed to continue now meant he needed to win. Something he was always unsure of.

***

Peter knew that piloting a vessel through the poles was going to take a lot of work. Most vessels would either drop people off with dogs, snow shoes or even hovercrafts, and then would have to return to those ships at the shortest distances possible. He even figured with his craft he could buy days or even weeks off other contestants simply by floating above them. He figured some ships would be used to break through the ice, which made them slower on the open oceans; and others vice versa, they wouldn't be able to cut through the ice as easily.

He went into his cabin. All the instruments read fine. He picked up the camera then began to document his journey thus far.

"Hello." He spoke into the camera. "My name is Peter, Peter Frontinac. The organizers have allowed me to continue in this race. Right now we are about 7,000 feet above sea level." He picked up the camera then walked outside.

"You can see some of the other boats from this height from the wakes they are leaving. We're travelling at about 14 knots which is pretty fast for a hovercraft, well flying hovercraft." He continued. "Hopefully the weather stays good during the pass over the North Pole, from there I can catch the North Atlantic drift which will bring me somewhere over Europe. I figure I can buy some time as others will be struggling with the weather, dogs, frostbite etc. I am hoping to reach the North Pole in just a matter of days."

"I guess that's all for now." Then turned off the camera and sipped from his flask. The whiskey brought a warm, sensation over his body.

CHAPTER 3.4

The following morning he was approaching the first batch of frozen ocean. He came out onto the deck from his cabin after sleeping for no more than a couple hours. He brought the craft down to about 3,000 feet above sea level to catch the cold air currents that ran across the arctic. Even though he'd only slept a few hours he was ready to tackle the first pole. Because it was March most of the bad weather from winter would be gone and was anticipating having nothing but clear skies for most of the journey.

He was still about 1500 kilometers from the pole with another 1000 kilometers or so before he'd reach the other side of the frozen ocean. To him that meant this was his chance to gain a significant lead over his competitors. He double checked his equipment then crossed his fingers that he'd be able to survive this crossing. Worst case scenario he could always land the craft, plus, he'd have enough food rations and clothing to weather out any emergency.

He walked out onto the deck of the vessel, and could see many other contestants had reached the icy shores. From his altitude there were at least twenty different boats near or within the icy beach that stretched for miles. He could see dogs and sleds, snowmobiles, but ice, frozen ice as far as the eye could see. He figured as long as the weather stayed nice he could keep the balloons inflated.

By noon he'd passed most of the other racers. They were nothing more than dots along the horizon. He went into the cabin and began to cook an easy meal, baked beans and bacon. Most of his food was easy to make, freeze dried meals and soups that were ready in minutes. At just under 19 miles an hour he was sure he'd catch up to the leader of the pack soon.

He got on the radio. "Peter to Melanie."

"This is Melanie." she answered.

"Can you tell me the weather forecast; I need to know what I'm up against." asked Peter.

"Should be okay for a little while but the weather always worsens as you get closer to the North Pole. And according to the GPS display you're third back from the pack, and there are about thirty people competing for sixth place. Can you increase you're speed? You might need to drop down to 3000 ft; but if a storm picks up you'll need to be at ground level. Are you tired yet?" she said into the radio

"Always tired, I have my watch set to beep every hour just in case I doze off." He said.

"Well we have the relay systems that will notify us of a malfunction if there is one, I built that into the computer programs. If I hear any malfunctions I'll be on the radio in seconds."

And for the time being Peter dozed off.

***

When he awoke the weather had changed. Not so much the temperature, the temperature was still the same, maybe slightly colder, but the crystal clear skyline had changed to a white background of snow and sleet. He hoped the engineering he put into the craft would pay off. He'd spent weeks on the blueprints fine tuning every detail before he even began to assemble a single component. The vessel itself was fairly high-tech. From the cabin of the craft he could monitor the weather, speed, height even the pressure inside the balloons and every pipe, pressure valve, and relay wired back to the central system designed to withstand the cold. The central computer system then relayed back to the computer where Melanie and Blanche were living.

Most of the metal began to freeze. The railing system around the vessel was almost completely frozen. He decided to take it down another 1000 ft as the visibility continued to deteriorate. Fortunately the winds were pushing him eastwardly so flying perpendicular to those winds would point him in the right direction.

He went into the cabin and picked up his book, Treasure Island and tried his best to recover from the cold. The cabin was well heated. It only took a few minutes for him to get warm. He wanted nothing more than to gain a lead during this polar cross. Apparently some of the sea vessels were quite fast. Fast enough to catch up to him or travel large distances over a shorter period of time. The advantage was his floating hovercraft through the icy cold snow regions of the poles.

He looked in a small mirror he'd brought with him. His beard was long. He hadn't shaved since he started this project. He smelled his underarms. He was sure he had bad hygiene. He melted some water in a cup and lathered some soap to try to clean himself as best he could, then brushed his teeth with one of the toothbrushes he'd brought. In all he had 10 bars of soap, four toothbrushes and toothpaste, six razors, although he wasn't planning on shaving until he was almost done the race; plus these same hygiene products in an emergency kit hidden throughout the craft.

He heard the radio, "Peter it looks like you just moved into second place." The radio squawked "Well there's still a long way to go." he answered.

That particular night was extremely cold. He'd sleep for a few minutes then the sound of his alarm would wake him only to doze off again.

The following morning came with a strong storm, strong enough to ground the vessel. He landed the vessel as best he could, although there was a large jolt when the vessel came into contact with the ground. He climbed out of cabin to make sure the rig or the housing for the balloons was properly tucked away from the weather and the winds.

He'd travelled almost 1200 kilometers or 932 miles in short while and was about 300 kilometers or 186 miles from the Northern pole. The storm ended up being so bad that he needed to weather it out, he could hardly see three feet in front of him and as such waited for the weather to cooperate. The wind wanted to carry the vessel away, so he threw down some anchors to keep him from moving in the storm. He deflated the balloons rather quickly, then, in the cold of the night packed the canopy and balloons into a compartment that could withstand the weather. Then he waited inside the cabin.

The next morning when he awoke, around five o'clock, he walked out onto the deck of the hovercraft. The craft was hardly visible and was under several feet of snow. The storm was so strong that he needed to double his efforts when removing snow from the bridge. Under the new weight he might not have the power to lift off; but since the weather was better he again hit the levers to inflate the balloons and was once again air born and continued to remove the snow from the bridge while continuing to his destination. He spent the latter part of the morning shovelling snow from the deck of the vessel. If his calculations were correct he'd arrive at the North Pole around midnight, then catch the strongest southerly wind towards the Atlantic Ocean. He began to look forward to temperate temperatures.

He wanted the vessel to travel faster somehow as the cold winter regions of the North Pole began to slow him down. Every minute seemed to take twice the time, to have the second hand revolve; somehow the cold made every second feel like two. It became a constant battle to keep the camera lenses cleared that were pointed at various locations upon the craft. As much as the ship was designed to be cold weather proof, the proof being that some of the equipment needed constant attention.

To pass the time he'd watch the snow blaze across the exterior of the craft, sometimes from the cabin and other times while scrapping the ice from the vessel. It was a white out; everywhere he looked was a snow filled wonderland of sleet and ice. His beard would protect him from the weather, but, every time he'd enter the cabin it would be covered in icicles.

He'd play solitaire to pass the time and sometimes chess against himself. He'd even brought a portable gaming system to play while inside the comforts of the cabin.

It began to turn dark. He was only 5 days into his journey, not counting the commute from Anchorage. He didn't like flying blind. For the most part he stayed inside the cabin, using only the sophisticated computer technology to guide him. He had night vision cameras that could allow him to see the rig, but as for the landscapes, there wasn't much to see. He kept one camera focused on the horizon and continued on.

The eleventh hour creped very slowly, but Peter was comfortable in his long johns and sweater, his sleeping gear. He figured the snow mobiles and dog sleds were travelling about 40 kilometers per day, provided there were no technical problems with the gear, but they also needed to stop to sleep which bought him 25 kilometers every hour.

He was right. Many of the entrants had a tough time with his mode of transportation, and were frustrated he wasn't disqualified. Several of them were on phones and radios trying to copy his wild idea, to get an edge on winning the race, while most just pressed on towards the first pole.

Most contestants were using dog sleds and snowmobiles. These were unloaded from the ships they used to travel the oceans blue.

Midnight came and he was forty kilometers from the first pole. Since there were little or no winds he upped the speed by just a few knots. He liked using the kilometers as a measure of distance because it could be referenced to specific times, per hour. 100 kilometers was often one hour of traveling so the math was easier to compute. When it came to cruising speeds he didn't want to cheat the naval community; as all vessels travel in knots.

The ship swayed back and forth as it travelled the route. He'd reinforced the balloon with strong metal strapping to reduce the swaying motion as much as possible but in these heavy winds the ship was at the mercy of the weather.

He looked at the clock he'd been awake a long time and was roughly 8 days into the journey and was nearing the North Pole. He sat in anticipation as he approached, watching from a GPS location system installed in the cabin of the vessel.

He began to line up his vessel, he didn't want to miss the target and circle around again, and getting it right the first time meant a direct line towards the next part of the race. He calculated his path, 2000 meters, 1500 meters, 1000 meters, 800, 500, 250, 175, 100 meters. *'C'mon, C'mon just a bit further'* 75, 50, 25, 20, 15, 10. He got on the radio, "This is Peter Frontinac, confirmation that the GPS marker was within range of the first objective." He waited, nothing. He repeated the message – nothing.

He put on his overalls and boots and went outside to check the communications antenna - frozen. In his haste to get warm from the long morning of cleaning the snow from the deck he forgot to break away the ice surrounding the communications antenna. He quickly went to his cabin and took out the first tool he could find; a wrench, and began to break away the ice. Accidentally, he snapped the antenna which fell deep down into the darkness of the night, towards the frozen earth.

He went to the spare parts compartment that doubled as storage for supplies and rummaged through the labelled packaging. He found what he was looking for *'Only two more'*. They had only prepared three replacement antennas; he quickly fastened the new antenna where the previous one was, then returned to the cabin.

"Peter Frontinac to base." He radioed, still nothing. "This is Peter Frontinac." He switched channels to Melanie's frequency. He didn't want to wake her but he figured they'd been waiting to hear from him. "Melanie this is Peter." He waited.

"Hi Peter, just wanted to let you know, someone called in frostbite and quit the race and had to be rescued, but there are still 162 other racers, that number should continue to drop."

"So how will the racers know when they get to the checkpoint?" Asked Peter

"Check the GPS beacon they gave you." Said Melanie

He checked around the cabin and couldn't find it. *'It's got to here somewhere.'* He checked the shelves, the cabinets but couldn't find it anywhere. He started to panic checking his pockets, his previous shirts and pants. Then finally found it, in the corner buried under some cushions. He held it up, it was green he was sure it was red when he picked it up.

"It's green." He radioed. "I guess I should use the camera to indicate I'm here with the GPS beacon, wasn't there a clause about being sure the captain was present with the beacon?"

"Yes there was, the camera also has a GPS beacon on it, by documenting your arrival to the pole, it should coordinate back to the race officials of your location during the chronicled footage." replied Melanie.

"I Hope you're all doing okay," he paused, "There's still a long way to go."

Melanie radioed back. "There's someone not far ahead of you, they haven't stopped for rest and are maintaining a steady speed." "It must be a submarine." He replied. "A submarine? I didn't see them at the start. There were so many boats on the water." He watched the sun rise that morning then dozed off to get some sleep.

CHAPTER 3.5

It wasn't long before he reached the end of the ice. The snow tundra horizon began to give way to the great big blue ocean.

He turned on his camera and began to detail his last few days. The ocean made him nervous. Frankly, although he hated the cold, he was much more comfortable with frozen water beneath him then giant blue unknown. He entered his next coordinate into the computer system then began to read his book.

By this point the media began to catch on. It started small, local stations from Alaska, and then Canadian and Russian broadcasts, even Great Britain and many American stations began to cover the event. Twitter, Facebook and Instagram had pages dedicated to the event. The news shocked some just as it was intended, and slowly people started to tune in to find out more details, but details varied from each news source, however the premise was the same. A few newspapers read "A Millionaires Challenge" and described the information they knew.

About four days later Peter saw the coastline. The last few days had been spent, for the most part, inside the cabin. He'd drift in and out of consciousness in a sort of hazy sleep. Eventually he did indeed get a fifteen hour sleep which made him feel regenerated. Because he'd stay awake for long, when he did sleep, it was usually for a longer time.

His GPS confirmed that he was somewhere over Norway and fast approaching Sweden. He needed to radio in to countries to let them know he was approaching their air space. He'd collected some of the details earlier in race; there was a code word he was to use as well as an exact GPS location, the vessel he was using, but mostly, he wanted to avoid having to ground his vehicle inside a given countries airspace. Having to stop somewhere over dry land would be better than making a stop over an open ocean.

So far, so good, he had clearance from Norway and Sweden as the plan was to pass through West Central Europe, Italy, then to cross in to Africa. He logged onto the webpage that displayed the GPS beacons. There were quite a few who hadn't even reached the North Pole yet, and the other half were still within a 500 km radius of passing the pole. Still, there was a beacon that was in front of Peter. '*It must be that submarine*' he thought. Because there is no land mass under the ice at the north it had a fairly easy time navigating underneath the frozen water. He figured although they might get a head start to Antarctica travelling to the South Pole would be much more complicated, as there is landmass under the ice. He tried to radio them just to give a little friendly competition, but there was no response.

Although it was still early spring, the weather was much more pleasant than the days he spent over the frozen ocean. He stepped out onto the deck of his vessel and puffed from his pipe. He began to realize how fortunate he'd been to hear about the contest in the first place, had it not been his mother, he'd still be sitting in his filthy coveralls and drinking the whiskey that made his life all the more difficult.

The weather definitely began to change as he continued onward towards the equator. Instead of being encased in ice the frame and body of the vessel were once again visible to the eye. He pulled out a lawn chair and fastened it to the deck of the floating hovercraft. Having revamped the rotor blade gave the craft some extra needed propulsion that allowed him to be a contender for the win. So he put on his shades and gazed in amazement at the European country side.

He found himself comfortably adjusting the altitude to coincide with the high and low pressure jet streams. When the winds were at his back the ship sailed like a catamaran on one pontoon and when the winds were in his face he'd take the vessel higher to avoid the incoming storm. So far so good, everything was working well and with the exception of the frozen antenna, was working fine.

In no time the southerly winds took him across the European country side and across into the Mediterranean. He was even welcomed by a small crowd along the Italian peninsula before the journey across Africa.

As soon as he crossed into Tunisia, he went straight for the binoculars. He picked up his satellite phone entered a few digits. The phone must have rang five or six times before someone on the other line picked up. He jotted a few numbers down then entered them into the GPS navigation system. About an hour later he'd spotted what he was looking for; a long time friend named Sal.

He adjusted the altitude and cut the power to rotating fan blade, and set down the craft right next to Sal and a truckload of needed supplies.

Sal shook his head as Peter placed his foot on solid ground for the first time in several weeks.

"When you said you were going to travel around the world in hovercraft, I thought you were joking." Sal uttered.

"She doesn't look like much but she's weathered everything that's been thrown at her so far."

"I would've known you were coming earlier but was afraid to log onto the standings website. I was sure I'd find that you'd plummeted to the ground somewhere over the arctic with no chance of rescue."

Peter chuckled. "Well... I didn't build this vessel to crash; so far, so good."

They chatted for a few minutes, and then began to load the vessel up with fuel, food and few electronic components.

"You know, that South Pole is going to be twice as hard to cross then that North Pole. The snow is deeper, more mountains, stronger storms, they say even the air is colder, frostbite in just under three minutes.

What are you going to do if you get stuck; it could take days before you get rescued. Are you sure you want to go through with this?"

'Don't let fear hold you back'. "Don't let fear hold you back." Said Peter.

"What is that supposed to mean?" asked Sal.

"Just something my mother always use to say to me." Replied Peter.

"Peter this has nothing to do with fear, it's damn near suicide."

Peter slammed down the last container of petroleum. "I know it's dangerous, it's just I've come so far, I've built this thing out of nothing, I wasn't even sure if it could fly – I need to keep going." He paused. "Just help me with the inspection! I need to make sure everything is still working properly."

Everything passed, in about an hour they'd properly inspected all the welds, bolts, even the electronic hardware and wiring. He handed him a bunch of folded bills to cover the expenses, then hopped onto the deck and was about to lift off. Just before he did, turned to Sal and said "Do you have any sunscreen, I wasn't sure I'd make it this far."

Sal chuckled then went to cab of his jeep, then tossed him a bottle SPF 55. "It's the only thing that will keep you from baking in the African sun." Seconds later, the hovercraft began to go airborne again. Peter waved as goodbye as the craft lifted higher and higher into the African skies. He engaged the rotor blade and was well on his way to completing the second leg of the journey.

CHAPTER 3.6

Now then, Africa is a hot, hot, place. There is a reason its people keep to shade while they can. Temperatures are recorded higher in Africa than anywhere else in the world. But with a new payload of fuel, food and supplies, Peter cracked a Coke as he sat in his fastened down lawn chair. The gentle breeze created by the moving craft kept him cool enough to savor the deliciousness of his soda.

Peter had never been to Europe, let alone Africa. It was as if, all at once, he began to see the world in all its beauty. He was startled to see how many farms there were along the European country side and now the enormity of the second leg of the journey. In fact he felt more confident now of his win then he did in the months of the vessel's construction.

Night and day he sat in his lawn chair only getting up to use the washroom or make some food. By day many people would gaze in amassment at the 120 foot monster balloon that travelled above their heads; by night he sailed as quiet as a hawk hunting its prey from the sky.

In the European skies he'd need to radio air towers who'd acknowledge his GPS position as an in flight craft. Over Africa the rules where a little different, it was more or less smooth sailing. Before long he was past the African Savannah well on his way to the Southern African peninsula. He kept a pair binoculars around his neck to gaze at the animals that inhabited that region. Hundreds of thousands of wildebeests, elephants, giraffes even crocodiles and birds. He tried to steer clear of any towns or cities since he was an unidentified flying craft over an unknown region.

On the eighth day travelling over the African plains he heard his radio squawk

"Unidentified craft please land you vessel or we will be forced to shoot you down."

A nervous rush entered his bloodstream; he gripped the radio in frustration.

***

I need to stop there for a moment. Most of you thought this was a story about a mouse. Well it is about a mouse, but it is also about so much more than a just a mouse. I will tell you what happened to the mouse but first I need to warn you; if you don't want to read anymore, and think this story might be too boring, I advise you put down this book and never read it again. For those of you who are brave enough to keep reading I will tell you the rest of the story.

***

A nervous rush entered his bloodstream; he gripped the radio in frustration.

"This is Captain Peter Frontinac, I am participating in a race, and I would like nothing more than to pass through your airspace without any conflict."

The response was less empathetic. "Please land your craft immediately."

Begrudgingly he entered the cabin and began to bring the craft back towards the Earth. For the second time he landed his craft in Africa, Just beyond the Congo, in the country of Angola.

As he exited the hovercraft, a dozen or so military men with assault rifles boarded and began to look around. He was immediately reprimanded and escorted to a military jeep in handcuffs. The jeep sped off down a dirt road and towards the nearest town. When they got there he was placed in jail.

About three hours later a large Angolan military man came to the door and opened it. He escorted him to an office down a hallway from the cells.

"What are you doing in Angola?" Asked the official.

"My name is Peter Frontinac, my vessel and I, are on route to Antarctica."

The official laughed. "Antarctica, and why would you be going there?"

"I entered a competition; it's a race around the world. I've been to the North Pole, across Europe and now Africa. I am on route to Antarctica then across the Pacific back towards Alaska where the race started. You must let me go on, and please do not mess with my ship."

The official wanted to laugh again, but wasn't sure if he was telling the truth.

"You are telling me that floating wreck is going to Antarctica because you are in a competition; a race around the world? Why should I believe you?" asked the official.

"Yes it's going to Antarctica, and yes I'm telling the truth."

The official got on the phone and placed a call to one of his menial military henchmen. He hung up the phone, and then made another call.

This time to a higher ranking official, they spoke for a few minutes than he hung up the phone.

"Okay." He started. "You can go." He pulled a key from his pocket then removed the handcuffs from his wrists.

"I will drive you back to your floating, ahh, what do you call it?" asked the Angolan official.

"Hovercraft..?" Asked Peter.

"Yes." He said. "I will drive you back there."

In no time they were back at the vessel. The whole debacle had taken just under five hours, and now the light of day was fleeting. Peter was surprised to see that his ship was still in working order, although his ship had been boarded they had not ravaged through the entire thing.

He entered the cabin, then pulled some levers and turned some knobs, than the ship began to take flight once again. He walked out onto the deck of the ship and waved goodbye to a handful of Angolan guards.

"Thank you." He said.

"Peter." The Angolan official said. "I hope you win this competition of yours."

"Thanks." He said. *'Me too'*

CHAPTER 3.7

He hadn't slept in long time. He programmed in the next few coordinates, then curled up on his cot and shut his eyes.

He awoke just in time to see the last of the African peninsula. Immediately he began to run a mental checklist of preparations before crossing into Antarctica. Although it was still a few days journey from South Africa, for the first time in almost two weeks he wouldn't have the comfort of dry land beneath his feet; and when he'd find dry land again it would be just as cold as the North Pole.

He also knew that storms that brew south of Africa and close to Antarctica are some of the worst anywhere, in fact landing the craft during any of those storms would almost be more dangerous than flying through them. Ocean swells can reach thirty feet while cold winds freeze the ocean water to surfaces almost in seconds; that most ocean going vessels avoid at all costs, travelling those treacherous waters.

Somehow his layover in Angola saved him from uncertainty. A monster storm some 1600 kilometers or 1000 miles off the South African coast was beginning to dissipate. Had he not been halted in Angola his ship would be just beginning to cross into that particular storm, chance by uncertainty.

Although he had just got some rest, he was exhausted. The African sun had turned his skin red, the sunscreen had worked for the first few days but now his tan had turned a painful red. He wanted to run his mental checklist again but instead found himself ready to sleep inside his cabin. He closed his eyes and fell asleep.

When he awoke, he realized he'd been asleep a very long time; some twelve hours. He checked his computer equipment, and then began to make some food. Because of the horrible weather, the ship was rocking, sometimes back and forth, sometimes left and right. He wanted to make some hot food, but instead ate a whole box of pop tarts.

He began to notice his altitude level was lower than he'd programmed. Immediately red flags went up inside his head. He exited the cabin to look around the deck. One of the balloons was not fully inflated. Instead, it was getting beat around by the wind and the rain. He realized he'd need to climb up the balloon harness if it wasn't something that could be fixed on deck. He grabbed some tools and began inspecting what he could.

He looked again at the balloon; it had not fallen out of the harness, which was good. He'd need to ground the craft to reattach it, if it had. He wasn't scared of heights but, he'd have to climb his rig to inspect it, to see if there was a hole, a leak, or a tear. He had brought some material for just this sort of accident, but fixing it in the rain was going to be difficult.

He mustered all the courage he could, then began his accent up the netting of the balloon. He looked down but could not see the ocean; the rain clouds, clouded his view to the water's surface. When he got halfway up the rig, he lit the flare he was carrying in his mouth. He took out a Swiss army knife then cut a small incision into the balloon. Then he placed the flare into the incision he had just made under the opening, until the smoke bellowed out from a tiny tear, another 20 feet further up the rig. He then climbed the remaining distance pulling a piece of patchwork and sealant from his pocket.

He desperately tried to reach for the balloon hands freezing from the wind while the balloon was still getting beaten around by the wind. With a lucky gust, he grabbed the balloon then adjusted his position to begin the repair. The sealant was strong enough to bind in only a few seconds even under terrible conditions. He added some extra, just to make sure the bond was airtight, then began his descent. When he got to the base of the balloon, he pulled another flare from his pocket then ignited it. This time there was no smoke leaking from the tear and the balloon began to fill the rig again. He patched the initial cut he made and hoped it would hold through the coming cold weather.

He continued his decent, but lost his footing along the way. The coiled rope hooked onto his foot and he fell backwards under his own weight. The flare he was holding onto fell into the darkness of the storm and its light slowly extinguished as it plummeted towards the Earth. Amazed he hadn't fallen off the craft he reached up to the rope ladder and pulled himself upright; then carefully climbed the remaining distance towards the deck. He brushed himself off then entered the cabin, still stunned by his close encounter with death.

Inside, he learned that this tiny tear had cost him almost a whole quarter tank of helium. His re-service with Sal gave him just enough fuel to finish the race, but not if there was a leak. He wasn't sure if he'd be able to cross the harsh lands of Antarctica. He pulled out his pipe and his flask to reward himself for his narrow escape and near tumble. It was getting late into the evening, he'd need to pull a double shift to make sure nothing else went wrong, opened his book and began to read.

Night turned to day and by daybreak the storm had subsided. That particular sunrise was one of the most beautiful he'd ever seen, by sunset the following day, he'd be nearing the Antarctic coast.

After he made himself some supper, he again walked out onto the deck of the vessel. Patches of ice began to appear, he knew he must be closing in on the coastline. He studied the route from a map, he'd be taking, due South from the African peninsula was the most direct route.

He logged onto the GPS website just to gauge his position amongst the competition. He was in third place, apparently there were some ocean vessels that were travelling faster through the oceans, his fairly large detour across Europe and Africa allowed for a few faster vessels to catch up to him. Surprisingly, many more had dropped out of the race. Perhaps they felt crossing two frozen wastelands was just a bit too unnerving. Besides, most had used sled dogs and snowmobiles to cross the North Pole and both methods of travel would be twice as difficult through Antarctica, since it's colder and more treacherous.

More and more the landscape began to change from ocean to coastline. Giant icebergs that had broken away from the main ice shelf were floating further out to sea. Somehow they concealed their fortitude beneath the frozen waters as only a small percentage were visible from the surface. Ice, was everywhere, the majestic ocean was gradually becoming more and more frozen the further south he travelled.

Only days ago, he was complaining about the heat, in just under five days he was beginning to feel the effects of the cold. The good news was that it was spring, meaning at least he didn't need to travel across Antarctica in the winter.

He stepped out onto the deck to inspect the tear he'd fixed earlier that day. All seemed well, and since the storm had subsided he made a nice warm pot of macaroni and cheese, enough to feed a small family.

The night was in twilight, and the majestic ocean began to conceal her beauty. It became tougher and tougher to identify where the ocean started and the icebergs began. Instead, the horizon took on, one of the darkest of dark blues before the twilight subsided with only the moon to bring light during the night. He spent that evening sitting in the same lawn chair that had coasted him over Africa. Although the night took away most of the visual spectacles, he felt like a space captain soaring into adventures unknown.

He awoke later the next day, but could not remember falling asleep. More and more, the ocean began, like a mystical game of dominos, to freeze at the surface and continue to freeze the further south he went. It was a sure sign that he was venturing closer and closer to the Antarctic shoreline. He noticed a few shipping lanes that had cut through the ice, although he could not see any vessels, instead the remnants of the ships were just large, broken pieces of ice, similar to the vapor clouds left behind by large airplanes.

He got into the cabin and decided to dress warmer for the weather, putting on some snow coveralls that kept him warm during the first transition across the North Pole

By dusk of that evening he was sure the vast expanse of Antarctica was somewhere beneath the vessel, but was hard to tell where land started since it was covered in ice.

The following day he was assured he'd reached Antarctica. He passed a small mountain range only visible by the tops of the hills, hills that were mostly covered by snow. He decided to radio Melanie and his mother - he hadn't talked to anyone in a few days and wanted to assure them he was okay.

Dusk turned to dawn and by dawn, the weather was starting change for the worst. He could see another huge cloud looming off in the distance. He made the reparations he could on the deck then made his way to the cabin, the place where he'd be weathering out the storm.

CHAPTER 3.8

Although he didn't mind being in such small quarters and the fact that the vessel could literally drive itself, made the time inside the cabin seem endurable. Although it was not much bigger than the largest of bathrooms, this 6' x 10' cabin could keep him warm and fed, even if he lost the entirety of the working parts within the vessel.

As he gazed out the cabin windows he could see he was definitely wandering into the storm. Ice, sleet and snow passed the window as if his hover-ship were re-entering the Earth's atmosphere. He lit his pipe and pulled his sketch book from his pocket. He'd been drawing interesting things that had caught his attention, finding it was a great way to pass the time.

Hours later, the bad weather had not let up. The cabin was a warm and wonderful way to pass the time, but periodically he'd walk out onto the deck to inspect the rigging and clear the craft of unwanted weight in the form of ice that could slow down the vessel. In fact, this storm was one of the worst he'd seen, had his vessel been grounded this storm would have completely buried his craft.

He could tell by the GPS locator page he was inching ever closer to the second waypoint requirement, the south pole; but judging by the web page, was still some 1000km or 621 miles from reaching the second way point, the South Pole.

Another ice storm began to creep up on the vessel; he'd chip away at the ice to pass the time keeping his body toasty warm with the snowsuit and gloves he was wearing. Once again his beard would ice up from the weather bringing snow covered icicles. When he'd finish or wanted a break, he'd enter the cabin, remove the snowsuit and brew some coffee or tea.

He'd collected quite a few cans from all the meals he'd been preparing during the voyage. Lucky for him he wasn't a fussy eater and could get by on the bare essentials.

Night turned to day and day to night, but still the storm raged on. The periodical removing of the ice became more and more lethargic and ever increasingly latent. He must have given thousands of pounds of ice back to the continent that seemed to do nothing but create ice. He tried to sleep but the uneasiness of something going wrong ever tormented his conscience, enough to keep him from getting any significant rest.

By the third morning, the storm had finished giving its devastating destructiveness, and the sun was clearly visible through the clouds. He learned that morning that another one the participants decided to copy his idea of using a balloon to traverse Antarctica, but was downed during the storm, as it lacked the motor from the hovercraft and generally the weight and power needed to wander the storm. He also learned that help was inbound as the organizers had foreseen this sort of predicament and had implemented a sort-of search and rescue team for those who were downed, or those who wanted to withdrawal from the race, but needed assistance.

He was now just days away from crossing the second way point and everything seemed to be working fine. It was as if mother earth was gently pushing his vessel towards a victory, a victory that only a year ago seemed as farfetched as any fairytale.

Instead of reading or drawing, Peter found himself just staring blankly at the computer screen, the website dedicated to letting the general population know who was winning the competition - he was in first place. He sat with his arms wrapped around his knees, watching as his little green dot inched ever closer to the pole.

By the time night came he was 100 kilometers from the South Pole. He wanted to sleep; his eyes drooped from fatigue and burned from exhaustion. He couldn't remember how long he'd been starring at the screen. He picked up his book, as reading kept him sane inside the cabin, but instead found himself watching very closely the little green dot.

He'd flown over the ice in Antarctica for two days followed by reaching the frozen coastline and continued through the valleys and mountains of Antarctica. It was colder than the North Pole or at least it seemed like it was, but soon he would be passing the second way point

An hour or two later he was nearing South Pole, again he prepped for the same routine, 3000 meters, 1000 meters, 500 meters, 100, 50, 25, 10 meters. He looked again at the GPS device issued at the start; it had changed from green to blue. He moved towards the camera then stated: "This is Captain Frontinac, I have reached the South Pole, 31 days after reaching the North Pole, I am on my way back to the start line, I, I mean the finish line."

He looked down at the scientists who'd been logging there and they all waved to him as he passed by them.

He entered some new coordinates and the ship made a hard right turn. He peaked out the port side window and noticed the wind would be at his back, making travel faster. He was on the last leg of the journey, the home stretch; 15,000 kilometers or 9320 miles to go.

CHAPTER 3.9

He went to the cabin and kicked the fan motor into high gear; just slightly above the travelling speed he'd maintained most of the way.

He walked back out onto the deck of the craft and began to shout, and sing, and dance. He taunted Mother Nature to do her worst, insisting that she could not break his spirit. After he was done he grabbed a wrench and began to break the ice that had collected on the deck, all the while whistling a merry tune. He went back to the cabin and puffed his pipe, sipped from his flask and made some supper still whistling the same tune. He tried to sleep later that evening but still had that stupid tune in his head, so instead he hummed that same tune, even while he slept that evening.

When he awoke it had been almost 28 hours he'd been sleeping for. The longest sleep he'd had during the whole trip and was even more excited to find the vessel was still in working order. Everything he did now was merry and almost orchestrated. The sandwiches tasted better, the coffee had a bit more perk to it, and this transitioned into everything he did.

For the next hour he threw a small ball at the wall, then played 100 games of X's and O's against himself, as it was becoming difficult to stay focused.

Night turned into day and day into again although being that he was at the bottom of the world it was hard to tell which was which.

Still, mountainous mountains seemed covered from head to toe with snow, enough snow to fill a whole football field a thousand feet high or so. He desperately wanted to see the ocean again, something under other circumstances he would've cared less about.

After two days more, he'd reached the coastline. Taking a route due North towards Argentina got him to the coastline as quickly as possible.

Again, the weather began to change and up-heave in some of the meanest storms this planet has ever seen, but this time Peter had strapped himself to the bow of the hovercraft. He wasn't going to sit this storm out in the cabin. However, the storm was strong enough to push him off course just enough for him to gain speed as he raced towards South America. The wind would blow him side to side and the rain and snow hit his face like pins and needles. He didn't care though he was having the time of his life.

Six hours later he entered the cabin, again triumphant over Mother Nature, yet freezing cold from head to toe. It seemed nothing could dampen his spirits. He was soaking wet and changed into some dryer clothes then puffed on his pipe and drank some coffee.

Hours later he'd reached South America.

Now the original plan was to refuel at the Southern tip of Chile, but since his last refuel had left him still with plenty of gas and food he decided not to, and motored on towards the Great North. He followed the coastline for three days until he came to the most Northern tip of Chile. Then took a bearing Northwest along the coastline of Peru.

He crossed into the Pacific headed towards the Baja, and then two days later arrived 100 miles off the coast of Cabo San Lucas.

That particular trip had been the longest of trips without rest. From Chile to the Baja he had not rested, nor did he want to, but since the temperature had been temperate he spent the afternoon snoozing on the aft portion of the hovercraft.

He'd lost weight, a lot of weight, probably 20 pounds since plunking the boat in the water near Alaska. But that did not bother him, what bothered him was that he'd been so merry after reaching the South Pole and excited about the last leg of the journey, that he'd forgotten to collect the ice run off from the vessel into water that could be used to drink, stay clean and cook with. He had devised a water filtration system that would allow him to collect rain water and snow runoff, but some nice fresh Mexican rain water would hit the spot just nicely, maybe even some tequila.

His ship followed the coastline of the Pacific from 5000 ft in the air. Then came across an old hotel located somewhere along that coastline and decided it would be a good place to refuel. He landed the craft on a deserted beach, placed a sign on the ship that said "back in five". He anchored the ship to the beach and walked a few kilometers to an old hotel. He went in and said, "I need to buy as much water as possible, and a sandwich." The front desk attendant looked at him funny, but didn't realize he was in a hurry.

It took some explaining but eventually Peter flashed a 100$ bill and receptionist was eager to help, as his English was not so good. By the time he left he was carrying 20 gallons of water, a ham sandwich and a small bottle of tequila and needed to hitchhike the few remaining kilometers back to his beach. Before he left he asked "Where am I?" The receptionist answered "The Hotel California, you're just outside of Todos Santos." "From the song?" he asked. "Yes" replied the receptionist.

He left the hotel but with too much stuff to carry. He stuck out his thumb as Jeep with a license plate from California came to his aid. He must have looked like a Neanderthal to them, shirtless, with shorts and a long scruffy beard.

"Where are you going?" the couple asked. "Just a few beaches over." he replied. "Where's your backpack man? How come you're only carrying water and chocolate bars?" "I'll explain later." he replied

The trip could not have taken more than five minutes to get back to the hovercraft. When he got back, a number of tourists had stopped at that beach to investigate the strange looking vessel on its shores.

"What the @#^*." Exclaimed the passenger as they approached the beach. They came to a halt near the side of the beach. Peter began to unload all the supplies he'd purchased at the hotel when he noticed the jeep was travelling with extra gasoline.

"How much for you fuel?" he asked. The travellers were still in shock from the docked vessel.

"Hey, hello? How much for you gasoline?" he asked again.

"I don't know?" said the driver. "There's enough here to get us back to California."

"Great!" he exclaimed "Will three hundred bucks do?"

"Well I guess so." replied the driver. Peter gave them the money then started to carry the water and supplies to the hovercraft. Some of the tourist suggested he keep away; instead he replied "It's my ship."

He ran back to the jeep, this time carrying the two oversized canisters of gasoline, then laughed as he found a place for everything he'd purchased. He hadn't had this much company since Angola. Within minutes he was floating five feet above the beach and waved goodbye to the on-looking crowd. Minutes later he was high above the sky looking back on that particular beach. Just then, a news van came rushing onto the scene and a reporter jumped out of the van with her camera man. Peter waved to them as he engaged the rotor blade and sped off North up the coast line.

Now he was ready to finish the race, that little bit of gasoline should be enough to get him back to the finish line, since he'd used a bit extra in engaging the motor to turn faster.

His vessel crept further up the coastline maintaining his bearing. Due to the topography, sometimes his vessel stayed close to shore and other times he could barely see the coastline, as the coastline shot in and out like a slow motion film of earthly proportions.

He walked into the cabin to gauge his position over the other racers. There was another craft that was gaining on his position ever so slightly *'It must be that submarine.'* Somehow, they'd managed to traverse Antarctica in just under three weeks and were cruising right through the center of the Pacific at a much faster nautical speed then he.

CHAPTER 3.10

Still about 800 kilometers or 500 miles from the San Diego - Tijuana border, spirits were still high. The submarine was right in line with Chile's, Santiago, but was thousands of miles from the coastline.

Peter sipped from the tequila he'd just bought. It immediately filled his body with a drunken sensation. Within an hour he'd drank the whole thing and felling queasy went to lay down. The cabin brought him very little relaxation as tequila is a far more potent drink than whiskey. In fact he thought he was going to throw up on more than one occasion.

He was drunk off the tequila. He grabbed a mirror and started talking to himself, "You" he said "You might win this race". Then he started dancing around the cabin in his underwear until he hit his head on the microwave counter and knocked himself out.

He awoke some twenty minutes later with a cut on his head. He was tired, the tequila was making him feel sick, so he decided not to drink too much more.

After another small, but dizzying rest he was famished, he ate chocolate bar after chocolate bar, in order to regain some calories. The stress of the journey was getting to him. He was thrilled to have stepped foot on the beaches of the Baja peninsula, because, ironically he'd never left the United States his whole life, and now had seen most of the world in one trip.

A few hours later he was nearing the border, he radioed the air traffic control towers, as the quickest route was over California towards Vancouver and Victoria.

They were angry, immediately they wanted him to land his vessel. "Land now, Land now" they shouted. It wasn't until a young man; a rookie within tower associated him with a news article he'd watched some six weeks earlier. After explaining this to his superiors someone came over the radio and asked him if was participating in this event. The answer was "Yes."

By this point the news officials, radio stations and TV networks started getting calls. "Someone is going to win 50 million bucks for successfully completing a trip around the world from pole to pole, and will be crossing the finish line in Alaska." The reporters started going crazy.

This time, nearly six times the amount of reporters were in the Alaskan town of Wales and still days from crowning a victor. Plus people were logging into the website to see who was winning. Twitter, Facebook had gone nuts with the pages dedicated to the race. It had become a phenomenon.

Peter knew nothing of how bustling the crowd was until Melanie radioed in. "Peter" she said. "The town of Wales has gone crazy with reporters and you're still in first place. You just might win this thing."

CHAPTER 3.11

The submarine was closing in fast, with a top speed of 25 knots it was gaining by the hour, nearly twice as fast as Peter was travelling. It was 4500 kilometers or 2800 miles of the coast Costa Rica and could maintain its speed day or night.

Peter was flying off the coast of the Sierra Nevada Mountains destined for the Port town of Vancouver, Canada. He was tired, just 500 kilometers or 310 miles south of Portland. He emptied the last of his gasoline into the flying contraption and once again puffed on his pipe and sipped his whiskey.

A few more hours into travelling it started to rain, he put on his rain gear and observed the storm from the deck. He couldn't see much the clouds were very low to the ground and he feared that he might get struck by lightning. Instead he took the vessel up to 10,000 ft. He thought he could get high above the storm, but it was still cloudy. For the first time he took the craft even higher to 12,000 ft. this time it lifted ever so slightly above; slightly bouncing from cloud to cloud. He took out his camera and filmed this orchestrated dance above the clouds. The sun was shining brightly and blue sky could be seen for miles. He sat in delight.

That evening he reached Vancouver.

CHAPTER 3.12

After a few hours of sleep, he was trudging up the British Columbia coastline and had returned to his cruising altitude of about 3000 ft. He was nervous, the submarine was inching ever closer towards a victory and third place was rounding the Southern tip of Argentina, with another hundred or so close behind in Antarctica. He'd learned that nearly 30 people had withdrawn from the race throughout the last two weeks or so, he didn't want to say it but it made his spirits run high.

The air was crisp, clean and dew set in all across the ship. Once in a while he'd conduct a systems check to make sure the dew wasn't effecting the computer equipment and relays. No sense in coming this far and having the craft fall to pieces.

Night turned to day and day to night again. He was above the Queen Charlotte Islands. He increased the speed once again as he neared the Alexander Archipelago. *'Not much further now'*.

The following morning he was just shy of the Gulf of Alaska. *'C'mon c'mon'*.

1000 kilometers or 621 miles left to go. He looked at the screen and the submarine made a sharp turn to the left try to avoid the Aleutian mountains.

Day to night, the landscape was baron and black. Although he knew there were trees everywhere they remained hidden in the landscape. No city lights just the blackness of night.

By morning he'd reached the Norton Sound he brought the craft down to about 700 ft. He wanted to cross the finish line without the giant balloon he'd constructed so long ago.

Then without notice something snapped. The rigging that had been supporting the balloon started to give way, in seconds the entire wire cage that kept him from falling began to heave into the sky, the balloon wanted to stay airborne. He desperately tried to cut power from the motor. One by one the rigging inched from its hinges the craft hung narrowly at a forty five degree angle. Peter hung on for dear life. He watched until the final bolt flung skyward and the craft began to hurdle towards the ground.

It weaved and bobbed as the air hitting the underside of the hovercraft punishing it, throwing it upwards and sideways. Peter could hold on no more, he let go and seconds later splashed into the freezing cold water of Norton Sound.

CHAPTER 3.13

He opened his eyes, he was under water. The fall did not kill him. He surfaced and looked around. He was far enough away from land that there was no safe shore to swim to. The waves crashed against his face. He looked up he could see the balloon slowly deflating as there was no helium to keep it afloat. He looked to the left and could not believe his eyes.

The ship had survived the landing, not only did it survive it, it was still sitting upright, ready to be piloted. He swam to it as fast as he could, given the water was freezing, his wet clothes were slowing him down and the currents were carrying the vessel ever-so-slightly away from him. The waves battered him as he swam as he tried to swim closer to vessel.

After a few minutes he got close enough to grab hold and climbed aboard. The ship was in chaos. Pipes exiting from the cabin were torn and mangled. The helium tanks were bleeding off helium. He went inside the cabin, most of the computer equipment was damaged, the radio, the navigation system. He climbed back out onto the deck then approached the helm. The craft was still afloat. Since the balloon and the hovercraft body were two different inflation systems altogether, he thought he might get the motor running again.

He inched lever ever so slightly and the motor engaged the fan. He pushed down the lever and the hovercraft was moving again. Since the navigation equipment was damaged he knew it would be roughly 300 kilometers to victory. Once again he was on the water, navigating the same part of the ocean where his journey began. Some of the landscape even looked familiar to him.

He quickly went inside the cabin and changed into a new pair of clothes, once again using a rain coat to quell the North pacific weather.

CHAPTER 3.14

He was on the water once again, the waves immediately made him feel nauseous as they battered him from side to side. Had he fallen from anything more than 700 feet, he would have died. Had he let go too early he would have hit the water with tremendous force also killing him. Instead, he hung on as long as he could and hit the water seconds after letting go of the craft.

He was driving blind, instead he headed towards shore due north on his compass. With an hour he'd reached Nome, Alaska. It was less than 100 kilometers or 62 miles to Wales.

He could no longer judge if he was winning, that the equipment had been damaged in the fall. Instead it was all about finishing this race in one piece.

Keeping the shoreline close, and travelling at 7 knots an hour, instead of 14, he rounded the corner towards Wales. *'Oh #%!*'* he thought. *'The GPS beacon'*

He'd kept it in the cabin but it looked as though it had been ransacked, he might not qualify for the win if he didn't have it. He cut power to the motor and went to look for it. Rummaging through the cabin he looked desperately for this piece of small equipment, lifting his bed, looking inside the cupboard, around the floor. Then he found it, it was on the floor under some old clothes. He put it in his inside pocket.

Grabbing a map from inside the cabin, he anxiously opened it while making his way back to the helm. Although the distance was small he didn't want to make a wrong turn. Wave after wave would hit the front of his craft, and every seventh wave or so would splash up into his face. Piloting the seas was much different than piloting by air.

He slowly approached the once very small town of Wales. Unbeknownst to him, the town was bustling. Thousands of media reporters had flocked to the scene. Cameras were set up for gatherings in and around small cities, who were relaying the feeds to the town.

As he got closer, he could see people with banners and posters lining the shores, at first just few then many, then thousands. He'd become a celebrity and didn't even know it. Slowly he approached. The finish line had been set up only hours before, as he took the craft out of gear it inched closer and closer until the craft cut the line.

Fireworks went off, a band played, and he was immediately greeted by the sponsors and organizers. Cameras crews pushed and shoved to get pictures of the man who circulated the poles and lived to tell about it.

"How does it feel to win that much money?" they'd shout. "Are you going to regale your tale one day?" Others would shout.

Instead he found himself looking for Melanie and his mother. When he found them he gave Melanie a great big kiss. It was the picture that made headlines, across the world, Time magazine, Rolling Stone, just about every magazine there was.

The following day he got his check, the unbelievable sum of 50 million dollars. Since he was a generous man, he refunded everyone half of their entrance fees; it just didn't seem fair to him, the entrance fee and such.

His friend from his hometown Dylan, never finished the race. Apparently he spent most of his time trying to get him disqualified from the competition, but was content on getting some of his money back.

Surprisingly, Peter Frontinac disappeared a year and a half after his insatiable win. Nobody knew where he went. It was like he just vanished.

CHAPTER 3.15

THE ELUSIVE MOUSE

And so, it was Peter that won that particular race. Although my family had paid the initial entry fee they decided not to participate in the actual race. Peter Frontinac ended up getting a ton of media coverage that went on well into the future, until his disappearance. Some say he was abducted for the money, others said he went to Nepal or Vietnam. I like to think he found some place that made him happy, away from all the media attention he got. If only he knew how to catch a mouse.

So where was I, ah yes, "ha, ha" said the crow.

It was about six in the morning and I went for a cigarette after not sleeping the previous night. There was a large amount of chatter from some birds; some particularly brave birds, birds that do not fly south for the winter. As the birds chirped it caught the attention of some squirrels and not just one or two, it was more like a dozen squirrels. Perhaps they were looking for hand outs like the rabbits got; a carrot or two to ease the cold of the night. But even the rabbits were cautious, to a rabbit every human is a hunter.

I went back into the house as the barrage of animals made me feel like I was being hunted. I began to cook some eggs and bacon a well deserved breakfast after braving the hellish nightmare of night which perpetually can get worse with no sleep and no dreams. Everyone knows there is no such thing as ghost or monsters in the night, but under the right circumstances it can appear as though these monsters exist.

The fact of the matter was this mouse had to be caught and soon.

But to my surprise a hunter who had been looking out for me stopped in to say hello. This particular hunter was just that, a hunter. Perhaps if certain monsters did exist during the night surely this hunter would hunt those nightmarish monsters. He was actually a friend of my mother's who'd decided to keep an eye on me, making sure I wasn't getting into any trouble.

"You're not going to put peanut butter on your toast?" he asked.

"No not today." I exclaimed "I think I'd rather use jam." And I quickly sat down to eat my bacon, eggs and toast.

"Did those rabbits eat the carrots you put out for them?" asked the hunter.

"Yes." I exclaimed.

"Have you caught that mouse?" he asked.

"Not yet, it continues to outsmart me." I replied.

"Maybe you need more peanut butter, or just use a mouse trap."

Just use a mouse trap easy for you to say. I'm trying to be humane, but instead I said nothing. Instead my attention was turned to the dog, who was insisting it was time for a walk. "Walk, walk" she'd say even though it came out as 'bark, bark'. Okay time to wash my face, once dogs start talking it's time for a reality check. Only a few more, what minutes, hours, days until I catch this mouse?

"Walk, walk." Okay little dog, let me get your leash and then... and then what?

I stepped out onto front porch. "Ha, ha" said the crow. Damn you crow, I picked up a rock with the leash still in my hand. With one quick toss the rock hurdled at an exceptional speed, which would be quite different for a rock something that usually stands still. It sped through the air, defying gravity and missed by only centimetres. "Ha" said the crow. It didn't even flinch; it just glared at me with the knowledge that it wasn't going anywhere.

I began to walk the dog who was now insisting we go for a walk; by gently pulling on the leash. As it would seem, I wasn't walking the dog, but rather the dog was walking me. The dog would pull on the leash trying to run to her favourite spots.

On the way back to the house a robin began to chirp. These bird brains are of few words, collectively, they usually agree with each other and say "yup." Somehow, agreeing that humans are seemingly less human since they often use cars to get around. But every once in a while they say "Sing." Now this was the case that particular day, the crow had somehow coerced these robins into coercing me to sing. So I whistled a tune, a tune that was playing though a radio earpiece impressed these robins oh so much that they hung around the house for days "Sing, sing." They'd chirp.

This in particular caught the attention of a magpie, a particularly intelligent magpie. Now, be it that I had a portable radio earpiece in my ear, the magpie did a particularly interesting routine to a commercial that was listening to. "Ahh yes." In French voice "the wonderful, yum, delicacies available at this particular time, are, oh yes, tantalizing to the mind body and spirit." Now I'm not sure but never in a thousand years would I have thought a magpie would do routine to a commercial and act it out in an almost perfect way; pecking at a food source every time the word food was mentioned. It was like I was living the commercial out in real life.

This of course made me think of one thing and thing only – I need to sleep. Instead I stood mouth ajar and a confused brow with the coldness of the morning gently burning my face. It was March but spring was late, the trees should have been blossoming with fresh leaves from spring but instead old man winter seemed to say he was still in charge.

Dazed and confused I walked back to the house with my dog pulling me along by its leash the whole way. Frustrated, I set some mouse traps with a bit of cheese and some peanut butter and said a prayer for the little mouse that would soon find its demise in the most lethal of none lethal mouse traps, then I waited.

Now day three without sleep wasn't much different than day two. I spent the evening drinking coffee and watching TV, even playing some video games. *'Mouse...mouse'* I began by making some breakfast some delightfully wonderful breakfast, bacon and eggs and toast, yes, toast with peanut butter. What a wonderful way to celebrate the greatest capture of a tiny rodent who was no longer welcome in 'Casa my house'. Forget humane, it was time to catch this devious rodent.

After loading the dishwasher I walked into the garage only to find that once again the bait had been taken with no evidence of a dead mouse anywhere. I sauntered to my bedroom and slept for a well deserved 20 hours. The only thing that followed me to bed that morning was my shadow. Ah yes my shadow the one elusive thing that Peter Pan sought to capture and reclaim, and for that reason got a name. I decided to name my shadow Peppercorn Ranch. I don't particularly know why that specific name, it's just as such it belonged to me. Once in while I wondered if I accidently woke with someone else's shadow this way, by giving it a name, my shadow would always return to me. I suppose it's not much different than naming an animal, a cat or dog, although mostly unconventional.

However, I had hurt me knee the day before. A small patch of ice had been particularly frozen and with an ungraceful step caused my foot to momentarily not work. Although designed to have five toes and support the weight of a full body, the frozen patch of ice turned out to be much more aggressive and caused me to fall on my back. My back did not hurt until the following morning when I realized the full force of the Earth had come crashing down on me during that fall, rather than me falling on the ice. My little dog poked her face near mine to ask if I was okay.

My back was sore this morning, but so was my head, I actually felt like kicking my foot since it allowed me to fall, but instead was rubbing my head as it too hit the ground hard. The restful sleep only postponed the pain until the time I awoke, but awake I was, and Peppercorn Ranch was nowhere to be found. As the sun illuminates most of the house by day I could only ever catch glimpses of Peppercorn Ranch.

Now this particular morning was not without incidents. A leaky dishwater hose decided it could no longer retain the hot water that fuelled the dishwasher. In fact, this hose was so lazy that it had decided to spew most of the dirty dish water out onto the kitchen floor, a floor that had no business being wet. So there was only one thing I could do, take this to the board of directors.

The board just happened to be some saltwater fish that I'd purchased. Although I was in charge the board generally agrees or disagrees depending on their fishy attitudes that day. Unfortunately the board generally decided that they were not going to clean up this fishy mess, that it would be up to me to clean the dishwater from the floor. *'Of course, how incredibly convenient for the board of directors but quite inconvenient for yours truly'* But with a wink and smile the board had spoken.

So, as I sopped up this dirty mess of rank smelling dishwater, who decided to poke his little head around the corner, that's right, the mouse. I immediately dropped the mop then tried to stomp the little bugger out of its existence only to discover it was much more cunning then I'd imagined. It quickly scurried into a hole it had carved out with its teeth allowing me to step into a swampy, swamp water collection of dishwater. Now then, this should not have bothered me, but given that the water broke the tension from foot and ground, for the second time in two days my full body weight hit the ground, with my clothes absorbing this swampy, swamp water mess; my back and head absorbing the rest. The last thing to fall was the mop which landed directly on my nose. While yesterday my other foot allowed me to fall, today the opposite foot caused me to hit the floor, with the inconvenient mop bopping me on the nose and my attire acting like a giant sponge, but what could I say, the board of directors had spoken.

To help me through these hard times I turned to a book, a book that is widely accessible, but rarely read. As I sat reading, with the rest of my body throbbing in pain, it made me think of this next story; and a story to be explained later.

CHAPTER 4.0

THE PRELUDE

For this next story to truly make sense, we need to travel back about 2000 years or so, say around 0 B.C, or 1 A.D. Now as much as people dislike religion or even have different views on the matter, they tend to believe in several truths, that this story is based upon a yearly celebration. This particular account is one account that may or may not have happened. For the purpose of this story we will assume this particular account to be true rather than fiction, even though it is a fictional event.

You need to imagine at this point in time somewhat of a lawless society, beggars, thieves, women having little or no rights, but especially the concept of war. That war was everywhere. That people were hungry all the time and often would go without food. That war was a way of life and it would seem that the largest, smartest army would always win. People fought because they had to and those who were better at it were treated better.

This story begins because the biggest threat wasn't from anywhere in the Mediterranean, at least not according to three wise men, but rather from somewhere in Asia. They came bearing gifts to a small child conceived of a virgin, a child who would make a great pilgrimage of peace to a far away land until, he returned some 33 years later.

To assure his parents that no harm would befall him, a small army would accompany him. That one day if he returned he would be made a king. He was taught languages along the way, as well as, any and all teachings relevant to, then, current standards. Because this was a war torn time, his loving family believed that a better future was possible for him. Through this, perhaps he'd have a better life then could be found closer to home.

And so it was by the age of two he'd already traveled further than most; on horseback to the Persian Gulf, by boat to the town of Karachi. Again on horseback across the land of India, stopping for supplies and rest as needed. After travelling just south of the Himalayas, they travelled into China headed for the city of Xi'an.

Now this pilgrimage was not for the faint of heart, in fact he'd learned about death at an early age. Many of those he was travelling with would fall victim to the weather, untreated wounds, snakes and snakebites. From a band of 60 men only half were left by the time they'd entered Zigong. He'd learned about thunder lizards giant reptiles that once ruled the Earth and even hoped to see some along the way. But rather in the dead of night it was another figure that frightened him more, a strange shadow. It was a shadow that seemed to be not from this world.

Eventually, the people began to look different as they gazed upon these unseen figures from an unseen desert. The locals spoke a dialect that hadn't been taught along the way. As a child and the voice of reason he sought not to have his remaining coterie engage in battle but rather to assure the hosts that it was in the name of peace.

"Can you tell me how to get to Xi'an?" he asked in his foreign tongue. Without words they'd point in the general direction.

By the age of 13 he'd travelled nearly 7000 miles, his teacher, also his closest companion was 55 years old by the time they'd reached the city. Of the 60 men that had accompanied him only 20 or so were left standing after the long journey.

When they reached the city they were met with awe. People stopped and starred as they entered the city. They'd never seen men like that before, and most of the men couldn't believe how peaceful a civilization could be. Instead of fighting for dominance they were working, farming, had homes. There was lush vegetation everywhere, roads, animals it was like arriving in Eden. The closer they got to the center of the city the more cause for alarm they caused. Eventually armed guards began to show up, as trespassers they were.

"Hands up, put your hands up" They shouted.

"We are travellers from a distant land," Jesush tried to explain.

But rather they were taken into prison. Now normally the army that was remaining would have fought to the death, however, they'd been travelling for so long and upon reaching their destination they found they were outnumbered. Rather than fight they decided cooperate only because they were planning on staying for some time, at least until they were ready to leave again.

Prison is not a place that is meant to be fun, especially if you are from out of town. For twenty days and nights the men were tortured, beaten and made bloody with only one of the men losing his life. In time, a multitude of people began to wonder their purpose, and talked their soldiers out of killing them. Over the next few months they were brought food, water and eventually let into the courtyard of the prison.

Once in a while the guards would shout and point at Jesush. The rest of the men would back off with him standing in the center of the courtyard, at which point a child roughly the age as him would enter. He was trained in the art of combat and would push him to fight. There first battle ended with Jesush a bloodied mess, the second not much different than the first. However the third time he'd learned just enough to defend himself against his distant counterpart; and this third battle near victory, the cloud of hostility had lifted and he, and the entourage, were welcomed more into the Asian culture.

***

The guests needed to learn their language. Simple yes, no and even thank you. Eventually it got so that they could communicate with each other, at least somewhat, as the guards of the keep also had trouble understanding what they had to say.

"What purpose do you have keeping us here?" The teacher would shout. They wouldn't reply just go about watching over the keep. Every once in a while, one of the men would fight back pushing a guard or stunning them with a swift punch until eventually a dozen guards or so would converge on him bringing him back to a cell until he'd learn to behave again.

In time, it was a young lady that took to fancying the young Jesush. She would enter the keep and make conversation with him. She explained,

"If it wasn't for you our guards would have killed you all." And sometimes,

"How many more are you?" She'd ask. Meaning are there more of you coming to this town.

"I don't understand." He'd reply.

Throughout the months that followed they learned much about each other, and as their friendship grew so did the liberties of the remaining group. He'd draw pictures in the ground trying to explain the lessons he'd learned during his travels and she, mathematics, art, ancient Chinese writings and song. She had a beautiful voice when she sang.

In time he became a young man and at the age 20 had learned much about their native culture. He could interact with his new found friends and felt accepted amongst them. His relationship with Xing, his female friend, had flourished into romance that captivated the city. It had been almost seven years since they'd arrived and Jesush had become deeply submersed in their culture.

Although his entourage had started with 60 men they were now just down to three. Guile, who'd come to love attention and celebrity status of being from a far off place. And then there was Joshua, his teacher who was getting ill from old age.

During his final months he'd lay in a small hut that was solely dedicated to him, and fed by those who cared enough about his worsening condition. During his final hours he called upon Jesush to tell him about a truth that he'd gone on living without.

"Jesush," he said. "You were born in a faraway place and to these people you've travelled with and protected you were sent, to learn in the name of peace." He coughed. "Someday, if you decide to return home they are to make you a king." And with his final breath closed his eyes and went to that eternal slumber.

'A King..?' he thought. He'd had no memory of the place his teacher talked about, the land from which he'd travelled from. No memory of his mother or father or even other siblings. His whole life the people around him protected him. He suddenly realized why he'd been chosen to make this pilgrimage, that one day he was to return and share the stories of his adventure to the people who'd sent him here. He suddenly realized why he was chosen, he was meant to return one day.

CHAPTER 4.1

By this time he'd made many friends. That same child who would beat him inside the keep, became a mentor to him. Over the years he'd learned many secrets of combat and the ancient secrets of meditation and tai chi and by the age of twenty he was indeed a man, skilled in Asian writing, art, song, mathematics and combat. It troubled him that he knew he'd have to leave these people one day; they'd become his family.

Things in his homeland were becoming quite difficult. Although at that time Israel was independent from Egypt, the Egyptian church sought to reclaim land and make slaves of a people who'd been free. Plus there was talk of a growing army to the North that could quite possibly overthrow even those from Egypt. Most people went about their own business but still paid homage to Egyptian authority. In fact most people forgot about Jesush and his travels. Although that particular story had brought much interest, and made jealous many would-be travellers, many believed he was indeed dead. It was only his mother and father that kept his memory alive in an attempt to accept he was all but dead.

***

At the age of 23 his final companion met his demise. Guile, suffered a heart attack and was entombed shortly after. But it was Jesush who felt alone. He was the last of his kind from a journey he barely knew he was to make. He'd been subjected to a language and way of life that was so different than the friends he'd been keeping, many of which refused to adopt, probably because they were too old to learn new things.

He began making trips to a waterhole where he could see his reflection. One day Xing decided to follow him there.

"I am different." He spoke in his adopted language. She turned to him and said

"The people here love you. You came to us a child and have grown into a man." "You were not as rude as the others who fought with us the whole time, although they were obligated to protect to you."

He gave her a kiss on the forehead.

"I have learned many things, but most of the teachings my teacher taught me I've forgotten." "My teacher said I am to be made a king if I return." He spoke.

This saddened Xing, she knew then that one day soon he'd leave to return home as she had learned to love him. She gave him a kiss and returned to the village.

He spent the next few days on his own, went out into the wilderness to talk with his spirit, to meditate, something he'd learned since arriving in Xi'an. It was then he decided to return home.

When he returned to the city a great many people had gathered to celebrate his departure. Then one of the elders spoke. "Your friend will accompany you during your journey. He is to watch over you during your journey." Peng bowed to his elder and accepted the task.

His friend was none other than the boy who'd beat him when he was to be disciplined, although it had been years since he'd struck him. They had eventually became friends. Peng taught him combat and the two competed in everything that had to do with battle, but he also frustrated Peng as he excelled at basic mathematics and language.

Jesush thanked the village for their kindness and promised he'd always value their teachings, but it also saddened him as he knew he might never return; and the two of them began their long journey back to Israel with no money and supplies.

It was Xing who followed him to edge of the city and sobbed as they walked past the last of the village huts. With a gentle wave and a heavy heart he blew her a kiss and gathered his strength for the journey ahead.

***

The first few days were spent following the paths out of the city. They were to rely on a map that his mentor and teacher had made while travelling to Xi'an. It showed a route through the forests for a long distance then a mountainous region and finally an ocean voyage. Neither of them spoke during the first few days.

"Did you love Xing?" Were the first words out of Peng's mouth. Jesush glanced back and said "Yes". He had never been in love before, in fact it was Peng that kept him from loving her; he could see that it was Peng that truly loved her.

And so, when it rained they put on furs to keep warm. They hunted for food and would make fire by night. They followed the stars as drawn by the maps and the sun by day. They collected fruits when they were available and carried as much as they could while they could.

It was during these nights that a familiar evil scarred him, that same unknown that haunted him as a child. He used to wake in the middle of the night while the rest of the entourage would slumber with the feeling that something in the darkness was watching him. A sort of monster that was unknown to human minds. This fear dissipated amongst the company of the village but seemed to return once he was alone again in the wilderness.

It is hard to imagine such a journey during this epoch of time; that an entire lifetime could be dedicated to a journey that was unequivocal even by modern day standards. At the age of twenty six Jesush was on his way to his home, a home he'd never even been to, only told stories from the company of his travels; but was still thousands of miles away from his destination.

***

Now at this point I need to remind you this just a story, it is one interpretation of an event that had very little information about it, at least its beginnings. It is history, perhaps, just the untold portion.

***

Along the way, he and Peng came across something very rare, very incredibly rare and no human eyes had ever came across anything similar. What makes this so special was the conditions that existed in a cavern and underground spring that allowed this anomaly to make it to the surface.

The water was extremely high in oxygen content, it was turquoise and this was not because of the rocks at a given depth, but rather the water itself. They had stopped there after weeks of travels, many relentless days of bush waking, as this was a road no man at this time had traveled, or any man since then. At first they were hesitant to drink from this fountain, as of course the water was turquoise when they cupped it in their hands. Jesush drank it first, his stomach felt queasy after drinking it, much like a stomach sickness. He looked at his hands and suddenly the protruding veins subsided within his hands. His hands looked younger. They had stumbled across the fountain of youth.

They decided to map their find, at least the best they could. It relied on a few visual makers, mountains that took on human forms, a certain amount of paces with "x" marking the spot. As they left Jesush glanced back, he couldn't help but feel something or someone was watching him, it sent chills down his spine. He turned back to look at the fountain this time positive that something was there, then in his brain, was whispered a little secret about the future. He panicked then began to run to catch up to Peng who was already off in the distance. He never forgot what was said to him.

He drank some of the water than began to run, he ran fast, faster than he'd ever run before. He passed the bottle to Peng as he ran passed him, but kept on running. Peng looked behind him then he too began to run. Peng couldn't keep up, but he ran till he was dehydrated then drank some water. He felt younger, stronger and this time caught up to Jesush. They ran for the better part of the afternoon without tiring and when they finally stopped neither of them felt tired. It was the water it made them stronger and younger.

CHAPTER 4.2

After the first year they arrived at the border of what is now Burma and another year later arrived in the City Chittagong. They then travelled to the city of Mumbai then onto the port town of Karachi which was on the map that had been written when their voyage began. From there their spirits began to lift as the route home was always closer than it had been the previous day.

The map that had been drawn for him showed travel by boat, so using furs and gold they purchased a boat from a fisherman in Karachi, who also taught them how to fish.

They set sail a few days after that, along the coast of now Pakistan and Iran. The map that had been drawn some 25 years ago was not completely accurate; it showed a passage, by boat, into the land of India. They followed the directions as best they could, however, instead of entering the Persian Gulf, they were side tracked and followed the coastline to Oman, then Yemen and into the Red Sea. The journey by boat took less time than walking. While Peng grew tired of the rocking motion and the sea sickness and cursed the water with every breath, Jesush on the other hand quite enjoyed the sea. Before reaching the coastline near Karachi, he'd never seen the sea. The last time he was on the water he was only a child and could not remember much of his early years. He did however grow weary of eating fish every day and only ate when he was very hungry.

By day they used the sails and ors to travel the lengths on the ocean and by night they'd camp along a suitable beach to sleep and rest. They travelled up the coastline until they reached the city of Mecca. It was there that their roles reversed, for the first time Jesush was among people who looked more like him while Peng on the other hand decided to keep his visage covered.

They docked their boat where they could and entered the slums of the city. It was a rundown place, rats, wooden shanties, the sick, the elderly, each glaring at the duo with eyes worthy of piercing the soul. Jesush began to wonder if he was home, or rather if this was what his kingdom would look like. How was he to help these people? He never knew exactly what his home would look like, but somehow the image of the village he'd travelled to, Xi'an, was more how he imagined it. He truly had no recollection of the place he was born.

Now Peng, needed to know the language, the dialect, and Jesush tried as best he could to teach Peng as best he could. In that sense their roles were reversed, because, there was a time when Peng tried to teach him as best he could, the ways of Xi'an. Still, the language was new to Jesush. His teacher, before passing away, taught him some of the different dialects; words which came in handy in the trek across India, as well as, now, in the great city of Mecca. He also had set aside some coins for Jesush provided he ever decided to return. In fact there was a time many sought to steal that small fortune from him and had been protected, always, from those types of oppressors.

They found themselves in a rundown bar of sorts drinking wine amongst a plethora of hooligans, each drinking to their hearts content. Among them all a girl named Ruth who watched them and danced a seductive dance. While tables were full of the inebriated she moved slowly and seductively behind these men, placing one hand on a shoulder or back then gently sliding it to the next man while keeping her gaze upon the two of them. They drank together, clanking their cups, as a measure of congratulation for their journey and their newfound good fortune. She used her finger to gesture to the duo to follow her and when they did they found themselves amongst not one but four belly dancing ladies, who welcomed them with open arms.

The next morning was a little hazy, they both had hangovers but neither could wipe the smiles from they're faces. They gathered their things and walked further into the town of Mecca. There, they came across a man by the name of Peter. He was to be executed for stealing from the shops in and around Mecca. This was not the first time he had been apprehended. The officials shouted "Does anyone know why this man should not be executed." The crowd was silent.

The officials asked again, "Does not one of you care enough, so that I might spare his life?" The crowd was silent again. Jesush and Peng looked at each other, and then Jesush spoke "What is his crime." The crowd gasped and awed as they turned to look at him.

"Theft of course, you thieves." The clergy said.

"Since when does a hungry man get sentenced to death for putting food in his belly?"

The clergy was silent.

"What will it take to set this man free?" Jesush asked.

The clergy laughed. "Do you not know, nothing can save this man from the sins he's committed"

Jesush walked to the middle of the crowd. "Suppose I were to defeat your best fighter in battle? Would you not say then his life would belong to me?"

The clergy laughed again. "As a high priest appointed by the lineage of pharaoh it is his law then mine. I will grant you request."

The crowd began circle around Jesush as a big giant soldier of pharaoh entered the scene. He was big, standing a foot taller and more muscular. His first swing was slow and lethargic; Jesush had no trouble ducking it. The second swing was as well, but this time was countered by a punch to the ribs, just enough to stun the beastly man. They circled each other, the ogre would rush in trying to bear hug his opponent; but time after time his offensive was avoided by the oppressor. Jesush was fast, blocking punches with ease and delivering stunning, quick blows to the soldier. The soldier began to feel embarrassed as Jesush using a fighting style he'd never seen, a fighting style taught to him by his friends from the East, continued to foil the giant. He backed away then did a series of spinning kicks that left the giant speechless. Jesush got close to the giant and got him in a headlock and squeezed so tightly that the giant could eventually barely stand. What the leviathan didn't know was that all that walking had made him very strong and that he'd been trained by the people of his distant land a few, shall we say, secrets in combat; a skill also mastered by Peng.

The giant dropped to his knees and with his last breath fell to the ground. The crowd cheered as Jesush emerged victorious. It took a few minutes for the ogre to regain consciousness, but he could hardly believe he'd lost to his underestimated opponent.

The High priests honouring their agreement removed the shackles from Peter's arms. He was bruised, dirty and had not eaten in days. "Thank you." He said. "You have saved my life and for that I am in debt to you. I will accompany you and your friend on your journey wherever you decide to go."

"You need not gravel before the man who set you free." He said.

He got up off his knees.

"We are travelling to Jerusalem. You can repay me by getting us there safely."

"Of course, but it is a dangerous journey, there are bandits, thieves, lucky for you I know all of them and know the way."

Peter grabbed an apple from a cart and tossed it to his new found friend.

"Tell me, why do want to travel to Jerusalem anyways?"

"I am a King, I am returning home."

"A King!!?? Well you can't go around saying that, the priest will make you suffer. For now you will be a carpenter."

"A carpenter?" Asked Jesush.

"Yes well, someone who works with wood."

"Wood?"

Although he'd been taught the language during the pilgrimage to Xi'an, he'd learned to speak and communicate in an Asian dialect. At least now he had a guide who could help him get to where he was going.

"What makes you think you are a King anyway?" asked Peter.

"I travelled to a distant land when I was young and was told I would become a King if I returned." said Jesush

"You!!?? I remember that, that was many years ago. That story was told across the land. But we, we thought you'd died. Ha Ha, but you didn't. Perhaps you are a descendent of David, that would make you a King, or a son of Pharaoh. And what of your friend, why does he cover his face?"

Peng removed his scarf.

"Oh I see, he is from the land you travelled to, well welcome to, not Egypt, that's somewhere else." Peter scratched his head. "Ah welcome to... welcome Israel, yah welcome to Israel."

Peter extended his hand only to have no response from Peng.

The trio began walking north towards Jerusalem. Along the way they both spoke of stories from their past. Jesush tried to explain the wonder and beauty of the land they'd travelled to, while Peter spoke mostly of the havoc in the homeland. How armies from the North were trying to take control, while the high priest of days of Pharaoh were trying to rule Israel. The country was in civil war over poverty and malnutrition and neither side had answers on how to help. Although he was amazed at a few things Jesush could do that he couldn't, including songs or psalms and art; two practices that were not in use in the Middle East at that time. Even the concept of farming seemed alien when Jesush would try to describe it.

The next day a man caught up with the trio. He followed them for quite some time before they caught on that they were being followed.

Peng quickly pulled a blade from his belt as the man approached from behind.

"Where did you learn to fight like that." asked the man. He was tall, taller than Peter and strong, built like an ox, his skin as black as night. He was asking about the fight the previous day.

"I have never seen a man fight like that before." continued the man, but no words came from the mouths of Peng, Jesush or Peter.

The man extended his hand to greet them. "My name is Mohammad." Both Peng and Jesush were unaware of this custom, but Peter was quick to greet him.

It was getting dark, so they lit a fire talked into the night sharing stories of their youth, some sad and others full of excitement.

"Perhaps." began Mohammad. "One day you will teach me to fight like that."

Jesush being a man of honor got up from the fire and began to show him some of the defensive fighting tactics he'd learned. Mohammad was eager to learn and the training amused both Peng and Peter. They laughed as they watched the two exchange fighting techniques.

"In the morning, I will be gone." Said Mohammad. "But I will always think of you three as friends." Shaking hands once more with Jesush. In the morning when they woke, he was gone.

CHAPTER 4.3

They hiked back along a route Peter was sure would bring them home, although he'd only travel the route once; which found him in great deal of trouble until his rescue, constantly insisting he knew the way.

Jesush was quite surprised at the way Peter would find means of survival. Every once in a while he'd distract a cart or vendor, then slide fruit or bread into his pocket, sharing with the rest of the group as needed.

Before long they came across a tax collector, who was taxing people on they're travels.

"Please pay the fee." said Mathew

"I am afraid we cannot." said Peter. "We are traveling with a carpenter and his friend from a faraway land; we have nothing to offer you."

"Perhaps your shoes then or the canteens you carry."

Peng caught on to the trap early, he noticed some rustling in some bushes not far from Mathew and went to investigate. There he found three, then four pirates and shouted out to Jesush.

"It's a trap." He said in his foreign dialect.

Peter was the last to understand but grabbed a stick from the ground. Mathew stood up, "So you see, you must pay the tax."

Peng raced back to rejoin the group, this time followed by four other men who drew blades in hot pursuit of Peng. Once the group was reunited they were surrounded by men who were trying only to rob them.

Mathew spoke up again, this time saying "Now pay the tax and we will let you go free."

He took his eyes away for just a slight second, long enough for Jesush to make his attack. He swung at his arm causing Mathew to drop his sword. Peng was next pushing one of the assailants then retrieving a bow stick from the ground with his foot and began to swing wildly at the would be robbers. One of the robbers tripped on a rock and fell to the ground. Mathew kept trying to retrieve his sword but instead found it was being kicked away by Jesush. Peter was the last to get involved, although generally humble had great strength and wrestled one of the attackers to the ground. They twisted in dirt, Peter hammering on the robber as often as he could. Then he stopped.

"Simone?" He asked.

"Yes that's me." He replied

Simone now had a bloody face and several bruises to the torso. Peng and Jesush battled on fighting, two to one, against the other bandits, unaware of Peter's long lost friend.

"I thought you went North, to fight the great armies."

"No." he replied. "I got scared then tried to head south to find you; these men have been helping me as we have been helping each other."

The battle slowly started to dissipate generally with Mathew and his group of bandits on the ground. They had been beaten by three men who would not pay the tax they asked for.

Jesush went and picked up Mathews sword, then returned it to him. "As you can see." he stated, "We cannot pay the tax you are asking for." While the rest of the bandits were still rolling around in the dirt from they're injuries.

Peter spoke up, "Jesush." he said. "Let me introduce you to Simone."

Simone stood up holding his gut then extended his hand to greet Jesush. Then Simone introduced him to rest of the group.

"Of course you know Mathew; the other three are Paul, Luke." They greeted him as well as they rose to their feet.

"We are on a journey to Jerusalem, I have been away from home for a very long time." said Jesush.

"It's not safe." Said Simone. "The armies from the North have been showing up in larger and larger numbers. They say they are here only to learn about our customs; but still, the high priests maintain the priests are still in control and still the main governing body."

"Then maybe they will listen to Jesush, he's going to become a king." said Peter.

The rest of the entourage turned their attention to Jesush.

"You." Said Mark. "You are the one who made a great pilgrimage. People were told you were dead. Ripped to shreds by the beasts not known to this region. Can it be you have returned to bring balance and prosperity to this once beautiful land."

"Perhaps." Replied Jesush. "It would seem that those in charge are not doing what they are supposed to be doing, given that people steal, and rob from travellers who are merely making a voyage."

"Perhaps you should join us." Said Peter. "You can be some sort of, what's the word, liaison."

"Of course, if it means changing the way things are now." Said Mark.

And just like that a group of three became seven.

That evening the sat around a fire, drinking wine and telling stories about their pasts. Jesush spoke of frozen lakes they had crossed in India, that he'd walked on water while the others told stories about their pasts. Some of love, some of pain, nonetheless, stories. Peng sat and listened, but said nothing all night, drinking wine with the new entourage.

The next morning, Jesush's hangover was so bad; he wanted never to drink again. He wasn't used to it like the other men were. He had never even drank before arriving in the small fishing town only a week or so earlier. Although the nights were merry, the following day was not always as fun.

***

The following day, they continued to hike North East towards Israel. Yet somehow, Peter had forgotten the way and took them on a path towards Alexandria, perhaps thinking it was the city they were seeking.

The next group of people they met were two fishermen, John and Bartholomew, Just outside the city of Alexandria. They were sitting on a beach starring off into the ocean. They had been fisherman their whole lives. In the last year or so had not been catching any fish, and creditors wanted to take John's boat, and, did indeed try to take his boat.

"I want to talk to the high priests or the Roman generals. It was not our fault, there are so many fishermen these days, and fewer fish to feed the masses. When they return they will take my boat away from me." said Bartholomew.

"Well you are in luck, I am to become a king upon my return to Jerusalem; I will build you many boats bigger and grander than any amongst these shores. Boats big enough to travel great distances in order find fish." said Jesush

John and Bartholomew were sold on the idea, but had trouble believing it to be true,

"If you are a king why do not have any wealth or armies?"

"These will be my generals." he answered. "I intend to make this kingdom as beautiful as the land I travelled from, and can see I'll have my work cut out for me. I just need to speak to those who knew of my travels and my teacher."

That evening while drinking the wine, four more people approached the camp fire, in search of food. The king topic was the number one topic of discussion all evening. Could it be that he was really a king?

The last person they met along the way was a man named Judas. He had gotten so drunk the night before that he'd punched a woman in the face and was still drunk when he was approached by the group. He had nothing to say as they asked him if he was okay.

"Are you okay?" they asked a second and third time.

There was barely a response. But in a drunken stupor he rose to his feet then attempted to pull a blade from his belt. "My name is Judas, and you may not pass." Then he dozed off again nearly falling to his feet. One of the men approached him and then slapped him, to try to have him regain his normal functions; still there was no response. Again he slapped him and this time he rose to his feet again. "My name is Judas and you.... may.... not." He fell asleep, in the middle of his sentence.

Although the rest of the group found this frustrating Jesush found it quite amusing. For once he gazed upon another who had suffered from the drink, just as he had, however it was someone else who was intoxicated. Rather than abandoning the man they decided to set up camp overnight until the group was ready to tread on the following morning.

Spirits were high amongst the group, they'd found a sort of camaraderie in each other's company, in all there were fourteen people in the group, including Peng and Jesush. The sat in awe as Jesush would regale them with the tales of his travels as most had not ventured to far from the city of Jerusalem.

In some way however, they were all criminals, most were thieves, some beggars but all of them could fight and fight they could, scuffles would break out if the wine was not passed or the food was being hogged.

That evening everyone slept soundly except for Jesush.

CHAPTER 4.4

They entered the city, news spread about his return. That a king was returning home. People lined the streets just to get a glimpse of the group. People cheered, and some of them even started to wave palm branches as the travelled the city streets.

That evening the group sat down to a dinner, it was the first time they had eaten like real men; just about every other time was around a camp fire, cooking meat over an open flame. It was a feast. For the first time in a long time Jesush began to feel like a king. He took some bead then broke it, and passed it around the table, then filled every cup with wine and offered a sort of thanks to his new friends.

The next day he travelled aboard a donkey to meet with King Herod, who he assumed would place a crown upon his brow for his heroic journey, as promised. Yet, he could not offer the royal divinity he sought, and sent him to see Pontius Pilate.

The next thing he knew he was being bludgeoned by men in army uniforms.

Then he awoke, he'd been asleep.

He looked around the camp fire, a fire that was burning much dimmer then it had before. Everyone was asleep soundly still. Some were sleeping back to back whilst sitting in an upright position, others asleep in the dirt. He wiped the sweat from his brow, it would be dawn soon. They would be using John's boat to cross back towards the land of Israel. Although a passage by foot was possible Peter assured him the route by boat would be much safer and take far less time.

He stood up, and then walked towards the beach unaware that that Peng was sitting, nearby, the shoreline.

"How come you are not asleep?" Asked Jesush.

"I cannot remember the way home." He replied. "We have travelled a great distance in very little time and cannot remember how to get home."

To make him feel better Jesush pointed in a general direction. "It is that way."

"How do you know for sure?" Asked Peng.

"I have been using the stars as direction. I was told on the way here that the stars are the same every night. That they are there for travellers to find their way home." said Jesush.

"What about the water we found? When I drink it I become stronger, faster, but know, there is very little left." said Peng.

"I too felt stronger, when I first drank of it, the blood vessels in my hand seemed to disappear, it seems to bring youth. Perhaps this water is like none other on Earth and perhaps we should not tell anyone of this, they may try to take it from us."

They agreed then talked until dawn broke.

"Your people say the sun is god, that it shines everywhere and brings life to everything it touches. Do you agree with that?" Asked Jesush.

"When I was younger, I believed it only shone upon our village. Now that I am older I can see that it shines down upon everyone equally."

"Perhaps." Said Jesush. "But why then does it disappear and reappear at different points on the Earth." Knowing the answer he stated "I believe it is because the Earth is round, like the moon, that somehow it circles us, to give us life."

CHAPTER 4.5

One by one the group awoke to the following day, bellies aching from drink and hunger. Feeding a group of 14 was becoming difficult. More and more they needed to steal to keep from starvation. Although Jesush never stole, the rest of the entourage were quite skilled at it. While Jesush spent his youth in travel and in teachings, at first as a prisoner then as a guest; the other new members spent their time avoiding starvation by stealing and trading stolen goods, it was their lifestyle. But, in these times did what they needed to do to survive.

Jesush started to wonder about his mother and father. His whole life no matter how hard he tried, he could not remember them. His teacher had once said that his mother was of great beauty, and his father an intelligent man, but Jesush had never met them. He wondered if they were still alive, still breathing the same air that keeps the soul inside the body. He missed them, he longed for them. Perhaps they would hear of his return and find him; if they were still alive.

The sun seemed to rise quickly that morning, and one by one shone lightly upon the faces of those asleep. They groaned and murmured as it hit their faces unwilling to return to light of day. But slowly, one by one, came back to life.

Peng had already caught three fish at dawn and began to cook them up for breakfast for the rest of the entourage. They hated fish at breakfast, it wasn't as wholesome as eggs or lamb but for the time being, it would do.

As day dawned, while the sun was one quarter from its noon position, the group boarded the boat bound for Israel. It was crammed, 14 men with very primitive sailing technology. John, a great fisherman, had taken the time to construct fourteen ors from a wooded forest. Although it took more than a few days to carry the wood back to the campsite and fabricate the ors from elongated trees; often fighting with the others who wanted to use it as firewood. When they boarded the boat it ran smoothly across the water.

Judas was the first to speak out from having to row. "It bothers me Jesush that you will not row with the rest of us."

"He is the captain." Exclaimed Peter. "It is not his duty to row; he will guide us to our location."

Jesush upon hearing this kindly asked to take Judas' place and continued to row until the sun set.

The rocky coastline made it difficult to simply beach the boat just anywhere, but as night dawned they went ashore to spend evenings on solid ground. Again the wine was passed and they drank to their heart's content and again everyone went to sleep.

Now, most were very skeptical about returning to Jerusalem. It had become a staging ground for the Roman armies and most were hesitant about returning, especially because of their take on thieves. They were very close, less than 200 kilometers from an Israeli port. Most dreaded this journey but not Jesush or Peng. Peng was eager to see the land his friend and new king would govern.

As dawn broke the following day, the ship set sail yet again and by noon the following day they had reached their destination. Jesush was the first to set foot on the beach and picked up mounds of sand and kissing it, falling to ground and hugging it with extraordinary content. He had never been so happy in his entire life. After 33 years of travelling the world, he was finally home.

CHAPTER 4.6

AT THE AGE OF THIRTY THREE HE'D RETURNED TO THE LAND OF ISRAEL.

"Your King has returned." he shouted as walked the sandy shores of the beach.

The other men grabbed the lines of the boat and began to pull it ashore.

Now unfortunately, there was no real plan upon his return, no prescribed battle plan, no meditated outcome of arrival, this was mostly for Jesush, he had returned to his home and was in a company of men that he wanted close to him should he become a king.

They walked for a few miles to a fishing town about five miles down the beach. From there everyone went their separate ways. Peter and Simone went to steal some food, some of the others were had their attention positioned to salesmen selling different items, but it was Jesush who found something different.

A fair maiden caught his eye. He had never seen such beauty before. She was carrying a small woven basket that had linens in it from the market. Their eyes met, but she looked away rather quickly. This bothered him, so he moved ever-so-gently closer to her. She looked up at him taking her attention away from the linen she was considering purchasing, then started to walk away.

Jesush followed her through the market, never once removing his glance from her. She was startled, afraid, but intrigued. He hid near some woven baskets and watched her as she moved through the market place. She moved so elegantly and gracefully. He had to speak with her, but didn't know what to say.

She had long black hair and beautiful blue eyes, almost something Shakespearean about her beauty. He ducked around the backside of the kiosks, so that as she moved slowly from one kiosk to the next, she would eventually run into him.

He stepped out in front of her as she went to walk down the dirt street. She had nothing to say, neither did he. He went to let her pass just as she went to step around him and found themselves again as the glimmer in each other's eyes.

"Excuse me." She said.

He said nothing then let her walk around him.

He watched as she walked off into the distance, looking back ever so slightly at him. That was his cue he needed to say something or lose her forever. He ran and caught up with her.

"Could I carry your basket for you?" he asked.

"No." she replied.

"Well perhaps I could walk you to your home." he asked again.

"No." she replied, but this time gave a smirk smile.

"Well what is your name?" He asked as she continued to walk away.

"Mary." She said.

He was in love.

"Mary." He said. "I shall make sure the world never forgets your name."

She smiled again, and then slowly walked away.

He was in a daze, and could hardly think straight. He watched her as she moved ever so gracefully along the road. It wasn't long before he heard someone talking but couldn't make out the words. Again words, but words with no meaning, he hadn't taken his gaze off her. But the third time the words sounded clearer. "Jesush." shouted Peter. He turned to him.

"What's gotten into you?" He asked.

"A maiden." he replied. "The most beautiful maiden I have ever met."

"Well there is no time for romancing now, tomorrow we travel to Jerusalem." exclaimed Peter

'My birthplace' he thought. *'My mother and father'* he longed for them, and wondered if they were still alive.

"But tonight we feast." exclaimed Peter.

The men had traded some fish for a fine pig which was roasted over a massive flame, which could be seen for miles. Even the libations were in plenty that evening. It started quietly, men stuffing their faces as though they had not eaten in weeks, until they were all full; followed by a debauchery that had been unmatched since the entourage had gotten together. Stories of laughter and sorrow filled the moonlit sky, and there seemed to be no end in sight to the good fortunes they encountered that evening.

Finally after weeks without saying a word Peng spoke up.

"I have found." he said, and the entourage went silent to listen to what he had to say. "You are a bunch of thieving, lying, Neanderthals." The silence remained for a second or two then was shortly followed by a huge uproar of laughter.

"Your friend." exclaimed one of the men. "He does speak after all."

One by one the party went to sleep from over drinking, and as dawn neared only a few were still in the company of the fire and wine.

That night Jesush had another dream.

He was sitting around a table with all of his friends, eating like a king, on bread, meats and vegetables. One by one all the people around the table stood and pointed to him, so he stood as well. He then walked through a corridor and found people shouting and throwing things at him until he came to rest at the base of a cross.

He opened his eyes and took a deep breath. He figured he'd been asleep for hours, but the sun still hadn't graced the horizon. Judas was still awake and was dancing to the night sky, yelling and screaming at the stars.

He walked over to talk to him.

"Ha, ha." said Judas. "They say you are to be a king, so tell me king why I should kneel to you."

Jesush did not reply.

"My whole life has been without purpose, so why is it that you bring purpose to my life now?" asked Judas.

Jesush replied. "Have I wrong you in some way?"

Judas fell to his knees and began to cry. "No, not you who has wronged me; perhaps never you who has wronged me."

"Why do you cry then?" asked Jesush.

"Because it is my life, that has been without purpose." replied Judas.

The sun began to rise and Jesush explained in words to bring comfort "It shines on us all equally, even in lands far, far away, this everlasting light."

Judas rose to his feet, and began to stumble back to the fire, a fire that wasn't much more than coals and ashes. "Perhaps." He said. "You are to be a king."

CHAPTER 4.7

The following day wasn't much different from the evenings of recent pasts, men sick from the drink, groaning, mumbling and passing gas almost habitually. The sun, however, was quick to wake most of them as the heat of midmorning became too unbearable for the men to continue their slumber.

Jesush didn't know it then but his story began to become regaled as the men in his company, over the previous few days had been telling everybody they were travelling with a king. Word began to spread far and wide about this new king, however, Jesush knew he had to seek out those who would make him king, as long as they were able to keep their promise.

As the sun sat nearing midday, the entourage finished off what was left from the feast the previous night. Several of them had already wandered into town to fetch needed supplies. Both Jesush and Peng realized it might become hard to keep track of everybody; when travelling together to a destination, they knew where they were going, but, without the destination they were free to walk about as seen fit.

Peter was right beside Jesush when he woke and said "It is time for us to travel to Jerusalem."

They gathered their things and the provisions they would need for the 30 kilometer trek from their ocean side camp. In less than half a day they'd travelled through sea town of Tel-Aviv and were on route to Jerusalem, all men accounted for, and some of them had gone on ahead.

There were many people making that same journey, in fact the trail looked more like a road, far different than any travelled during his distant travels. But with backs turned to him he'd constantly catch up with the women travelling in front of him hoping to catch a glimpse of Mary, the beautiful maiden he'd met the previous day.

It would seem luck was not on his side that day, every time he'd approach a women from the back found disappointment that it was not the maiden he sought and longed for. Until, he recognized at first the basket, then the dress, he was sure it was her.

He followed from a distance then picked a flower from the side of the road and quickly caught up with her.

"Don't you know, it is dangerous for women to travel alone." He said while walking behind her.

She turned immediately and looked at him. "You." she said. "Have you not the courtesy to leave a woman be?" But then she smiled when she saw the flower.

"Can I help you to carry you things?" he asked.

"No." she replied. Then slowly began to change her mind. "Oh, all right" she said. "But if you steal from me I will, I will, I will have you apprehended" she was a bit flustered.

They walked for a while without saying anything.

"Mary." he said. "I have never met a woman as beautiful as you." she smiled nervously.

"Enough about me." she said "What about you. Where are your mother and father?"

"I have never met them." he replied

"Oh really, and how is it you have never met them before." she asked

"Well" he replied. "I was asked to make a great journey in the name of peace to a distant land, and now have returned to take my place at the throne."

She had heard the story from years past but never believed it to be true.

"I have heard that story." she said "But that is not a true story that boy died during his travels and was never heard from again. And even so, if you are him whom you say you are, this land has been suffering for a long time, war is everywhere and the high priests are likely to lose their power to govern since the soldiers from the North have taken hold of this land."

"Then I will ask of both of them to hold true to their promise to make me king."

She laughed. "A king and where is your army." He stopped and pointed to some of the men still lagging behind him.

They walked and talked for the remaining journey, he eager to mystify her with stories of travels, cities, villages and cultures beyond this seemingly boxed in area of the world, and she would speak mostly of her youth, her parents, brothers and sisters.

By the time they'd reached the city of Jerusalem they had been talking for nearly 2 hours. When they got there, she tried several times to leave to return to her home, but he was persistent wanting not to part company. Eventually, she told him where she could be found and hurried off into the busy city. Jesush chased after her, took her in his arms and gave her a kiss. She blushed, then wandered in the direction home, looking back only to meet his gaze of love and admiration.

Peng and Judas were not far behind and teased him a bit about his new found love, but he didn't care, he wanted only to see her again.

CHAPTER 4.8

Unbeknownst to Jesush, his story was travelling far and wide. His entourage had been spreading the word of his return, but over time, the story began to change, to manifest itself into talks of revolution and of peace.

This story was particularly interesting to one woman who years ago gave her only son to the government of the time to make a great journey to a far away land. Her name was also Mary and had been a virgin before she gave birth to a young healthy child she named Jesush. For years she had been waiting for this moment, but, often felt her prayers for his safe return had always gone unanswered. She would listen to the townspeople then ask very kindly where this person could be found.

Peter had been missing at least a few days since they'd arrived in Jerusalem. The entourage found themselves eating dinners together but by day Jesush was telling a different story. His was trying to help his fellow man and was treating the sick and elderly was medicine not practiced at this particular time in this part of the world.

The fear of revolution had been brought forward to the local magistrate who could easily put an end to the magic he seemed to be performing should they feel the need. Ironically, it was the armies to the North, from Rome who were ever so slightly more in control, during that time, as they sought to govern in a more peaceful manner that ultimately gave them more control.

When Peter finally made his appearance the following morning, he had with him a donkey, obviously stolen or traded with stolen goods.

"If you are to be a king." he began "You should at least try to act like one." then gave the donkey to Jesush.

The following day he rode through the streets of Jerusalem to a crowd that waved palm branches for him as they travelled towards the office of the magistrate seeking his crown promised to him so many years earlier. He entered the town a hero, a hero who'd been forgotten and thought for dead.

Peng the closest of friends, aside from Peter, kept his face covered. For the first time in his life he was somewhere completely foreign to him. He had already been shunned for the way he looked several times since beaching upon the Red Sea and was at times afraid, afraid for his life, afraid of never returning home, afraid of being different.

Now, I suppose I need to stop there. Most of you have heard what happened to Jesush after Palm Sunday. He was bludgeoned, crucified and left for dead only to have survived and lived, as not only a legend, but a god. But I will tell you what happened after the crucifixion.

The mother Mary was reunited with her son after he fell off the cross under his own weight.

The disciples were asked to, in their own words, recount what had happened over the brief time they knew Jesush.

Most of the writings went to Greek philosophers who studied the writings and number system still used to this day.

Peng never returned home, but found a fondness for the Indian people of India and lived there until his death fifty seven years after the crucifixion.

Jesush went on to have a baby with Mary, his love from the moment he saw her.

Many of the disciples went into exile, as did Jesush and his family. Most of the disciples built houses for travellers that were far from home. Places they could visit and pray for safe travels.

CHAPTER 4.9

Something had been puzzling me, why was it, this mouse could not be caught. Had it gone to super mouse school, a school for rodents, rodents who could evade capture from mortal men? And why had this particular mouse brought so much misfortune to a single mortal man.

So, I did what any man would do, grabbed a pencil and a piece of paper then designed as many mouse traps I could think of. My house transformed into a battlefield, man against mouse. Weeks of hearing this mouse scurry through the rotten timber of the attic had left me with little or no sleep. I found a case of black mascara left behind from a female friend some years earlier and painted the underside of my eyes, war paint. But it didn't stop there; I found some old army clothes and fastened a bandana around my head, big boots to keep my feet warm, but most importantly army pants and an army shirt. Surely, I would catch this mouse.

I need to be clear about something, although I say this was my house it actually belonged to my mother and once in a while friends of hers would stop in to see how I was doing. This particular morning the hunter friend showed up.

"What the fuck are you doing wearing all those army clothes?" I barely had an answer. Sort of like a dog who gets caught stealing or doing something they're not supposed to be doing, or perhaps a deer in headlights.

"I'm trying to catch that mouse." I stated.

"That same mouse who has been trying to catch for the last few weeks?" he asked.

"Yes." I replied.

"Well I am going to meet with your mother who is out of town for a while, it will be your job to look after the house while she and I are away." said the hunter.

"No problem." I replied. *'Perfect'* I thought to myself. No longer would this house be a house, but a battlefield, good versus mouse.

"Do you want breakfast?" he asked. "I was going to make some peanut butter toast."

"Sure." I replied; a bit frustrated with my answer.

After he closed the door behind him leaving me alone with my dog, the winged bug and my thoughts I began to revise the battle plan. *'Three mouse traps in the attic, three in the garage, two in kitchen and living room...'* "Perfect." I said out loud. Now to wait.

As any man might tell you waiting for something is not quite as rewarding as getting it, parents might say the waiting is the best part, but I disagree, the waiting can create madness.

Unbeknownst to me the queen bug or rather the little winged bug inside my house had given birth to a plethora of smaller bugs, all with the god given job of decomposing things that they come into contact with. The house I lived in was not that old, and was in no, or was at no point, ready to start decomposing. So one by one I caught these bugs inside a glass then released them into the wild. I felt my heroic duties had been completed for the day so I went about tidying up the rest of the house as best I could.

Night after night I heard the creature scurrying around at first in the attic, then in the walls, then somewhere in the floor. Every scratch opened my weighted eyes like a fulcrum or lever would on a much heavier object. I walked out of my room and unintentionally set off one of my mouse traps to a great big bucket of sand falling on my head. After spitting out the remaining granules, I went into the basement tripping on the two final stairs. Tripping on the stairs set off a series of unfortunate events. I landed on a rake, a rake that sped at tremendous speeds towards my head, and a head that incurred a brutal impact from the rake. I stumbled knocking a bunch of shelves that relieved a bowling ball from sitting upon it. The bowling ball then rolled off the shelf hitting the hot water tank, forever damaging it, and, as a result I got no more hot water.

'Idiot' I thought to myself. The problem was I was on a budget that could not allow for a new hot water tank; no more would I be having hot

showers let alone clean dishes and hot running water. Truly the mouse was winning.

To make matters worse, the noise had been enough to frighten my little dog, who would no longer hang around in my company, rather she lifted her chin and found a comfortable spot to not speak or have anything to do with me. When I went to the mirror, I would have wiped the mascara out from under my eye as it had metamorphosed into army face paint, but with no hot water decided rather to ensure the gas to the water heater was turned off.

I was angry, angry for not catching the mouse after weeks of attempts, angry for unexpected damage inflicted on me because of the mouse, and of course the first mishap, the water heater.

I tried to find my Zen place, ready to use yoga, tai chi and all those arts that calm the nerves and tend to the soul. I sat down to find my happy place, when there it was, the mouse. It poked its head out then scurried down the wall. I closed my eyes, crossed legged and imagined the mouse finding its way into one of the traps set by yours truly.

That's when it happened, a loud noise from inside one of the rooms with a trap. I jumped to my feet and ran into the room from whence the noise came, eager to see this mouse trapped in my most humane of mouse catching attempts, only to find the mouse had scurried off with some peanut butter and no mouse was inside any of the traps.

CHAPTER 5.0

THE UNFORESEEN SPY

John Torvald had volunteered for the army at the age of twenty four. He'd studied German in university which made him an ideal candidate for operation deep cover.

"You know German?" his superior asked.

"Yes I'm fluent in it."

The year was 1934 and the American government was nervous about Germany remilitarizing.

"You're government wants you to go undercover."

"Undercover?"

"Yes that's right. We want you to change your identity and spy on the Germans; we don't want another World war to break out. It could be of great interest to you."

"Well what do you want me to do?"

"We want you to change your identity, to relay information back to us, to change your name to Aldawin Zieger. Ideally, to enlist in their army to keep a close eye on what's going on there."

"This mission sounds dangerous."

"Yes it could be, we're sending five operatives in and you meet the criteria."

"And if I except?" asked John.

"If you accept this mission we'll send you overseas immediately."

He looked at the dossier that been handed to him just minutes earlier. It had all the necessary documentation for him to change his identity, plus the formal description of the op.

"So what do I do if things get bad there, or if I'm discovered as a spy, they'll kill me won't they?"

"That is something you need to think about yourself, in my mind both of those outcomes are potentially possible, it'll be up to you how to handle those types of situations when the time comes. You do have significant training though."

"Yes sir," he began "I enlisted after university. I excelled in all the strategic training categories, I guess that's what happens when you live on a farm in Iowa, I always had a significant amount of training, shooting gophers and elk."

He lit up a cigarette. He didn't usually smoke but he found the rush to be similar to a hunt back on the farm. The first few seconds were always a rush, but after it was gone he felt he could think clearer, especially when his life was on the line.

"Alright, I'll take the job."

The superior smiled and walked out of the room.

John waited for a few minutes. The room was empty just a few painted pictures, a few other smaller black and white photographs. He stood up and walked over to one particular picture and picked it up off the shelf and began to chuckle. Just then his superior walked back into the room. This time he was accompanied by an even higher ranking official.

"John." He said "This mission is of top importance. As soon as you walk out of this office you, your identity, you're past, everything about you changes. You become Aldawin Zieger. The only way to relay information back to us will be an issued and addressed mailing address that only you will know about. If this information reaches the Germans you identity will be compromised. We expect you to serve your country till the utmost end."

"Sir." he said smiling "You got yourself a spy."

Over the next few days he studied every page, every scribble, and every picture of the dossier until he knew it like the back of his hand. By the time he got to the boat yard he'd become Aldawin. But for the first time in his life knew he was going to miss being John Torvald.

The trip across the Atlantic was without discourse. He spent most of his days reading one of his favourite books, 'Of Mice and Men' but knew Aldawin would have to read German literature. He figured it might be a while before he got the chance to read great American novels again.

He spent most of the nights aboard the deck of the ocean vessel, starring off into the great abyssal of the majestic ocean. The waves seemed to disappear into the darkness of the night.

After 12 days at sea they arrived in the port of Nantes France. His destination in France was Strasbourg but he was in no rush to get there. He took in the sights and the people, knowing what little French he knew. Although John Torvald wanted to take pictures and buy souvenirs he knew Aldawin Zeiger would have limited pictures and such in his world. He had a fist full of money more than enough to get him to Strasbourg so he decided to have a little fun along the way.

CHAPTER 5.1

Aldawin was German who studied in Reims. His next task was to join the German army and hopefully not go to war. He figured in a few short months he'd be a ranking official and could send his letters back to America. So for the second time in his life he enlisted in an army and in June of 1936 graduated to from soldier class to Second Lieutenant.

Now, being a spy in an army is not as easy as it sounds. For one he needed to carry out orders that were given to him, especially if it completely contradicted his moral beliefs as an American. But in the fall 1939 everything changed. His cushy office job became his worst nightmare as Germany invaded Poland. Prior to that he'd been writing his letters to the American government, coded, as specified in the dossier he'd studied some 3 years earlier. His most recent letter suggested an attack on a neighbouring country but he prayed it would not come to fruition.

But it did, a borage of soldiers invaded Poland to regain a small section of land that belonged to Germany before the First World War. He could not believe that for the second time some twenty years later they were looking at another major conflict. Most of the time he believed that America was crazy for sending him here, that there was no and would be no future conflict. But the more he learned during his months and years as an officer the more he began to believe a crisis was brewing.

As mentioned being a spy in enemy's army is not an easy task. He often stationed the soldiers beneath him to easy jobs, jobs that didn't interfere with his conscience or his real intentions for being there. He had to put on an act any time he was around other superiors and even the soldiers that that followed his orders. They were generally frustrated with him, at the time they wanted to see some action, but instead were patrolling neighbourhoods that were predominantly not threatened.

By 1939 he'd already sent a letter stating the names of a few brilliant minds, minds that were offered amnesty from the Nazi tyranny. And somehow by the summer 1939 most of those names and people had already fled. It was then he realized he wasn't the only spy in the German army, but also, that conclusions might be brought forward as to who was aiding these people. For the first time in 3 years, after enlisting, an internal investigation suggested spies in the German front. This made him all the more dedicated to being Aldawin.

Trouble began to brew personally for Aldawin that year as well. He'd been frequenting a bar near his station and a lovely lady began to take a liking to him. He'd seen her several times over the last few years but needed to keep his true identity from her. If she got to close he might forget, or slip up during a conversation, then get handed over to the higher German authorities; no, for the time being he'd avoid any chance of getting discovered.

Germany at that time was much different then corn fields he'd grown up with in Iowa. He missed America a lot, his whole life that had been his home. The roosters crowing at sunrise, the stream that ran past the acreage where he'd play as a child; his mother who would cook meals for him, even though the depression left them extremely poor. She could have made a living off her beet recipes, beet soup, beet stew, beet pie; beets were the only thing that grew of plenty near the old creek. That was the only reason he left home to join the military. The depression made his home feel like they were the only house in all of Iowa. He'd never even seen the ocean until he was asked to cross it as someone else.

Being somewhere else and someone else gave him a sense of security, even if it was a false sense of security. Things were different here, food was of plenty and a whisper of victory kept the people occupied. The papers constantly spoke of victories on all fronts; it was the Nazi flag he detested. It wasn't the red, white and blue he'd been so patriotic about.

The papers at that time spoke highly of victory, polish workers who'd be manufacturing materials needed to win wars; but he knew, for the time being at least all was quite on the western front.

The invasion of France was next. It was met with a more difficult resistance than Poland, but even the French Army could not compete with the German offensive. As an officer he instructed his soldiers to take prisoners captive rather than opening fire. At least that way he could keep his conscience clean. He'd volunteered to occupy a small city on the former French and German border, and day after day watched as troops marched further past his post and deeper into France. By this time he'd already transferred three soldiers who were fed up with his complacency, or inadequate action to the front lines. But still, he managed as best he could given the circumstances.

It was only a few months later when soldiers around him began talking about insubordination, but specifically of a British or American spy who'd been captured after failing to comply with a superiors notice. This frightened him terribly, he wanted to research it more but felt he needed to let this go. So instead he walked to the local bar and downed a few pints. This routine continued for more than a week. At first he was silent as he sipped his beverages, but, as the days and weeks drew on he became somewhat of a local celebrity as soldiers were fascinated by his music, personality and humor. Even to the point where superiors were amazed with his talents.

"Do you know how to play this song?" They'd ask in German.

If Aldawin didn't know it he'd shake his head, but once in a while he'd heard of the song, just as John Torvald had planned. The people would smile and raise their glasses even join in to merry singing enjoyed by all.

That summer he wrote what he thought might be his final letter. It described in detail of further attacks on either Great Britain or Russia. He also described the, shall you say, the net that began encompass him, in terms of security within the German administration, and how further letters could compromise his identity. He sealed that letter then sent it to the usual address. It was weeks later, the first of the air bombings began in Britain. He feared even if they had received the letter, it would be inconsequential or too late, to help the people of Britain.

That summer he was also promoted once again and accepted his rank cordially, but whole heartedly felt awful about the promotion. He knew more people would be counting on him which made him awry about his stature. But his stature may have been the only thing that saved his life that year.

10 months later the push began on the Eastern front. Nearly 3 million men marched day and night into in what was thought to be another glorious victory for the regime. Aldawin was one of the few who were fortunate to make the march by horse or by car, as many other soldiers were forced to walk the seven hundred mile journey. In fact Aldawin could not believe the scale of the operation. Everywhere he looked men were marching into position.

He was once again fortunate to be assigned to a small city bordering the Russian lines. His job became to interview the soldiers and outline the directives assigned from Berlin.

In some of his previous letters he'd outlined the dangers of Russia allying with Germany, but now didn't know to feel about being at war with the Soviets, after-all his real identity was an American. But, he was an American who'd been away from America for so long. Not for a second did he want to admit it, but he'd grown tolerant, at least somewhat, of his enemy. Most of his memories had become him as Aldawin Zieger, rather than John Torvald.

Wave after wave of infantry, tanks and artillery passed through the small town. The Russians were slow to meet the oppressors. The Soviets who were limited to ammunition, were met with devastating force, as wave after wave, of Soviet troops, were shipped by train to meet the German onslaught. And wave after wave were shot down in the name of combat.

Aldawin could only imagine the newspapers in Berlin, "Germany conquers Russia." At least that's what he imagined they'd read. They were advancing on average 20 miles per day, with no forcible opposition in sight. The number of Russian prisoners numbered in the tens of thousands as they threw down their guns rather than fighting the harsh and tyrannical advance; as some of them thought being a prisoner to the Germans was better than facing the Soviets defectors firing squad.

The borage was eventually 30 miles from Leningrad when German intelligence suggested they could have control of the city within a week, and that there was, little, or no, Soviet resistance upon reaching the city.

The fight for Leningrad was on, but the intelligence proved to be wrong. Nearly two hundred thousand Soviet soldiers were still ready to fight for the city. The German supply lines began to cover great distances and getting troops the necessary equipment got more and more difficult as torrential rains bogged down most of the supply trucks and tanks.

CHAPTER 5.2

Still stationed at the former Ukraine – Russian border, John Torvald began to wonder the outcome of his choices. For the first time he realized he might not ever get to go home. For nearly five years he'd been serving his country, America, but had trouble rationalizing the outcome of his decisions. He also felt for the first time he might have to be Aldawin Zieger for the rest of his life, or perhaps die as him.

He knew his superiors had broken the non-aggression pact by marching soldiers into battle some six weeks prior and victory seemed imminent.

In the weeks and months that followed, the soldiers began to lose their moral. He soon learned that Russians were more tactful then his superiors had anticipated. Although the assault began strong the tenacity and perseverance of the Russians eventually led to a complete standstill of the German push. The Germans sought to capture Moscow in one massive push, but were met with a hostile resistance. The Red Army, the name of the Soviet opposition was proving to be, under the circumstances, more resourceful as an assailant; and well into the winter months both sides refused to give even an inch.

That particular winter was colder than any other in history and both sides dug in, refusing to let the other break their lines. Aldawin got word on November 28th that more and more Red Army troops were being sent to Moscow while the German supply lines seemed to be breaking up. In fact, even the winter supplies that were on route in early October still hadn't been distributed to all the German troops. Many were freezing or cold, prone to disease or generally unable to function due to the harsh climate that was, unequivocally, unexpected. The supply lines stretched an overwhelming 1000 miles from North to South and every day, artillery and supply trucks were stopping short of their intended destinations, sometimes hundreds of miles away from the destinations.

***

Aldawin spent most of the days sitting at his desk in the comfort of an old wood burning stove that generally staved off the cold effects of that winter. He continued to read any and all dossiers sent to him and generally knew the assault was not going as planned. Instead, he sipped from a flask of whiskey that had been on route to another post. As a high ranking official he was able to commandeer supplies that were on route to the front lines; mostly chocolate, alcohol, food rations, and warmer clothing. He wished each soldier that passed through his office the best of luck as these supplies were rarely making it to the designated outposts.

On December 8th he was shocked to read about an assault the day before. Somehow a paper printed in Berlin made its way to his desk that read only one day prior, the Japanese had bombed Pearl Harbor. He gripped the paper in anger; it seemed that this war was everywhere. He strongly feared, as John Torvald that America was to be targeted even more.

He demanded to have more information relayed to him and followed the story as best he could given his stature and rank. Day after day the papers continued to read about France, Russia and Berlin and very little information was ever printed about an attack half a world away, or even the camps that held the prisoners of this war.

He knew Iowa was a long ways away from Hawaii, but somehow the images of his German soldiers gave him the impression that California and the west coast was under an impending attack. This caused him to lose his temper especially to the people around him. He'd drink from his flask then would argue with people that didn't need to be argued with.

He began to wonder what John Torvald would do, and more importantly what should John Torvald do?

He started to write his superiors, this time his German superiors, stating the offensive on Russia was a doomed failure and requested to be transferred back to his station in France. The weeks turned into months and there was little or no reply.

Eventually a familiar face entered his office. It was the same man who he'd entertain in the pub, a man who'd also been promoted several times during their distant time apart. He was a superior officer back then, but was even more of a superior to Aldawin now. He entered the office, placed his coat on the back of a chair, a chair that many a soldier sat in during the last few months. He removed his hat and placed it under his arm.

"What do you think of all this fighting?" he asked.

Aldawin stopped to think for a minute. There were plenty of words that flashed through his mind. Instead he answered. "I don't think the German front can survive for long."

"And why is that?" he again asked in German.

"The supply trucks are not getting to their destinations, the men are freezing from the cold and Leningrad still has not fallen. Russia might still have plenty of soldiers who haven't been drafted yet."

"And why do you want to go back to France?"

Aldawin needed to answer carefully. Suddenly the information about spies re-entered his brain. He began to wonder how long he'd been being watched, or even if he'd been being watched.

"I think by spring..." he paused. "The red Army will be too strong."

"Then perhaps we should send you to the Eastern front lines" The officer stated.

Aldawin stood up, then moved towards the window then glanced out at the frozen terrain. He needed to say something, anything...

"There is a woman. She was there at the pub, when I would sing and entertain."

"Ahh..." he said. "And did she study with you at Reims?"

He was stumped. He'd already given away some clues as to his true identity. He turned back to the officer, then, picked up a cigarette from his drawer. It had been a long time since he'd had a smoke. He casually lit his cigarette. He was half expecting to have the letters he'd written since 1936 to be slammed down on his desk. After a few seconds he decided to change his approach.

"Since the invasion has been going so well, I was hoping to be transferred back to my former station, in hopes of finding her again." Said Aldawin, all the while crossing his toes.

There was an awkward silence. Then the commanding officer stood up, put his coat back on, and then said. "I will consider your request." He quickly exited after placing his hat back on.

Aldawin sat back down, his heart still beating wildly from his close encounter. Then he turned his chair to once again face the window.

That winter seemed to drag on. He knew the Russians were continually getting stronger, even though it appeared they were outnumbered, at least that's what injured soldiers were saying, soldiers who were returning from the front lines. That winter a Nazi flag flew in the capitol of Leningrad, but was later reclaimed, only days later by the Red Army.

The battle of Stalingrad in the south faced similar shortfalls, all the while; the siege on Moscow was the main priority. The city of Kiev was the only penetrable hole the Germans had to try to push through. As such, soldiers were being relocated to from the fights at the North and South without having full control at either end.

***

It took six months, but eventually Aldawin was transferred back to France.

It was the summer of 1942, and Germany was facing a large number of Allied resistances, in and around Moscow. Unbeknown to the Germans the number of Soviet troops had nearly doubled from the time the invasion began, but still they were ordered to continue the invasion.

CHAPTER 5.3

Aldawin was met with mixed emotion as started to settle down in the province of Courtisols, still 160 kilometers from his original station.

German soldiers saw him as a, sort of hero, being that he'd been close to the frontlines in Russia. Meanwhile the people of occupied France gave blank or resentful looks of anger.

It was then he learned, from a soldier, assigned to his command, about the prison camps holding both Soviets and Polish workers, and that their numbers were in incomprehensible amounts. Pleasantly, the soldier kindly stated where they were being held, but that he'd heard there were many camps across the European continent.

John Turner decided to write one final letter, even if it meant this scenario was a trap. This time a map was included along with a letter how to decode the map. It included the locations of the camps, some of the factories where weapons were being made, as well as, weak points in the German front lines. To further conceal this particular letter from the Germans he wrote other letters as well, and sent the letters to addresses of people he'd never met, that way they might not intercept this particular letter.

For Aldawin, the drinking continued. It was from the emotional stress of the war along with the combination of being someone else for too long. He tried, yet again, to entertain the people of his company, but this time, emotions were not running as high.

He asked kindly, of his superior officer, to travel the former French country side, to ensure there were no spies within the administration. That his new role would be to interview soldiers and to make sure they always had the proper documentation. His request was met with great anticipation from his senior officers; all but one, Sebastian Hokenan, the same man he'd entertained in the bar, the same man who sat at his desk, before he was transferred to France. Sebastian began to look into Aldawin, since his prediction about the Eastern front lines proved to be correct. The number of Red Army soldiers nearly doubled that year and Germany would soon be forced into a retreat. Yet Aldawin, never knew of Sebastian's inclination towards him, other than the conversation they'd had only months prior.

Three days later, a German vehicle was commandeered and both Aldawin and John Torvald felt as though a great burden had been lifted off his shoulders, because his request had been granted. It was nearing summer again, 1942, the papers printed from Berlin these days were not as assertive as they had been in 1939. The push at the Eastern front was failing, the plan to take Moscow was proving more deadly than anticipated as Germany was losing more soldiers, from battle, and Moscow and the Red Army were gaining more soldiers during the communist drafts. The papers rarely spoke of America or the war in the Pacific Ocean, but once in a while would mention it, or at least what they knew of it.

As he drove around former France, he could see the devastation. The French who were left looked at him with evil glances. Many of them frustrated with the Germans since they'd destroyed their houses, their families, their lives. He wanted to say "Don't worry I'm an American," But instead would rev the engine of his vehicle to release his frustrations.

He drove back to the small town where he'd once entertained so many German troops and began to ask questions about the whereabouts of his prolonged passions, this lady he fancied so. Unfortunately, nobody had ever heard of her. Puzzled, he return to the small house he'd been living in before he was assigned to the Eastern front. He'd hidden a bunch of pictures under one of the floor boards; cautiously he lifted those boards and retrieved the pictures he'd hidden away. Sure enough, she happened to be in one of the pictures, only one of them from a dozen or so. He spent the night sleeping in the same bed he'd used so frequently before being reassigned.

The next day, he returned to a small pub for breakfast. The mood was different during the day than in the evenings. Somehow John knew they were up to something, something they were trying to keep hidden from Aldawin. After his meal, which was complimentary for any German officer, he again asked the bar keeper if he had seen the lady in the photo. He shook his head 'no'.

It seemed as though, now, he was looking for a ghost. She could be anywhere, and could probably, simply, disappear in the chaos. The last few soldiers he'd requested papers from, all seemed to state, the mentality of the German occupation was one of fear, but also disrespect and anger. That there was a general consensus of a growing opposition towards the German occupiers.

Still, he travelled from town to town, spread apart only by a couple kilometers. Every time he'd come across stationed soldiers, he request their documentation, but always asked if any had seen the lady in the photograph. Most would shake their heads no, but once in a while would point him in the general direction of her known whereabouts.

As it turns out, she had become a member of the French resistance. A small social club dedicated to the liberation of occupied France. A hush, hush organization that frowned upon their German occupiers. Every time Aldawin was getting closer to finding her, a secret network of associates were letting her know a German officer was looking for her.

CHAPTER 5.4

It took almost three weeks before anybody had heard of her, but much like Aldawin was searching for her, Sebastian was searching for him. It turns out the name Zieger belonged to a family of aristocracy before World War I, all of whom were presumed dead from the first conflict. That there was a Aldawin Zieger who'd studied a Reims, but none of the surviving alumni recognized Aldawin's photo, and on more than one occasion stated the man in the photo was not the man they'd attended university with.

Sebastian felt the German army should've been in a fanatic frenzy over infiltrators within the regime, however the growing problems with the occupied Soviet Union, the questionable outcome of the prisoners of war, along with the general needed perception that all was well within the regime kept more than most people unaware of the circumstances; especially since he seemed to be such an apparent asset to the regime.

It wasn't until October of 1942 that Aldawin finally had located the woman he sought. She'd changed her name more than once to avoid detection by the Germans, and was currently going by the name Penelope. Although Aldawin hadn't approached her yet, sources had identified her known whereabouts, and both sides feared confrontation.

She had been living with a group of women, about five or six, in an area that had a heavy German presence. The town was Vezelay, France and was roughly 250 kilometers from Strasbourg, the town where he'd first laid eyes on her.

He approached the house, but three years is a long time without seeing someone. The women inside thought he was nothing more than another German captain seeking solace from the confusion that had disrupted their lives in the first place. If she was part of the resistance, it was disguised as a brothel. As Aldawin approached the door, several would-be friends of hers were, ready to intercept his cordial meeting. He removed his hat then repeated to knock or rap upon the doorway. It took several knocks but upon the third or fourth try an old lady opened the door.

"Yes??" answered the old lady.

"My name is Aldawin, Aldawin Zeiger, I have reason to believe this women is living here" and displayed the picture that had been taken almost three years prior.

The women cordially looked upon the photo, and then claimed, "That woman no longer lives here, and she left more than a year ago, to search for her father who was presumed dead. Good day to you," then closed the door, closed the door upon his foot.

"Madame if you please, I have reason to believe she is here, and will not leave without speaking with her, if you don't let me in I will be forced to call the Gestapo." A cleverly disguised anecdote, surely to not let a would be German into resistance territory.

The old lady slammed the door again, this time catching the arch of his foot between the doorway and the 300 pound door. She put more than her weight into the exertion, enough to cripple even the toughest of German tough guys.

"Madame!!" he exclaimed while jumping on one foot. "I am here to seek information about her family" suddenly there was a change of heart. Perhaps the inclination of finding her long lost family made the old French lady a tad more compassionate towards his cause.

"If you try anything stupid, I'll kill you myself." She exclaimed as the door was for once opened to an opponent they wished not to entertain.

He walked through the house from the entrance into the dining room, then up the stairs towards where cynical eyes were pointing him. Penelope was washing a pair of clothes, with a washboard from the late eighteen hundreds. Although long extinct from that time and era, it seemed quite suitable to do the job given the unfortunate circumstances.

"Do you remember me?" Was the first question he asked her.

She looked with the corner of her eyes then shook her head "No."

"Didn't you work at a pub, near Strasbourg; I was stationed there several years ago."

Again she shook her head "No."

He held up a picture, "Isn't this you." He asked in French.

She looked at the picture, and then changed her mind.

"Yes, that is me. The Inn keeper at the pub let me live there after your German goons destroyed my house, murdered my family." She spoke softly.

"Surely it was not me who did that." He again spoke in French.

"No, not you, but your friends they did that to me, my family."

He sat down on the bed. The conversation continued for quite some time, he explained where he'd gone to school, Reims, his station near Strasbourg, moving him to the Eastern front and that he'd been searching for her so, and that every day since then he thought about her. He also talked about the war, that he'd enlisted because he wanted to help people, not regain German territories or fight a war he never wanted to be part of. In the end she started to smile changing her mood from a frustrated resentful type to a calm, and concerned, almost loving type, it was her eyes that lightened up, and he could see she cared.

Over the next few weeks he went about his assignment, checking documents, while she, the housework for an overprotective landlord. He'd drop in to see her every chance he got. But was often shooed away with a broom or stick the landlord kept near the front door. Although the winter was another cold one, just like the year before their love continued to blossom and kept hearts warm in the company of friends, and friends of those as well.

Penelope left the house early one morning. She walked down the alley, across the street, walked a few blocks then down another alley. She jumped through a small hole in a fence then, up some stairs and into a building missing a roof. She entered one of the rooms then closed the door behind her, just like she had every few weeks or so. She tapped on the wall until she found a loose brick then removed it from the wall.

Inside was a letter, a letter written to her every few months outlining the next move of the resistance. She opened it, started reading, and then she dropped to her knees. She tore off the bottom half of the letter, tucking it into her bra, then with a match lit the upper half aflame.

She exited the building, and continued walking down the street towards the market. She bought a few vegetables then started walking home, with the food under her arm. She returned to the house, and then went about preparing dinner for the rest of the ladies, as it was her time to cook.

Aldawin showed up on Saturday, with flowers and chocolate as it was Valentine's Day. Instead being greeted with a hug, or a kiss, she was angry, and she was never angry. She dismissed him then walked up the stairs to her room; he followed her into her room then closed the door.

"Who are you really?" she asked.

"What do you mean, I'm Aldawin, I've been living here since..."

"Don't lie to me." she exclaimed.

He sat down, and then looked at his uniform. He removed his hat, followed by his coat.

"My name is John Torvald, but I haven't used that name since I got to Europe. I've been undercover since I agreed to this mission almost ten years ago. I often believed John Torvald was dead."

She didn't say anything; she was just as shocked to hear this as he was.

"It appears you have a friend, your government wants to bring you home."

She removed ripped portion of the letter then handed it to him.

"This is an address, if you get to it there will be another letter, telling where and when to meet your ride home."

He was shocked, "But how did...?"

"My contact" she exclaimed "Another spy has been helping us until help arrives."

"So go!" she said.

He didn't want to. He wanted to stay, to fight.

"Come with me." He said

"I can't my place is here." She said.

"But, your family, they are probably dead, and if someone already knows I'm an American they won't be nice about it. Come with me, back to America." asked John.

She didn't know what to do. She sat down on the bed next to him, and then started to cry. He held her in his arms, until the tears subsided. She wiped the last one from her eye.

"I will go with you." She said.

He spent the night, that evening both locked in a loving embrace.

CHAPTER 5.5

The next day came far too quickly, a crowing rooster brought a morning that was different than the others over the last few years. They went downstairs, to a breakfast that was already being prepared. They weren't sure if the others heard their argument the previous morning but assumed they didn't. After breakfast Penelope was the first to speak.

"We want to go to America." She said.

The rest of the ladies looked at each other, but were excited for her. Aldawin was not wearing his uniform.

"You cannot say anything." Said Penelope.

The old lady spoke up. "Aldawin, you wish to defect." She asked.

"I defected a long time ago." He replied.

"How will you get there?" The old lady asked.

"We're not sure, but we need to leave soon. There are Germans that might be aware of Aldawin wanting to defect. We beg you not to tell them anything."

The old lady gave Penelope a hug, and was hoping the best during their travels.

They needed a plan. Since women served in the German Army perhaps they could commandeer another uniform. Then just drive to the next destination before getting picked up and heading for home. So the next day Aldawin drove to a supply center for the German army, requested a new uniform since his old one was tattered and ruined. He then drove back to the house with his old uniform still waiting for him. The old French lady was master seamstress and altered the uniform to fit a woman. The only thing they lacked was the proper documents for Penelope.

The plan was almost fool proof. On March 1st 1943 they set out towards home. He drove north about twenty miles towards the hidden location of the next letter. Aldawin didn't want to say it but he was nervous. She was the only one who knew his true identity. Suddenly the emotions from the early years came back to him. What if he was wrong about her, what if it was a trap? Surely he'd be tortured or sent to camp or maybe even shot. He looked at her and she smiled at him.

They came to the first German crossing. It was guarded by several soldiers and a giant road blockade that would only open if they had the right documentation. Several soldiers approach the vehicle.

"Were are you going?" They asked in German.

Aldawin handed them his papers. Since he outranked them as a superior, they apologized and opened the gate. The military truck was quick to speed through the border check, and continued to its destination. The destination was a suburb near Lyons.

The vehicle passed several convoys travelling the opposite direction. Each time Penelope would sink into her seat.

"Sit up straight." He'd say, and she would comply. She must have been just as nervous as he was, but he was better at concealing it.

As they approached the next destination on what was left from the original note they parked the truck. She took the lead as she knew the hidden emblems and sketched secrets to look for. She walked down a stone cobble wall, looking for anything out of the ordinary. Aldawin looked around the landscape as well, all seemed quiet, if she was going to turn him in, it sure seemed as though the capturers forgot to show up. Although passing through the last German checkpoint provided enough comfort as to think she was telling the truth.

She continued down the cobblestone wall looking for any prying eyes that could compromise there escape efforts. She couldn't see anyone, and then she found what she was looking for; an arrow, pointing the direction. She followed it until she came across another arrow, made with tiny rocks then used her foot to break apart the formation. Then finally a third arrow made from a few soda bottles. They kept walking, this time Aldawin was right behind her.

Then they found it, a shovel, sitting next to a recently dug up grave. "I think they want us to dig this up." She said.

"We should wait until it is dark." 13 years in the army wasn't for nothing.

A half hour after sunset, they started digging, with a lantern to help them in the darkness. They'd angled the light towards the nearby forest rather than the road which was a hundred yards from the dig site. Finally they found what they were looking for, a small wooden box, but not a coffin. In fact there was never a coffin there in the first place. It was a piece of rock near a small town graveyard, highly worthy for hiding secret information. They walked towards the forest with the lantern then opened the box. Inside was a letter, it stated,

Dear John,

Although we have not spoken since we've left I wanted you to know I am still alive. I have decided to stay until we have won. Rest assured I am still fighting to be a patriot. In the final letter from our government they stated your ride is waiting for you. Provided you have found this letter your departure home will be waiting for you on March 20th 1943. I have been told if you fail to be at this location on that specific day they will be forced to leave without you. I hope this letter finds before your transportation departs back for America. It turns out Penelope learned about you before you knew anything about her. I am sure she will help you get home.

Your Brother,
Fletcher.

"You see." She said. "He wants to get you home."

John couldn't believe it. He was sure he was dead. All that time checking lists of the dead soldiers names. He didn't even know the name his brother was given for this assignment. But apparently Raphael knew his as Raphael was the new name his brother was given. He wanted to cry but he held back the tears.

Penelope began to rummage through the rest of the box.

"There is still a whole bunch in hear, pictures, secret documents." But was all held together by a German dossier.

"I think he needs you to get this back to America."

It turns out his older brother earned a higher rank, and was looking out for John. Making sure his posts were easy and would not get him killed. Although Aldawin and John never knew the name given to his older brother, it was always part of Raphael's job to know his. Somehow he'd amassed a huge amount of German intelligence that was destined for America.

They walked back to the truck. Suddenly both John and Penelope were afraid. It would be two weeks before they needed to be at the extraction zone. They needed to lay low for a while. She knew of a cabin somewhere deep in the woods, just north of Marseille and Nice. So they drove most of the evening until they arrived there just before day break.

The resistance had a list of safe houses that could be used by resistance members if need be. They'd stayed at that house for seven days and nights. The problem was it had been a week since Aldawin had checked in. It could be that he'd been flagged, or perhaps presumed dead, he wasn't sure. They'd have to go around most road blockades from now on rather than through them. This safe house was miles from most roads and was just as isolated as she'd promised. Surely they could lay low until it was time to go.

There was no food inside the house, aside from a few canned goods but that would not last for the two weeks. John went hunting the following evening and caught a deer; it would feed them for the rest their stay. Plus he'd collected a few things before leaving the old ladies abode, some chocolate and whiskey.

As the days turned into weeks, fear began to set in. It was the final leg of their journey that frightened them but with all the dossiers and the unissued notion that they were wanted, red flagged within the regime, every breath was full of apprehension and anxiety.

On March 16th the couple were having dinner planning their route to the ocean, when he heard a noise outside the house. He walked out the house and looked around, didn't appear to be anything of importance. Then a figure stumbled out from behind a tree. John immediately went after him striking him.

"Who are you, what do you want."

He was bleeding; he'd been hit a few times in the face.

"I want to go to America."

He raised his fist again "Then how did you find us."

"I was posted outside the brothel. You were the only person coming and going. The day after you left Sebastian was at the door looking for you. He was so upset that he had not found you, screaming he's a spy. He told me to follow him, so we tracked you. The convoy said they saw you, the guards at the road block said you'd passed through. We tracked you to the cemetery, and then lost the trail."

He struck him again.

"He'd determined you hadn't gone North or East or West because of additional roadblocks. When I told him I was too far from my post, he reassigned me to a post 20 kilometers from here. When I got there the soldiers, they said if anyone was hiding this forest could keep them hidden, but neither of them wanted to investigate; and I did not tell them why I was there. When I got close enough I saw the tracks and figured you were inside. I've been helping the revolution"

"I'll kill you myself if you're lying, how many more are coming!" said John.

"None, I'm not lying, I've always wanted to go to America."

"My papers?" asked John.

"You are to be reprimanded at the next road blockade."

"What is your name?"

"Tucker, Tucker Harpe."

He went back inside. "Get your things." He said to Penelope. "We are leaving tonight."

He had no choice, he had to trust him. They left on foot burning all three uniforms in the wood stove making sure they were completely gone before leaving. Then they cleaned up the place, as though no one was even there. That evening they slipped into the darkness and headed towards the coast.

CHAPTER 5.6

They hiked south towards the ocean. The mountains made it easy to hike, since the range ran north to south, and on the third day arrived in Toulon. From there they dodged main roads, jumping fences and avoiding the soldiers. It was occupied but not as bad as Marseille to the East or Nice to the North West.

"Are you sure you want to do this?" Penelope asked

"Don't let fear hold you back." He replied.

They waited till the sunset, and then made a dash for the ocean. They sequestered a boat, then headed due south until midnight. By midnight they could hardly see the lights from the shore. By morning, they were lost somewhere in the Mediterranean.

"So this is how we get to America." Joked Tucker.

It was met with only smiles; somehow they'd already done the impossible.

"What is your real name?" Asked John.

Penelope shook her head she didn't want to answer.

"You're not going to tell us?" Asked Tucker.

"I will tell you when we get to America." She replied.

The day dragged on slowly into the afternoon. By noon, they were feeling the effects of sea sickness and dehydration began set in. The boat was not much bigger than a small yacht. Only 13 feet long at most. It made the threesome feel a little overcrowded. By four o'clock they began to hand out chocolate rations. There was not much left since most of it had been eaten during the hike, even the water rations were running low as well.

March 20th had come and gone and there was still no rescue in sight. All afternoon they'd been waiting to see a boat or a ship something useful for a rescue, but there had been nothing. No ship, no boat nothing. By evening there were still no boats in sight. They lit a lantern to make life aboard this vessel liveable. And they tried to sleep as best they could, the waves made it difficult to get any shut eye.

Tucker enquired. "So this letter you found told you to steal a boat, and then paddle into the Mediterranean, and then what?"

"This is it, it said to paddle out beyond the lights that they'd find us." Replied John

"Do you think a boat could get here; I mean passed the Germans?" Asked Tucker.

"I hope so, if not we'll be paddling to Africa." Joked John.

"How did you know we were heading to America?" Asked Penelope.

"They said you were a spy, and you weren't trying to get to Britain, nor back to The Soviet Union, I thought perhaps, maybe you were from America. I always dreamed about it, living in Montana or Wyoming, far away from this war. My parents laughed when I told them I wanted to be a cowboy."

'I will tell you the truth but not yet' thought John.

The night turned once again into day. They'd been at sea for 32 hours and were starting to feel the chances of rescue were getting slimmer. Day then turned again into night. They were hungry, dehydrated and becoming restless. The lantern had been burning all night and was running low on fuel. John gripped the lantern then tried to pump fuel back into it. It ran about another hour then began to lose its glimmer. It seemed there was no hope for the would-be sailors. They had exhausted every glimmer of rescue after a daring, but heroic escape.

Submission began; every wave that crashed against the side of the boat brought them further and further from reality. As time went on the chance of being rescued became more and more of a dream rather than a reality. By the following morning all hope was lost. Adrift for days, the trio began to contemplate their fate. John had learned the ocean could be a far more devastating foe then any he'd met on land.

Tucker was silent, asleep for hours; Penelope could hardly keep her eyes open, her head bobbed from left to right as the oceans surge continued to batter the boat. By day break the following day all hope was lost. No one aboard the vessel had any recollection of any of the events that had occurred. Eyes drooped and optimism was all but a distant dream. John hung his head in defeat as the rest of the crew bobbed silently to the Mediterranean tale of conquest.

Then life gave way. The ocean surged as a giant form emerged from the ocean depths. The lantern aboard the vessel had been the cue to finding there location. The ocean began to move. It gave way to a submarine that surfaced meters from the boat. The initial thought was that it was a u-boat but the sailor on deck shouted.

"John, John Torvald.?"

He hadn't heard that name in years.

"Yah." he said "That's me."

They paddled closer and they were helped onto the surface of the submarine. It was an American submarine crew that had been assigned to this mission. They'd travelled nearly 4,000 miles to make this pick up. The captain knew it must have been of some importance, since it had come directly from the highest order of the navy, received almost a month earlier.

CHAPTER 5.7

He was eager to shake their hands then welcomed them aboard his vessel.

"Welcome aboard." Said the Captain.

He was tall, black and handsome, enough to make any German nervous in his presence. Once aboard the captain gave instructions to close the hatch.

"Well John," he said "It appears you've done the impossible."

Both Tucker and Penelope looked at each other, not realizing the severity of the events they'd been through.

John was walked off to a room near the captains' chambers while Tucker and Penelope were escorted to the second mates' room. What the captain had to say was in secret.

"We are in enemy territory." he said. "And frankly, these men have been at sea for months and they think it's bad luck to have a woman on board. So I won't tell them. We knew we were to rescue you, but we didn't know you'd be bringing company. But really, the only thing that scares me more than dragons or werewolves is passing through the Gibraltar Straight again. We were posted for days just observing the ships passing through."

John didn't know what to say. "You're efforts have been heroic, maybe one day they'll write stories about you."

This made the captain laugh and he didn't laugh often. "Well." he said, slapping John on the back "Welcome aboard. You're lady friend needs to stay in her cabin and your other friend, can stay in one of the quarters."

"With all due respect Captain, Tucker should stay in the holding cell for now until it can be established that he has truly defected." Said John. "You mean you just met him?" Asked the captain. "Yes, but he had a convincing story, and I guess I believed him. And captain," he added, "I have information that needs to be returned to the American government as soon as possible. It needs to stay hidden from peering eyes until it can be returned to the proper authority."

The captain escorted John to his private quarters then opened a safe for John and only John to reprogram the combination. The several dossiers were placed inside and John reprogrammed the combination. The captain shut the door to his quarters, and then escorted Tucker to a holding cell. Tucker wasn't angry, but cooperated unwillingly without putting up a fight.

John spent the afternoon walking and meeting the crew as he was free to move about the submarine.

The crew seemed angry; they had travelled a huge distance, passed through dangerous territory and for what, to simply rescue a single American. That they had all put their lives on line just to rescue one other person. Sensing this apprehension, John spent the next few hours sitting in the company of Penelope who it seemed was also in a sort of detention.

When he awoke the next day, he was instructed to be extremely quiet. They had neared the Gibraltar Straight and were preparing to pass through. The Straight was only eight miles wide and the enemy assumed no ship or submarine would be stupid enough to pass through. Although they had snuck passed days earlier, for the second time were travelling into an enemy bottle neck.

All was silent, minute after minute the crew communicated silently. The sub was running just below sonar detection, about 3 or 4 knots. The sonar specialist signalled there were no immediate U-boats in the vicinity. The coast was clear and the ship inched forward ever so slightly.

After what seemed like hours, the engines began to speed up, slowly but surely. John assumed he could speak to the crew but instead they just told him to hush.

The submarine glided through the straight, unbeknownst to anyone or anything at the surface. They stayed steady at pace of about 5 knots for a while. As the ocean began to give way, slopping slightly towards the abyssal trenches of the Atlantic, the sub submerged lower and lower, dipping from about 100 feet, to 125 feet then 150 feet. It seemed they were in the clear.

After almost, what seemed like hours, the order was given to have the sub return to normal status, meaning to go about their regular routine.

The captain made it his duty to interrogate Tucker, who'd been locked in his cell for 24 hours. The captain brought him some food from the galley, it didn't look appetizing but he was so hungry he decided to eat it anyway.

"Why did you enlist?" Asked the captain.

"My parents." He exclaimed, biting down on a piece of chicken. "I didn't want to; I had heard about the first war and thought it would be stupid for that to ever happen again." "My parents, wanted me to because I was part Jewish, that they couldn't find me if I was in uniform."

"Where are your parents now?" Asked the captain.

"Not too sure, they went to the work camps to build weapons for the Germans. That was almost 3 years ago."

"We have reason to believe the Germans are massacring the people in those camps. You need to know there is a good chance that you're parents are dead."

With saying that, he stood up and began to fish about his pocket looking for a key to open the cell. Finding it seconds later he opened the steel gate and Tucker was free to move about the cabin. He instructed him to stay clear of the other men working on the submarine. It is not a place for guests; it needs to be proper and orderly, all the time, no funny business and no fooling around.

CHAPTER 5.8

Penelope was still in her quarters, she had not left them since boarding the sub. One of the second mates had given her his cabin, still feeling that women were bad luck on submarines. John was in her company and had been since the previous evening. The cabin was small, but luxurious as it belonged to the second mate. The second mate had been bringing food to her at mealtimes, although starving from the original boat ride into the Mediterranean; she had eaten her share of food to make her full and had been eating very little since.

She was nervous, starting a new life somewhere else with someone she had just met, but mostly because she was on a submarine and had never been on the ocean. However, it was much more appealing than being involved with the Germans. The other problem was, her family. She was much like Tucker in that she had not seen them in years. She wanted to believe the worst was behind her and wanted to believe they were still alive.

Tucker had been sleeping in a bunk bed that was normally reserved for the submarine crew. Since space was limited it was either the keep or the bed he was in, although, the keep was proving to be a bit more spacious. He wanted to help the other officers and crew, but knew he did not have the training to do so, at least that way, he wouldn't be feeling like he was doing nothing.

Sitting in his bed for far too long made him anxious and apprehensive. His plan was to find John then try to talk to him. He was so bored and had not brought any books with him to read and there was very little to do to keep him occupied. He thought mostly about his new life, and getting home to America. He'd been gone almost nine years.

John did the same routine, he'd been in Penelope's company for at least a full day, although it was hard to gauge it since there is no sunlight aboard a submarine. He opened the door to exit the cabin, while putting on a shirt that had been provided to him from the captain. He exited the cabin then gently closed the door to not wake her. Pulling a hat from his pant pocket he placed it on his head.

Then, with a giant heave the sub shook. It knocked him to his knees.

Seconds later he was lying on the ground. Crew members were running around him trying to get to their posts. He stumbled to his feet.

"What happened?" He asked a passing crew member.

"It was a U-Boat." He exclaimed. "We've been torpedoed."

He opened the door back into the room he was in. Penelope was shocked; she was practically in tears but had been through enough as to not let herself fall to pieces.

"What happened?" She asked.

"I think we've been hit by a torpedo." he replied.

"Are we going to sink?" she asked.

"I don't know." replied John "But I'm going to find out. Stay here unless it is absolutely necessary to leave this cabin."

CHAPTER 5.9

Tucker had been making his way through the quarters and into the dining area of the sub. When the sub was struck he stumbled to his knees then got to his feet. People were running past him to get to their posts. One of the senior officers approached him and removed some hand cuffs from his belt. Without any hesitation, just a disgruntled look on his face, he put his hands out and was hand cuffed to a table in the galley.

Seconds later John entered the galley. He looked at the officer who'd hand cuffed Tucker to the table and said "Good."

The officer was needed elsewhere and quickly left the galley.

John looked at him and screamed "Did you have anything to do with this?"

"No of course not." Replied Tucker

He asked him a second time "Did you have anything to do with this?" this time striking him in the face.

"No!" he replied. This time a tear fell from his cheek.

It was believable.

"I am needed elsewhere." Said John then quickly hurried off.

When John got to the subs main control center the captain was screaming orders left right and center.

"Get those leaks under control; I want every last man closing off pipe to keep this submarine from sinking."

"Captain." he said. But the captain was too busy to hear him. "Captain." he said a second time.

This time the captain looked at him. "Captain, is the sub taking on water." The captain momentarily paused from speaking into the handset.

"Yes." he replied.

"Is the ship going to sink?" asked John.

"We're not sure, we're doing everything in our power to prevent it from sinking." replied the captain.

"Captain." He said. "Make sure this ship does not sink, those documents could help us win the war."

He exited the main control center then through the galley once again. Tucker had not moved, instead looked as though he knew he was going to die, that he would be going down with the ship. John passed him and continued through to the aft end of the sub where the torpedo had struck.

When he got there he was knee deep in water but was surprised to see the water was everywhere, given the slight pitch of the sub as the aft end was sinking and water was heavier at the aft end.

He quickly asked "Who is in command."

There was panic in his voice but someone replied "I am."

"How bad have we been hit?" Asked John.

"It's not as bad as it could have been, the torpedo detonated just before impacting the sub, the impact caused the sub to keel sideways suggesting it was not a direct impact."

"Can the sub be saved?" Asked John.

"Yes, but we need to reroute some of the ballast tanks and fast before the sub takes on more water and we are taking on a lot of water."

"Good." replied John.

Then John went to the head and grabbed a piece of soap and did the only thing he could think of doing. He walked back to knee high water and then took off his shirt. He looked around, everyone was shaking and panicking. Water was spaying from pipes like it was a Fourth of July water party.

"Alright." Said John. "I don't know much about submarines, that's your job. But here's what I know this bar of soap is not going to lather in salt water." People stopped to listen to him. "No matter what this bar of soap will not lather, now I want you to carefully think about what you are doing to save this ship from sinking." He was up to his knees in water, the crew was wet and shaking and could not focus. He thought that if he could convince them they weren't going to die by getting the attention focused on something else they might do what they needed to do.

It was a morale boost. He continued to use the soap against his body not having it lather up at all; all the while the water levels slowly rising on the ship. Because he stayed so calm many of the crew got a sort of second wind and began communicating better with one another and focused carefully on the task at hand.

One by one, pipes were closed off to prevent the water from leaking in. John just stood there trying to lather soap on his body. The crew had forgotten about the torpedo and were focused on saving the vessel.

After a minute or so all the pipes had been closed off, suddenly John felt a stinging pain on the back of his head and slowly began to pass out.

***

When he awoke, he was sitting across from Tucker, hand cuffed to another table in the Galley. Then he heard another voice coming from down the hall, it was Melanie's voice.

"Get your hands off me!" she continued to shout but with little or no hesitation, or dismay from the submarine crew. They threw her down at another table, and hand cuffed her to a table beside Tucker but across from John.

"Together again." Joked Tucker.

CHAPTER 5.10

The submarine came to rest in about 450 ft of water on the silt and sand bottom of the Atlantic. As it impacted the sea floor completely listed to one side rocking the entire crew off their feet.

Inside the galley, John was now hanging from his cuffed hand looking down at Tucker and Melanie who were both in a much more comfortable position then he. Water began to pour into the galley as the slight pitch of the sinking sub became more horizontal and began to flood the side of the sub, which was now the floor position.

It was quiet. The moaning and groaning of the sub as it was sinking was enough to frighten anyone to stay out of the water. But now silence.

The captain entered the galley and proceeded to ask John the same questions John had asked Tucker only ten minutes earlier.

"Captain" he said. "I had nothing to do with this!"

The Captain took a set of keys from his belt and detached the cuffs from John hands, then turned to Tucker and Melanie and said. "You two need to stay here for now. The crew is stark mad at me for letting a women on the ship, as its very bad luck, and for letting a former Nazi soldier aboard as well. Right now we are this close to having a mutiny aboard this vessel. Although, I am a righteous man, if we take on more water I'll un-cuff you myself before we drown"

They started to walk along the now side of the ship and the captain began to bring him up to speed. "We think the torpedo detonated before impact. And I heard what you did to keep the crew focused, very ingenious if I do say so myself. If it weren't for that, you'd still be cuffed to that table, but now we have bigger problems."

"If you don't mind me asking how come the U-boat wasn't detected." asked John.

"We think it was beneath us, camouflaged as debris on the ocean floor. We also think it fired on us more than once, it was the third torpedo that hit us." Said the Captain. "We couldn't surface because we are in enemy waters and this place is crawling with German boats."

"But it detonated before impact?" asked John.

"Yes, luckily." replied the captain. "But, just barely. It cracked the hull near the aft, so we think the water got into two of the aft rooms, the same room used to control the bilge pumps but it was sealed off shortly after impact."

"Are there any casualties?" Asked John. "None so far, everyone has reported in and we aren't taking on any more water that we know of. The biggest problem is that since we hit the bottom of the Atlantic the working bilge pump is above water and the second was damaged by the torpedo. We think there is an air leak only accessible from outside the sub. Second, it appears we can stay here to avoid the U-boat, they might think we all drowned. The problem is I'm not sure how long we can stay here at the bottom, these walls are under a lot of pressure, more than they were designed for and we could take on water at any minute."

"Is there any chance of making it to the surface, you know, by swimming?" Asked John.

"Not without drowning first, we're roughly 500ft from the surface and your lungs would rupture before you even reached the surface, assuming you didn't drown first."

He knocked on a steel door, now twisted sideways from the listing of the ship. Once it opened they climbed through it into the subs main control room. Immediately he was met with stares of anger, then he remembered what the captain had told him about Tucker and Melanie.

"Alright" began the captain, "Who wants to volunteer to close off the leak." Nobody did, they just looked at each other

"Captain!!??" said John "Let me do it."

"Alright." Said the captain, "However, I am disappointed that the members of my own crew will not volunteer for this assignment."

Then one of the other men spoke up "Captain, I can do it." He was an older man, possibly twice the age of John and maybe even older than the Captain.

The Captain smiled at him, "Good work." he insisted.

Minutes later the captain, John, Dieter - the man who volunteered for the repair and several other crew members were standing near the hatch that went topside. But there was another problem, once they flooded the hatch exit there was no way to pump the water back out, meaning Dieter, the volunteer was going to drown if he couldn't repair this fix, however, he knew very well of this danger. The downside, if he did not fix this problem the crew would have the sub flood eventually and probably use the hatch to exit, provided that was the final option.

"Once you get outside the ship," started the captain "the water is going to be very cold, low visibility and possibly currents along the bottom, and be careful not to kick up too much silt, it'll disorient you."

He handed him a canister of air, military grade for the time. The crew looked on with sad and weary eyes, they were sure they were going to die here.

After about 45 minutes from the initial torpedo impact, Dieter with his flippers, layered clothing, and military issued goggles, a torch, and a tuque, to keep his head warm, flooded the escape hatch; and opened the other hatch into the cold Atlantic. The water was near freezing, it hit like a series of needles as it flowed down around him, his breathing rate nearly double from the stress and anxiousness of departing the sub. Once the water was all around him he moved towards the hatch exit. Once he poked his head out from the sub he could see just what the captain meant. There was little or no light being 500 feet from the surface, at that depth only 1/25 of the suns light can penetrate, towards, the murky bottom meaning practically no light at all. He could feel the current already pushing against his mask. He was scared, he wanted to scream.

He oriented himself towards the aft of the ship then with a big breath exited the hatch. Immediately the current began to fight him. He kicked and kicked but was getting nowhere, almost moving backwards from the speed of the current. He changed his game plan and swam down so that he wasn't fighting the current. At the bottom things were a little easier except for the silt he was kicking up, but it too was being washed away by the current.

He swam parallel to the sub until he reached the aft of the sub, swam around the rotor, and then began to swim towards the gapping gap that had disabled the submarine. It wasn't a big hole, however, because of the way the submarine had settled on the bottom only a portion of it was visible, and barely enough to fit through. He dug his hands into the Atlantic soil removing silt to make the opening more accessible, until finally it was enough to fit through. He positioned himself to fit through the hole, and then carefully worked his way back into the submarine. He was cold, his hands were crying out in pain because of the glacial temperatures of the water, all the while trying to put out of his mind the effects on the rest of his body.

By the time he entered the sub, he was nearing hypothermia but relentlessly carried on as only a military man could. He approached the air leak, a series of bubbles streaming out from a pipe along the side of the ship. After cranking the valve it seemed to fix the problem. He approached the console containing the bilge pump mechanisms and turned it on. The red light changed to green, then he knew he had succeeded. He then swam towards a giant steel door, and opened it, swimming into the next room, while closing and locking the door behind him. Immediately he could see the bilge pump was working and surfaced to a tiny pocket of air created by the pump. He was relieved but frozen. Minutes later, the tiny pocket of air turned into larger breathable space. But Dieter didn't care about breathing because his body was so cold, just breathing was torture.

It took almost ten minutes for the room to empty of water, every second an immeasurable amount of pain. Finally, the water was low enough to open the door. He opened to cheers and congratulations from the people on the other side but was too cold to care. They quickly found him blankets and warm clothes then moved him a part of the ship were they could care for him.

CHAPTER 5.11

Tucker had been hanging from his handcuffs for well over an hour. He tried to think of something funny to say to lighten the mood but was still in shock from the events that had occurred in the hour past.

Neither he nor Melanie were content, being hand cuffed in the galley. It took time but eventually one of the crew members came in and removed the hand cuffs. They were both interrogated then quarantined to a part of the ship that wouldn't interfere with the rest of the crew.

The captain waited as long as he could along the silt bottom. After four and half hour went by, they decided it was time to surface; thinking the U-boat had long disappeared from the site. The bilge pumps had been working none stop since they were turned on and most of the water had been pumped back into the Atlantic.

Like reviving Frankenstein from the dead the ballast tanks were engaged and the steel ship began to hoist itself from the sea floor, once again all was quiet aboard the submarine.

The captain gave the order to level off at 50 meters then plotted a course south for half a day until they knew they were clear of the enemy. The ship surfaced then radioed in their distress call to the Navy fleet explaining the damage and the scenario. They were ordered to dock at an undisclosed African port to make repairs to the semi-damaged submarine.

Again they plotted their new course taking only a day to arrive there.

Upon arrival the submarine underwent the surgery needed to cross the long cold stretch of the Atlantic. The crew counted their blessing that the ship was not permanently sunk in the Atlantic and Melanie, John and Tucker were escorted to a second ship that would bring them back to America. They too counted their blessings.

The captain was sad to see them leave and they parted ways as professionally as possible, some of the men even decided to salute him.

The trip home was mostly silent. John had been through a tremendous amount of pressure since accepting his mission. He'd left his brother behind; although, his brother had brought him an incredible amount of information, part of the deal for his return home. At times he'd forgotten the pledge he took to protect America, but after reuniting with Melanie got his priorities straight. It had been nearly ten years since he'd set foot on his native soil.

He spent the ride home studying the documents he'd been in charge of safeguarding. Mostly it was full of maps that showed prison camps and enemy strongholds and factories. It even included some maps of legend and lore. Hitler had wanted to use relics from the past to win his war, as seen in some of the Indiana Jones movies, but nothing could prepare John for one of the maps said to hold the directions to the ark. He made a copy of that map, for his keeping but would eventually return the rest to his government, just slightly altering the original.

When they arrived back at port along the Eastern seaboard all three were apprehended. Although the documents were immediately turned in to the higher authority the three were again questioned.

John spent three more years in a mental hospital until he was deemed not responsible for the attack on the submarine and was cleared of all wrong doing by the United States government and eventually awarded several medals for his undercover work.

Melanie became an American citizen 8 months after arriving in America and waited for her future husbands' release.

Tucker too became an American citizen and to this day he and his family continue to fight for the rights and freedoms of all people.

Fletcher managed to stay hidden within the ranks of the Germans until they were brought to justice for war crimes nearly 40 years later. John was always told he was still alive.

The information brought back to the American government gave them the edge they needed to win the war.

CHAPTER 6.0

THE MANIACAL VILLAIN

I suppose no great story would be complete without a proper villain. Well it just so happens that this villain or rather race of villains have been to Earth long, long, ago. Through a technology not quite developed by our own brilliant minds.

These beasts were so frightening that they wanted to feast on an intelligent race and a race that would know they were being hunted. So frightening in fact, they covered they faces when they arrived here first 50,000 then 5000 years. They taught humans the basics of mathematics so that in our future we would be worthy opponents to feast upon. They were so frightening, they wanted to eat our reflections first so that we'd have nowhere to run when the time came for them to eat us. The beasts of Sirius B, the name we gave their planet. Creatures who had evolved in the night, whereby it is said you can see their reflections in windows and mirrors, if one were so inclined to do so, however, most of us go about our days without the slightest inclination of their existence. But there plan was flawed by a line who first visited our planet 50,000 years ago.

These beasts had continued to evolve without any sort of apocalyptic catastrophe, unlike what happened to the dinosaurs of Earth, upon their planet giving them the technological advance through no depletion of species. It has been said that only the smartest of smartest humans could see or know of their ploy and plot to eventually eat us all. They had a tactic to seek out those who would not sleep because their minds were already full of fear from entering the dream world and not resting their brains.

However, 50,000 years ago during their first visit to Earth a line of compassionate beasts wanted not to eat us; they accounted for less than 0.000001 of their total population. During their last visit to Earth a portal, or stargate, was destroyed, destroying the link between our world and theirs; damning the beasts of Sirius to a doorway that could not be opened, locking it away deep in the sand somewhere in the Sahara desert.

This meant that one of them lived amongst us, hunting the beasts of our planet to spare us from becoming a favorite food. Stories of werewolves originated from this beast, far more intelligent than any man and far hungrier than any beast known to man.

Back on Sirius, the beasts vowed to kill and torture eternally all those who helped destroy the gateway and swore they'd return to Earth one day to finish the job. But the nights on Sirius B were growing thinner and the sun much hotter than any day here on Earth. They spent their time migrating with the darkness to avoid the light making them stronger, faster and hungrier than ever before, all while building a vessel to return them to Earth.

It was said that a young man had seen him years earlier chosen to help fight these beasts through his story as it sought its favorite drinking hole, water extremely high in oxygen - one of the secrets to everlasting life. He became one of the few people to have seen this beast and lived to talk about him. He felt the beast had been reading his thoughts rather than speaking, a trait known to exist amongst the beasts of Sirius.

This water was common on Sirius but only existed in two locations here on Earth, both known to be frequented by the beast. It lived in the shadows on Earth but coached Earthlings from a distance helping them prepare for the coming storm, however the beast remained so frightening that most that looked upon it died from the shock.

It would find people who would help him and feed on their livestock to survive.

But after all these years of living in the shadows one thing was for sure, the beasts of Sirius would be returning one day to take their vengeance.

CHAPTER 6.1

'Mouse, mouse' it had been almost a month of trying to catch a mouse, a creature with little or no purpose except to make my life difficult. The hunter had been gone for almost a week and my mother at least six months. I would have showered to remove the war paint from my eyes but with no hot running water life was becoming more difficult. No showers and no hot water to clean dishes, no baths, just me and the ever growing insanity of not living up to my expectations.

Because it was free to move about the house, it kept me from getting any sleep. Surely if there were unknown creatures that hunt in the night I would be worthy prey since my mind had not fully rested in weeks.

Time and time again the peanut butter would be removed from the traps without catching any rodent. My brain had been so overloaded from lack of sleep that even television, yes television my greatest ally seemed to be turning on me. Commercials of happy couples, peanut butter even working washing machines and tires, programs seemed as though they were being beamed through time and space just to humiliate me.

My little dog had taken to sleeping more everyday and seemed to like me less and less. My war wounds were taking their toll, keeping me from healing completely from this so-called tragedy. I started to envision the routes the mouse would take through the house; rodent roadways with signs saying if you don't want to get caught go this way. I was the Wile Coyote and he or she the road runner.

Like any cunning military man I began to place blockades in front of known passages the mouse might wander then set traps right in front of or near those blockades.

But something eluded me, my shadow. I hadn't seen Peppercorn Ranch in almost two weeks. The funny thing was prior to this mouse hunt I was philosophizing about the world around me. How important the breakdown and interpretation of colors of the rainbow could be applied to undiscovered planets. Could all blue planets be blue and red ones red and so forth and given characteristics that follow color theory. That not all planets had the same genetic makeup as our so-called Earth but rather these laws could be twisted ever so slightly depending on some given circumstances. For example, all trees being blue instead of green because the chlorophyll from that particular planet was in fact blue instead of green.

I'd even come to the conclusion that time travel might be the last thing ever invented by humans provided we didn't kill each other all first. How first we would need a teleporter, like the ones used in the movie 'the Fly' to first move an object. Then the machine would need a specific almost, 4th dimensional positioning system to travel backwards and forwards. I was already going crazy thinking, trying to figure out things that I believed hadn't been thought of before.

The truth was I was fascinated to have found a series of documents and maps that meticulously fallen some weeks earlier from inside a box in the garage. My father had always been sort of a collector of rare antiquities. Inside a dossier, one I had never seen before, were maps that dated back thousands of years.

There were two maps that seemed very interesting to me. One of them was purchased at a bazaar in India titled "The Well of Life" in Chinese translation, but it wasn't the original copy, just a duplicate. The other hand been handed down to my grandmother who worked as a nurse at a mental hospital. She always said the patient had stole it from the government and insisted it was only right to give it away, rather than to keep for himself. Supposedly, this guy was some sort of American hero, but I never heard anything too much about it. She almost threw it out except she thought it might have some value and kept it throughout the years.

Apparently my dad had gone to investigate some of these maps, but I had never heard too much about it, just that he sought to seek his fortune from them. He'd assembled a team years ago to explore the world but I had never heard from him much. He'd sent me a package some years earlier that had a single ring in it, it look tarnished and hardly worth anything. I was always disappointed there was no gold or anything, but apparently one of his finds went to a government facility, which I guess was pretty cool.

CHAPTER 7.0

INTO EGYPT

C hristian, Bella, Mark and Hakim all studied archeology at the University of California and graduated top of their class. Going into the final semester it was unsure what or where they would be going once they finished but, it just so happens, that an offer had been made from an undisclosed party who wanted to research the authenticity of some maps that had found their way into the undisclosed parties possession. Christian was the first to examine the maps, he declared that one of them was authentic, dating back 2000 years or so, the second couldn't be older than 60 years tops, but was made to an interesting likeness of what appeared to be somewhere in Egypt.

Then the offer was made, Christian was asked to assemble a team of new graduates for an all expenses paid trip to research the locations on the maps. At first he was hesitant, but the more he thought about it the more he thought he could work with Bella and some his friends that he'd made during his studies at the University. Most other students were already offered jobs from companies around the globe. Christian liked the offer but wasn't sure if his friends would go along with him, although they would make a great team.

He kept his mouth shut for the remaining semester until they had finished their exams and earned their degrees. He made the offer after some graduation photographs were taken; they were all sitting around a picnic table talking about their new found success.

"What are you all going to do now?" He asked, keeping his intentions a secret.

Bella was first to answer. "I might go stay at my fathers' cabin for a few months until I can find some sort of work."

"What about you?" She asked Hakim.

"I want to return home to India, there are still many secrets to our beginnings buried away in the Earth." said Hakim. "What about you Mark?" asked Hakim.

"Not sure. I guess I'll keep bartending for now, I've sent resumes to dig teams all over North America but have only heard back from a few, you know paleontology. My job pays pretty well, but the lease on my apartment doesn't expire for another few weeks, then maybe I'll take one of those offers."

Christian listened to all of this, then spoke up. "A man came to me at the beginning of the semester; he wanted me to investigate the authenticity of some maps he'd collected. After I told him the answers he asked to hire me upon graduation, its expenses paid for me..." everyone looked at each other. "...and my team."

"Where did you meet this man?" Asked Bella.

"I'm not sure, I mean, he found me."

"So what do you think?" He asked the group.

They looked at each other. "Where would we be going?" asked Bella.

Christian replied. "Somewhere in Egypt, I think that's where the newer map was from, the other was older, much older, but I had no idea where or what the other map was showing." "So what do you think?" he continued. "Are you in?"

The group looked at each other, Bella was the first to reply.

"I'm in" she stated.

"Me too" said Mark.

They looked at Hakim; he wasn't convinced "I don't know."

"C'mon." said Bella. "You said you always wanted to go to back to India, this is the next best thing."

"Alright I'm in too." replied Hakim.

"Great!" said Christian. "We leave from LA to Cairo in a weeks' time."

CHAPTER 7.1

By the time they had arrived in Cairo they were exhausted, the year was 1981 and the world was becoming a busy place. They exited the plane and followed the walkway towards the baggage turnstile, gathered their belongings the exited towards the main terminal.

Once in the main lobby of the airport, they saw a fellow holding a sign, Legamond it read, Christian's last name. They introduced themselves then followed the man out of the airport and into a van.

"So," the man said. "How do you like Cairo?"

"So far so good, but when can we eat?" asked Mark.

"Anytime." the man replied. "I know the best restaurants in town." he continued

"You want me to stop to get food?" the man asked.

"Yes." replied the group.

Minutes later he'd pulled over to a small, hole in the wall kind of place, but the group was surprised how good the food tasted. Once they were all finished they loaded back into the van which drove them to a hotel.

It seemed as though the reception people had been waiting for them, they were greeted with courteous smiles and shown to their rooms. They weren't sure what would happen next. Each took their time changing into new, lighter clothes then met in the hotel lobby for a drink.

Some of the group were still unsure what they were doing there. It seemed a little unorganized but everything so far seemed to be working in their favor. After a couple hours of conversing in the lobby, one of the receptionists approached the group and asked for Christian saying he had a phone call.

He got up and answered the call then came back and sat down with the group.

"We leave in the morning." he said. "There will be another van waiting for us to take us and some supplies to our destination."

The group had mixed emotions about hearing this, but ordered one more round then went to bed.

The following morning came rather early. By 5:30 the group was in the lobby ready for adventure. They travelled east towards the Suez

Canal and the Red Sea, then South along the Red Sea's shoreline. By midday they'd stormed the cooler for sandwiches and bottles of Coca-Cola stopping every once in a while to take pictures to document their adventure.

As the evening approached they set up camp along one of the beaches and watched as the sun set into the Sahara desert. The camp fire kept them warm as the temperatures dipped substantially from the heat of the day time.

They all slept soundly that evening and the following day, tore down the camp and loaded into the van again to continue their travels towards an unknown destination. The van had a hard time navigating through the desert, the infrastructure was far less modern, the further one travels into the desert. People they passed were riding bicycles or sometimes camels as very few people were using modern transportation. Ruts and desert pot holes were quite common and the van left a smoky dust trail that rejoined the desert after it settled down.

The ocean kept the insanity of the desert from creeping up on them. Had they been travelling directly into the Sahara the attitude might have been different, but, for now, the desert kept from causing the insanity the desert is known to cause.

The trip was taking much longer then it normally would have, in that, the van was not travelling at a very high speed. The desert was making sure it was respected and seemed to want to pull the van right into its metaphorical gaping mouth. At 40 kilometers an hour the 600 km journey was taking twice as long.

There was little being said inside the van, the group generally kept to themselves.

As nightfall approached they set up camp once again. Then the driver said "Tomorrow, I get you to where you are going."

As morning dawned, Mark had already prepped a pot of coffee, and one by one as the group withdrew from their slumbers, they filled up on the fresh pot of coffee. Within an hour or so they'd torn down the camp yet again and were packed inside the van.

Their curiosity peeked as they learned they were approaching the destination.

"They found something you know." said the driver

"What did they find?" asked Christian.

"Something, I am not sure, but everybody laughed because the desert hides all. If you lose something the desert it will never be found again."

Bella looked to the group with big eyes, as if to say *'see, perhaps this will be worth it after all.'*

The ocean sparkled from the van as it drove along the shoreline; it was hard to believe the root modern civilization originated from this general area, it was like they were in the cradle of life. The van began to slow down as it approached a series of erected tents. It was just after 11:30 in the morning and they had finally reached their destination.

CHAPTER 7.2

A man approached the van as they pulled in, and he looked like an archeologist, if one were to say that indefinitely that an archeologist stereotype existed. He was an older man, with a long white and red beard, dressed in big boots and clothes made to tackle the desert.

"Welcome, welcome." he said. "We have been awaiting your arrival for some time now"

They exited the van and began to gather their things.

"Leave it," said the man "We have people that will set up your tents."

He brought them into a tent probably used for eating as it had several large tables and many chairs.

"How was your journey?" he asked.

"It was fine." began Christian. "We were glad you were able to set up accommodations for us which were very nice of you."

"Not me." he said. "Christian the man you met has also set up this dig for me; he has been paying for everything. He even got approved for a grant, but put some of his own money into it."

"So why did you choose us?" asked Hakim.

"Well" said the old man "I am getting older and my mind is not as sharp as it used to be, I asked for additional help was told the best would coming to assist me. How long have you been archeologists, how many digs have you done?"

"We've only been archeologists for a couple weeks now, we just graduated."

"Oh I see." Said the man. "Well let me introduce myself, my name is Walter, I have done many digs and researched many finds here in Egypt; but this, this is truly exciting." he exclaimed.

He didn't waste any time and pulled an artifact out from a locked chest.

"We used a map to find this, when we first arrived there was nothing here, then we realized there was a cave here buried in the sand. After we dug out the entrance, we realized it was a very old cave and once we went inside of it we found this." He handed them the artifact. It was made of stone and had an etching of a shark, a snake and a wolf. The artifact was passed around the group.

"How old is it?" asked Bella.

"Not as old as we were hoping, the stone dates back about 50 years or so, but it wasn't that that surprised us."

"What was the surprise?" asked Mark.

"Here, follow me." said Walter

"What about the artifact?" asked Christian.

"In time." replied the man. "I will let you investigate it later, but first you must follow me."

They walked five or so minutes down the path. It was a busy place, bustling with Egyptians who'd earned an income working for Walter and the rest of his team. Finally they approached the mouth of the cave. It was easy to see how the mouth of the cave had been excavated and reopened to allow in the rest of the world.

"Although the stone and the age of the cave don't seem to match up, that wasn't the most intriguing discovery." he said "See look here." Then pointed to the ground "We were able to carbon date the footprints, these ones, look to be from biblical times."

"So the cave dates back that long, but the tablet didn't" asked Bella.

"That's correct, but look, there is another set of footprints and these ones are not that old." said Walter pointing to strange phenomenon in the sand

The group looked at the prints

"Are those even human?" asked Mark.

"Precisely." Exclaimed Walter

"This must be some sort of hoax." exclaimed Hakim

"I assure you, these prints are hardly even 50 years old, but this was not our doing, once we opened the cave these are the prints we found." said Walter.

"So you are saying something, not human, entered this cave, but why." asked Bella

"Well because of the authenticity of the original footprints, we believe there was a relic of some importance in this cave and if I'm correct, something entered this cave to retrieve it."

"Then why not take the tablet?" asked mark.

"Perhaps not take but leave; it could be a map to find the original relic."

The group was shocked after only a few weeks of graduating from their classroom, everything they'd learnt just went out the window. Talk of aliens or monsters, ancient relics; in no classroom whatsoever did any teacher ever talk about aliens or monsters. They were in a league all of their own.

Astounded of the archeologists claim, they went back to the camp and began to search for instruments and tools to begin their archeological discoveries. Lunch had been prepared and was just about to get underway.

"He's crazy." said Hakim. "There is no way I'm going to believe this is not a hoax. They probably faked all those footprints then brought us out here to try to justify the claim."

"Well we are archeologists." said Christian. "Perhaps we should use what we've learned and try to determine as much as we can while we're here. After all, the entire trip was paid for plus a big salary. I think we should hang around and find out if any of this is true."

"I agree." said Mark. "If Walter isn't lying it could be one of the biggest finds in archeological history. I say we stay."

"Me too." said Bella.

After lunch the spent the rest of the day investigating the claim, until night fell and even worked well into the night. It had been a long day by the time they went sleep and were anxious about the following day.

CHAPTER 7.3

As dawn broke Christian was the first to wake and was followed shortly by Bella. They went down to the ocean to talk to one another.

"I'm glad you decided to join me on this adventure." said Christian.

"Me too." said Bella "I guess it helps that I always had a crush on you."

Christian turned red from a blush, and she leaned over and gave him a kiss on the cheek. He tried to muster up some words but she was already on her way back to the camp before he could say anything.

The rest of the day was spent authenticating the claim Walter had made, a series of lab tests, research and deliberation. Bella spent most of the day right beside Walter inside the cave listening to what he had to say. Christian was fixated on the tablet. He studied it over and over again trying to determine if it had any significance. The more he pondered its secrets the more he wanted to believe what the Walter was saying was true. That evening they sat around the dinner table taking turns talking about what they'd found that day. Hakim stayed skeptical of the whole thing but the rest of the group was becoming more enthusiastic about the short time they'd already spent in Egypt.

Christian was the first to wake again the following day. He walked down to the beach just like he did every morning since arriving at the Red Sea. He was dumbfounded about the relevance of the artifact. He sipped from his coffee starring off into the ocean and walking along the sandy shore. This routine continued for about a week. Waking, walking to the beach starring at the shoreline from the water, going about the rest of the day.

One afternoon, he joined fishing boat to catch some fish for supper. Suddenly, he noticed something familiar about the shoreline like he had seen it somewhere before, but he couldn't quite how or why he'd seen that shoreline before. Around lunch time, Christian began to study the artifact once again. It was the shape of the snake, the shark that seemed to bite his tail and the wolf, large and standing on two feet. Then he remembered the shoreline. It mimicked the contour of the snake, which had a specific number of scales. He decided to bring it to the group.

"Look at this." he said when he returned from the boat. "The snake matches exactly the contour of the shoreline. Do you think that's what it could be?"

"You mean, the snake is supposed to represent the shoreline." asked Hakim.

"That could be, and look exactly 11 scales on its back, I thought maybe it represents a prime number equation, but it could be a distance." said Christian.

"So you think there is another cave or artifact buried along the shoreline?" asked Bella.

"I guess it's possible, but look." said Christian holding up the artifact and a picture he took of the shoreline form the boat. It matched it almost perfectly. "I think if we go eleven kilometers or maybe miles we might find another cave and hopefully get some answers about this one."

They brought the claim to Walter who suggested first thing in the morning they take an ATV and investigate whether this claim could be proven. Walter was almost more excited than Christian because he believed what he found was not a hoax.

That evening their spirits were high and they even opened a case of beer to celebrate their findings. Walter was great at regaling tales of his youth and even Hakim and Mark shared stories of their youth. Eventually, everyone went to bed, some slept soundly from drink and others too excited to sleep from their latest and most excellent archeological discovery.

The next morning Christian was the first to wake as usual. He followed by Mark and Walter. They started gathering supplies to make the trek along the ocean shoreline, filled up on gas and even brought some extra supplies just in case.

By six o'clock A.M. the two left on their ATV's with as many supplies as they could carry. They scurried along the shoreline dodging rocks and following the desert path as best they could. They were well beyond any towns or cities, meaning only desert as they travelled forward. They used the instruments as best they could, calculating the distance between the starting point and the relative destination.

They counted both miles and kilometers as they trotted through the desert. By eleven o'clock they'd travelled 10 kilometers and began to take in their surroundings with a little bit more awareness. After exactly 11 kilometers they came to rest near a giant outstretch of rock heaving up towards the heavens.

"Well would you look at that." said Mark.

His gaze was fixated upon the upheaval of rock that looked surprisingly like a shark, a gapping mouth with serrated rocks that looked just like teeth. They walked up towards the desert dune and began to investigate further.

Mark began to kick the rock formation. "It's solid stone, it won't move an inch."

Christian referenced a rubbing that he'd done from the artifact. "The only thing I can think of is that one of the teeth might be an opening." He referenced the rubbing and showed Mark that one of the sharks' teeth was out of place, extending out from its mouth rather than up.

"That means there might be a doorway somewhere." He started tapping along the rocky surface looking for anything that meant his idea was plausible. It seemed possible; they'd got this far on just a hunch. Mark walked one way across the plateau and Christian the other, tapping, tapping, tapping.

Then Mark yelled out "I've found something. Look here." The rock was pliable like sand and broke away easily, unlike the other material that made up the peak. Christian walked back a few feet and glanced towards the hill, it fit the picture, and it looked like one of its teeth. He ran back over to Mark and the two of them started to hammer away at the semi porous matter shattering it more with every strike.

They got some tools they'd loaded up on the ATV's and continued to break away the solidified sand, striking, striking. After one particular hit the sun shone through the dark, dreary cavern hitting the floor of the cave, the first time light had been in its presence in years. Bit by bit the lighted hole crumbled away allowing more and more light to shine through. In no time at all the entrance to the cave had been excavated and was once again allowing in the human presence.

Christian got on his radio and said. "We found another cave just like the artifact said; maybe you guys should get here to see this for yourselves."

He grabbed a torch and entered the cave, Mark wasn't far behind with and flashlight.

The cave was dark, he was sure there hadn't been people in it for years, maybe even hundreds of years. He shined the light on the ground. "Look at this, same footprints that were in the other cave." They were big, had four claws and toes, probably a full foot without the claws and toes. They followed the tracks, careful not to step on them the torch guiding their way through the darkness.

The light came to rest on a chest, or treasure chest of some sort. It was old decorated in gold and jewels, Christian was eager to open it. He walked up to the chest and began to slide of the top. It crashed to the ground breaking the decorative stone in two. He quickly shone the light inside. There were two more stone map artifacts and a ring.

The ring looked futuristic and shone like no other, he went to pick it up then it quickly changed its appearance, to tarnished silver look. Christian quickly dropped it into his pocket then turned to check on Mark.

Mark was amazed by the chest as he approached it. "Well would you look at this." he said walking up to it. "What do you think it is?"

"I'm not sure; we're going to need a second opinion." Said Christian.

CHAPTER 7.4

As evening dawned and the sun was set to cross the Sahara, two jeeps pulled up outside the cave. Walter, Hakim and Bella were among them as well as some additional help.

"Well done young man." said Walter as he approached the cave. He lifted up the original artifact and could see the likeness to the newly discovered cave. They walked inside the cave to find their newest discovery. Walter was dumbfounded "Can it be?" he exclaimed. "Have you found the Ark of the Covenant?"

"It's cladding is very decorative, but inside I found two more stone tablets; just like the one we found in the other cave." Said Christian.

Walter began to study chest "This might very well be the biggest find in archeological history. I want to alert the press but first we need to study the authenticity of this find."

Christian walked over to the stone tablets inside the chest. They were different then original. It had giant numbers at the top of the tablets then a sort of 3D mapping technique. It was like looking at miniature model carved in stone.

Bella commented on the chest. "What happened to the lid, it's broken in two."

"I opened it when I came into the cave. I didn't mean to break it when I opened it." replied Christian.

Christian walked back out of the cave and into the desert he reached into his pocket and felt the ring he'd just found. Hakim was just leaving to go pick up the gear to spend the night at the new location, a find like this could not be abandoned during the night.

Walter exited the cave and stated "It turns out you were right the stone artifact was a map that lead us to this new find. Your name will go down in history for finding this, not bad for a rookie."

Christian had mixed emotions about this new find. *'What did it all mean'* he thought to himself. The tracks in the cave, the ring, two more tablets. It seemed like this new adventure was just about to begin. They were going to be here for a while, to figure this all out.

CHAPTER 7.5

One week later, the team had been busy day and night documenting every possible aspect of the new claim, and its relation to the old one. Mark was a bit of an artist and sketched a number of drawings of the treasure chest. Walter and Bella had been working side by side the entire time leaving Christian a bit jealous and frustrated. That evening as they sat inside the foods tent they had a discussion.

"It seems," began Walter "That we have made a significant find in the archeological community. When I took this job I was sure that nothing would be found. The original map had been handed down from a mental patient who had stolen the information from the Nazi's of WWII. How they never found this remains somewhat of mystery, possibly because their map was stolen."

"But whatever was in the original cave," continued Walter "seems to have been moved to a new cave by some-sort of alien or monster, which drew a map to find what we believe is the ark spoken of in the Old Testament. The problem is the scientific community will never accept this account, nor will the general public. As such I want to stay here to try to find a more conventional story, one that doesn't involve monsters or aliens. Can you see the problem brewing?"

"I didn't believe you at first until I saw the same tracks in the new cave, but what could have made them. You say aliens, but there has been scientific explanation." Said Hakim.

"Precisely, young man, which is why I want the four of you to investigate further the new artifacts located from the new cave. How would you feel about that?"

"An alien scavenger hunt, seems dangerous." Said Christian. He paused reaching into his pocket then decided to speak up. "There is something else, something I didn't tell the rest of you." he was ashamed.

"Well what is it young man?" Asked Walter.

"I found something else inside the ark or whatever; when I reached for it, it, it glowed like the stars, then after I picked it up turned to the color it is now." he handed Walter the ring.

"I'm sorry, I should not have tried to keep it for myself." he paused. "But I do believe it was alien, nothing on Earth can glow like that then change its appearance, it was like a hybrid metal."

Walter looked at him with disappointment.

"I do think we are on an alien scavenger hunt, and do think going after any artifacts we find through a stone tablet, left for us to follow would be dangerous; especially if we think it was conjured up by some alien." continued Christian. The group went silent. It was a difficult concept to except.

"Well," said Walter. "I was going to tell you the university has decided to further our funding as did the original owner of the map; the man that spoke to you Christian and the man that decided to hire me. If you so choose to embark on this endeavor it will be paid for, but the rest is up to you."

"I'm always up for adventure." said Mark

"Me too." said Bella

"I think we are all in, again." said Hakim

"The numbers at the top of these artifacts correspond directly to GPS coordinates. I've taken the liberty of researching where these coordinates correspond and these are the results. One is somewhere in Mexico, and given that the artifact details square pyramids it is only logical that whatever is there is buried under an ancient city or civilization."

"I've heard stories about aliens that helped build some of those cities" began Bella "Could it be that an intelligent race helped them to build those cities."

"Precisely my dear." exclaimed Walter "Perhaps those alien architects placed what we've found here."

It sounded ludicrous, still, but after everything that had been found in the last two weeks it started to add up to Walter's conclusion.

"The second artifact" he continued "Looks to be an island East of Fiji; and judging by this 3D model is located inside a sunken ship of some sort." said Walter. He was sure the stone tablets did not lie.

"I think it is only appropriate that Christian and Bella go to locate the items marked from this, the Fijian artifact, since they have experience in scuba diving and underwater training, while Mark and Hakim go to investigate the other stone scripture in the Mexican town of Chichen Itza. I will make arrangements tomorrow for your travels and wish you all the best of luck in researching our latest find. So with that I say good evening to you all and we shall discuss further in the morning"

Walter exited the tent. The team was apprehensive again, this meant they would be further investigating stone tablets to some sort of treasure. It was difficult for the team to sleep that night as their minds pondered the events that had already occurred and the journey they would be undertaking in the near future.

CHAPTER 7.6

Hakim and Mark were the first to arrive to their new destination – Chichen Itza. Walter had made arrangements for the two of them to explore the surrounding area with a sort of archeologist pass. The year was still 1981 and the public was allowed to tour the ancient civilization without guides or without hassle from the government, however, guided tours were still available.

They had taken four different planes to arrive in Cancun, two to get to France and then another two planes to arrive in Cancun. Mark was exhausted; he spent the entire trip trying to sleep but the noise from the plane kept him from getting any significant shut eye. He'd already solved almost half the puzzles in a crossword puzzle book he purchased before leaving the city of Egypt.

It was difficult to say goodbye to Bella and Christian who were heading towards the South Pacific, but was glad he wasn't travelling alone. Unlike Mark, Hakim seemed to sleep most of the way there. He snoozed almost elegantly, as the plane crossed the Atlantic and was in tip top shape while travelling the airports, from plane to plane; but was glad to finally be at their destination.

First on the list was to get some food, second was to travel the three hour drive from Cancun to the Chichen Itza pyramids build long ago on the Yucatan peninsula. The air was significantly humid and not quite as dry as in the desert, but it was June and the hot season was well underway.

They arranged for a cab to take them to the pyramids and managed to negotiate a cheap fare with one of the drivers. But because there were no hotels in the area the duo would needed to bring tents, along with a huge checklist of necessities they made before leaving Egypt. Once the cab was on the highway, the tension from inner city traffic and general stress, causing frustrations that come with heat and travelling, were subdued.

Mark kept one hand out of the vehicle moving it, like a dolphin in the water, making his fingers and hand wave up and down with the fresh Mexican air. He was happy but tired. The trip had made him forget about all the significant finds he and his friends had made in the last couple weeks. He was sure glad Christian had asked him to join the expedition; after all he was only a few weeks away from being homeless and unemployed.

But Hakim was different. Everyone always believed his family must have been rich although he never talked about it. He was always the first to buy the books, was one of the first to move into the dormitory at the university even got to buy his lunch everyday instead of bringing a lunch to school. But even he was glad to be part of the expedition, somehow and for some reason he didn't really want to go home.

The cab driver tried to make conversation with the group as they sped down the Mexican highway, but his English was poor and neither Mark nor Hakim spoke Spanish very well. The trip from Cancun took three hours through the Mexican jungle and since it was nearing the summer, temperatures by day were extremely high.

Mark wiped the sweat from his brow then reached into the cooler they'd brought to get a cold drink. He cracked the top of the bottle, and then finished the entire thing in just a few gulps. But that wasn't enough; he reached in again for a second cola, given that the he was sweating from every pore in his body. He motioned to both Hakim and the driver to see if they wanted anything to drink. Hakim was eager to have a soda and drank from it while wiping his brow. The driver reluctantly refused, he was okay just driving in the summer heat.

The jungle carried on for miles and if modern scientific achievements hadn't already dismissed the notion of jungle monsters Mark would have believed it, as though the Earth still had mysteries that hadn't been discovered yet. But Mark was one to know, he'd spent several evenings in the Montana outback before he started university. He always felt no matter who you were the world was still a scary place and not so much because of other humans, but rather the fear that can set in when the imagination dismisses intellectual reasoning. Mark was one of the few who'd gone on a vision quest originally developed the native Indians hundreds of years ago. By the third and forth days he hadn't slept, had barely eaten, his imagination ran wild with the notions of monsters, and of hallucinations that would baffle modern science. But he never talked too much about it; people would call him crazy for the things he saw during those five days in the wilderness. But when he finished, he considered himself a man.

Time went by slow as they neared the ancient village; every turn of the tire brought them closer to their destination. The road was not nearly as bumpy as it had been Egypt and was even paved to allow most cars to travel along it. Mark was tired enough to sleep but rather kept his eyes on the jungle, that passed in a hurry, while in the moving car.

Around four o'clock that evening the cab reached its destination. The pair paid the driver the agreed upon amount then started to unload their belongings from the vehicle. Mark threw his backpack over his shoulder then began to take in his surroundings. Hakim stretched, reaching for his toes then placing his arms behind his back continued to stretch.

"So where do we check in?" joked Hakim.

The cab driver quickly sped away once all the gear had been unloaded from the car.

"I'm not sure where we're supposed to set up camp, but Walter said we could stay within the park a slight walk from the main pyramid."

For those of you who don't know Chichen Itza is an ancient village with a pyramid at the center of it. Many buildings have been built in or within a short walking distance complete with cenotes (large round cylindrical cliffs with water below) and ancient architecture.

Since they had time before they needed to start digging, they left their bags with the administration office and decided to take the last guided tour of the day of the ancient city.

They learned that the ancient civilization was quite barbaric - sacrifices, deadly games of ancient basketball, but above all the use of mathematics in all the structures surrounding the pyramid and the pyramid itself.

When the tour was over they spoke to the tour guide in hopes of learning where they would be setting up camp. She brought them to a map that showed the entire site of the Chichen Itza city then showed a small clearing on the map where archeologists where allowed to camp, provided they were permitted by the government; something Walter had arranged before they left.

They gathered their things, and then headed towards the location on the map; everything else would have to wait until the morning. They got to a small clearing in the jungle, currently being excavated by the government. It was easy to see stone entwined by roots from the jungle floor. They set up their tent, made some supper then went to bed for an early morning start.

As morning dawned, the heat inside the tent became unbearable; by 7:30 it was enough to awake the duo to their morning duties. It started out simple, make some breakfast and some coffee then they got to reading the maps they'd brought with them.

"It looks simple enough." began Mark "Although we don't have the original stone tablet, I made several drawings as precise as I could, but, I do also have a photo of the tablet." "Look," he continued "Right here, that should be the pyramid and the other buildings are corresponding to the map as well, the tomb of the high priest plus even the observatory. Right in the middle of all three is our 'X' assuming 'x' marks the spot."

"What about those pathways, we can follow them to the 'x' since they all seem to converge on the 'x'."

"Agreed" said Mark. We'll start from the pyramid then follow the angled trajectory of the 'x' maybe this pathway is a river or creek so we'll follow it from El Castillo, the pyramid."

Mark wasn't all dressed, he put on his socks then his hiking boots. Hakim a bit more of an early riser was already dressed for the job. The park didn't open until nine o'clock so that gave them almost a whole hour and a half to conduct the research they needed to do.

They walked back down the rocky path for almost a quarter mile or so, since the camp site was a fair distance from the rest of the city. As they approached the courtyard they were overwhelmed with grandeur and scale of the city. Although there were walls and buildings they were all decorated in stone sculpture depicting stories from the past and gods who gave knowledge to humans.

After a fifteen minute hike through the city they finally reached the pyramid.

"If we turn this map to orientate with our location, then we should head South Easterly to find our buried treasure." insisted Mark

They began to walk in that direction, at first a hundred paces then a few hundred more until finally they got to, roughly, where the 'x' had been indicated on the stone tablet.

"If this where we are supposed to be, there is no 'x' marked anywhere, at least not on the ground" said Mark.

"What about the first tablet." began Hakim. "There was a bit of mystery to it, remember?" The scales of the snake indicated a distance, a distance that lead us to a cave that looked like a shark. Maybe there is a riddle of some sort we need to solve, in order to find the treasure."

Mark was dumbfounded. He wasn't very good at riddles.

"We could definitely use Christian right about now." he stated. Then looked back towards the pyramid, then at the map, then at the ground and continue to do so for about a minute or so. Hakim took a seat on the grassy plain cupping his hands at the knees.

"I don't understand." said Mark "We're right here, right exactly where we are supposed to be, so why isn't there any indication or clue for where we are supposed to go next."

"We could try digging." said Hakim.

"But where are the pathways?" he pointed again to the picture of the tablet "These definitely look like pathways or creeks and there is nothing here."

The time was 9:30 and tourists began to flock in to view the ancient city. They didn't look like archeologists, they looked like treasure hunters who'd been led astray.

"What should we do?" asked Mark.

"We can come back tonight and try digging, maybe the treasure is buried around here somewhere." replied Hakim.

"We could dig for days and not find anything, besides our passes are subject to the preservation of this site. I don't think the Mexican government would like it very much if we are digging holes in one of their biggest tourist attractions."

He'd lost hope. Either the map was a dud or they'd been on a wild goose chase from the start. Mark looked at the ground then began to fold up the map and put it in his pocket. They walked over to the pyramid then took a seat at the base of it.

They sat there for about twenty minutes watching other tourist taking pictures of the pyramid and every once in a while a tour group would pass by with a tour guide talking about who, when, and how these pyramids were built. They were thirsty and tired, after all, they'd hit a complete dead end.

"I'm going to go buy a soda from the vendor, do you want something to drink?" asked Hakim.

"Yah sure, get me a Coke or Seven-up." replied Mark.

Hakim got up then started to walk back towards the entrance to the park, the only place that sold beverages.

Mark sat starring at the ground his hands cupped upon his face. He was ready to admit, he'd met defeat.

He listened as another tour group walked within range. The tour guide was talking about the complex mathematics that went into the construction of the pyramid. "And." she added "There is a complex series of tunnels that run beneath the pyramid and some of the other buildings. They connect just about everything inside this city."

Mark raised his head from his hands. "Could you repeat that." he asked the tour guide "Yes of course." she said "This site was built on a series of tunnels that run through the entire city. They connect the cenotes, the pyramid and even extend through to most of the buildings that have been built here as well. But we don't allow tourists down there it is too dangerous"

He was thrilled *'That's it'* "Thank you so much." he yelled, then began to chase after Hakim.

When he found Hakim he was standing in line for a drink, just about to order from the lady behind the counter. He saw Mark running up to him out of the corner of his eye, then turned to face him just as he approached the kiosk.

"That's it" said Mark. "That's it."

"What's it?" asked Hakim.

"Tunnels." said Mark. "There are a series of tunnels that run underneath the complex. I'll bet you if anything is down there that's where to find it. So let's go back to camp then tonight, with the proper gear we investigate the tunnel system."

Hakim agreed then the two of them walked back to their tent sipping from some well deserved soda beverages.

CHAPTER 7.7

They waited right through till the evening. Judging from the night before, by 5:30 there were only a hundred or so people left at the archeologist site, but their doors were closed by 6:00 to anyone who wasn't an archeologist. In fact they were lucky, they were the only two archeologists around for miles. Mark figured it was because everything that had been needed or intended on being found had already been found.

Hakim had occasionally walked to the end of the path that emptied into the plains where the buildings were constructed. Each time he'd return stating that fewer and fewer people were still around to take in the park, and by 6 o'clock they were the only two people left in the park.

They began to gather things they'd need to explore the caves below, headlamps, ropes, additional flashlights, hiking boots even onetime use scuba bottles in case they needed to travel any distances underwater.

"Do you really think you'll need that?" asked Mark.

"A machete?" replied Hakim. "I wouldn't even consider going anywhere without it."

They'd spent a good half an hour prepping for their journey into the cavern systems underneath the ancient city of Chichen Itza, until they were at last well on their way. They had a couple more hours of daylight available to them but that wouldn't make much difference once they entered the caverns system. They walked one foot in front of the other, in single file, from their camp until they reached the open plains of the city. The city was barren. There were no tourists around and the duo felt a little bit like they owned the ancient city. They headed straight for the pyramid and began to climb the steep ascent to the top of the pyramid.

Once at the top they took a minute to view the magical city from an elevated height. They could see for miles, but the jungle surrounded the outskirts of the city much like an ocean surrounds an island. Mark took a couple shots with his camera then followed Hakim.

Hakim had found a set of stairs that led into a small room at the top of the pyramid. It was built inside the pyramid and the only light came from the four stairwells that bordered the four magnetic directions, North, South, East and West. From there, there was a railing system that kept tourists from a four by four hole in the pyramid that descended into to crypt of the city.

Mark reached into his gear bag and found a glow stick, broke it to activate it, then dropped it down the shaft. It fell, illuminating the shaft of the crypt as it fell, until finally it hit the ground.

"That's at least two hundred feet down." said Mark.

"Good thing I brought plenty of rope." replied Hakim. Then he began to fasten the rope to a stone pillar to allow for their descent into the caverns.

"Are you scared?" asked Mark.

"No, not yet. Are you?" asked Hakim.

"A little bit, we don't know what's down there." replied Mark.

"That's why we're going down into this thing, to find out what's there." answered Hakim. Then he threw the rope down into the hole. "By the way Mark, you're going into this thing first."

Mark was already to go, his harness was on but he was a little skeptical about being the first into the caverns. Hakim fastened the rope around the harness and Mark stepped over the edge and into the descent. First only a few feet at a time, then got comfortable with descending and went some ten feet at a time. In just a few minutes the light from the glow stick was feet beneath him. He rappelled one last time until his feet touched the cavern floor.

The floor was a little bit wet. Apparently this cavern had been carved by an underground spring that barely flowed anymore.

"I'm at the bottom." he yelled up to Hakim but there was no response.

He reached behind his head then turned on the light that was wrapped around his head. The light seemed to shine everywhere and Mark found he was in a rather large cavern. Upon further inspection he saw there were three other passages that went in different directions underneath the city.

He began to walk around slowly and cautiously looking at stalactites and stalagmites and other limestone deposits inside the cavern. Every step he took was educated as he navigated through the darkness. Then he looked behind him. The rope was moving and he assumed Hakim had begun his descent into the cavern system. He waited and watched as Hakim rappelled down the shaft into the underground chamber. Suddenly he could see the light from his headgear and watched as he rappelled the final few feet into the cavern.

Hakim could see the light from Mark's headgear. He was already navigating the cavern. Hakim pulled the rope from his harness and began to follow the light emitted by Mark's headlamp.

"There's three passages." Mark called out to Hakim. Hakim took a second to look around and could clearly see there were in fact three passages that lead deeper into the cavern system. He walked closer to Mark and began to pull the map from his back pocket. He oriented himself north and then adjusted the map to correspond.

Mark was already heading in the direction of the cavern that lead towards the "X".

"Wait up." shouted Hakim in the darkness. He walked through the sunless grotto and caught up to Mark.

"It's this way isn't it." asked Mark pointing his headlight in the direction of one of the tunnels.

"I think so." replied Hakim.

They began walking towards the tunnel which started to descend even deeper into the darkness. Again they moved cautiously through the darkness carefully stepping from foot to foot. It was hard to judge exactly where they were according to the map but continued on through the tunnel.

The day before they had established that the drawing was accurate to its scale, meaning the buildings were proportionately spaced from one another. Using that deductive logic they might accurately determine the location of the "X" wherever it might be.

They counted their steps as they walked through the tunnel until finally they reached what should be the location of the "X". They looked around for any clues, on the floor the ceilings, but could find nothing.

Hakim decided to continue through the tunnel and followed it another few hundred feet then decided to turn back towards Mark.

Mark had found a small stone to sit on and was focused on one of the walls of the cave.

"Come quickly." said Mark and motioned to Hakim to rejoin him.

Hakim made his way back through the darkness.

"Look." said Mark, and then pointed his headlight at one of the walls.

"I don't see anything." replied Hakim.

"Look closer." said Mark.

He turned his light towards the wall then noticed some of the stones were darker than the others.

"They make the shape of an "X"." said Mark.

Hakim walked towards the wall then placed his hand on the wall. It was brittle and watered down. He pushed lightly against the wall, then with some force and could feel the wall wanted to give way.

"Help me push." said Hakim.

Together they placed their hands on the cold, wet wall and began to push. The wall was ready to give way. Hakim took out his machete and chipped away some of the stone with the handle of his blade. It weakened the wall enough that it started to collapse inward. With one big push the upper half of the wall fell inward. Their lights shone into the grotto for perhaps the first time in years and saw it was not much bigger than a large bathroom. It was still too difficult to fit through, so Hakim and Mark began to push on the lower half of the wall until it too was ready to give way.

Mark was the first person inside; he swung one leg over the wall then straddled it, allowing him to bring his other leg into the grotto. He fix the light on his head then began to look around. Hakim wasn't far behind he used the same technique to enter the grotto. They both looked around and at first thought there was nothing there. Then they noticed a small metal case, probably from the time of the First World War, hidden under a few rocks.

He shone his light on the chest and began to remove the few stones that guarded the treasure inside, and then he opened the chest.

Inside was a ring and a watch. The ring and the watch again shone with a brilliance of no other stone, and then faded to a tarnished silver look. The watched looked like it was from the future but had stopped ticking a long time ago. It too was made from the same material as the ring and shone brightly only to tarnish seconds later.

"Another ring." said Mark. "Do you remember Christian saying it shone with a brilliance then dissipated." asked Mark.

"Yes. He said it shone brightly then turned to the color it was, well the color it is now."

"Exactly." This ring did the same thing when I opened the chest. And look." He continued. "There is a watch in here as well."

"Maybe someone buried this stuff before it was a park. I mean before this city was found by western civilization." Said Hakim.

"I suppose, but that shine wasn't a coincidence. I think we found something special, something not discovered before." replied Mark.

"Well we should bring it all back, the chest, the watch, the ring back to Egypt where Walter can have some people look at it. It must be of some importance, otherwise why build a treasure map out of stone to find it." said Hakim.

"Agreed." We need to tell them what we have found and probably travel back to Egypt with our findings." replied Mark.

CHAPTER 7.8

In just two days they had found a treasure buried from light and time. A stone tablet discovered in a cave in Egypt had led them to their present situation.

"Let's get out of here this place gives me the creeps." said Hakim

"What if there are more artifacts to be found down here." asked Mark.

"We can notify the park of our discovery, but, they might try to keep it. We should state these caverns are worth having future archeologists explore for relics and such but claim we found nothing. After all, this stuff probably belongs to the Mexican government and we are stealing it to keep them from getting their hands on our findings." said Hakim and was sure Mark agreed.

And with that, both exited over the fallen wall and back into the cavern system that existed beneath the ancient city except, under Mark's arm was a treasure chest, complete with a ring and a watch. They began to walk back through the cavern system, Mark leading the way with the treasure under his arm but Hakim could not shake the feeling that someone or something was following them. Time after time he'd stop dead in his tracks looking back into the darkness to see if there was in fact anything there. Just as they were entering back into the cavern, the large room they had descended down into, Hakim turned to Mark and said.

"I think there is something following us."

"Don't be silly there is nothing down here." replied Mark

"No I mean it." replied Hakim "I just saw something moving behind us."

Mark turned his light towards the direction they just been walking from but couldn't see anything.

"There is nothing there." said Mark. He continued on towards the rope that would bring them back to the topside of the city. He latched himself in, all the while carrying the case that would eventually go back to Egypt, and then began to climb back out of the cavern.

Hakim was left alone in the darkness, with nothing but his torch on his head as his eyes to darkness that now encompassed him. Mark was well on his way to the surface carrying the chest under his arm. Hakim's emotions began to get to the best of him; he started to believe that there was something following him inside the caverns. He began to sweat, beads of sweat, pouring down his face and under his arms. He was fidgety, every sound echoed through the dark labyrinth and shadows danced across the horizon as he looked from side to side. He began to tell himself he was alone in the dark, that it was only his imagination that was getting the better of him, all the while suspicious of his over active imagination. Then he heard something, like an echo on the wind; something he wasn't meant to hear, something that meant they shouldn't be down there.

Hakim glanced back at the cavern they had exited with the chest. There seemed to be nothing there but he wasn't convinced and continued to study the passage. Then something moved, it was only shadow but was enough to cause a panic. He began to hyperventilate and screamed for Mark, but there was no answer.

He continued to study the area. First he saw movement but it seemed as though there was nothing there. Then again he saw, a shadow, a shadow that crept. He realized he was not alone and quickly moved to the rope to exit the larger cavern.

"Mark." he screamed "I'm coming up." but there was no answer.

Then he saw something in the darkness. The way darkness gives way to light, two silver strands, eyes.

He quickly looked with his torch and could clearly see it was a serpent, a large snake, with a head as big as a bear's or a lion's; long and thick bigger than anything documented in books.

He panicked and tried to wrap the rope around his waist, but his hands were shaking too bad. He was helpless, with a giant serpent stalking him. It slithered around stalactites moving ever closer to Hakim. It was big, at least 50 feet long. Every time it moved, Hakim was forced to take his eyes off its head, which made him lose track of where the beast was heading. He was sure of only one thing, that he would be lunch.

The snake was closer now, it had managed to slither through the cavern and was inching ever closer to Hakim. He couldn't think. He was so panic stricken he couldn't move, a sort of paralysis from fear, hands trembling and legs feeling numb. He tried hastily to find and attach the rope but was too afraid. Instead he found his machete and slowly began to grip the handle. It slowed the adrenaline running furiously through his body and gave him temporary comfort given the immense size and swiftness of the creature pursuing him. He slowly pulled the blade from its sheath, hand still rattling, like a loose roof in a hurricane. He kept his eye on the snake, who slithered this way and that approaching ever closer. In a moment of courage, he pulled the blade from the sheath and held it in front of him, gripping it with both hands.

The snake rounded some stalactites ever focused on the prize. It slithered closer and closer then reared its ugly head upwards preparing to strike. Hakim stood frozen he couldn't scream, he couldn't yell, he just stood his ground staring at the massive beast.

The snake reared upwards then in a silent second unleashed all its power in a single bite.

Hakim closed his eyes. He thought he was dead. He looked around, he was still alive.

The snake had lunged directly onto the blade Hakim was holding on to. Perhaps his torch had blinded the beast just before it struck. Hakim was puzzled yet grateful to be alive. He began cursing and shouting at Mark who'd left him in the darkness with this monster. He approached the rope then fastened it around his waist, all the while the snake's tail still moving from shock, crashing up against the rock formations along the cavern floor. The blade had lodged itself inside the mouth then brain of the serpent, in a moment of paralysis Hakim had won the battle.

He began pulling on the rope that hoisted his heavy body up through the narrow tunnel and back towards the top of the pyramid, one slow pull at a time. Finally he reached the surface. Mark was dumbfounded.

"How did you get all that blood on you?" he asked. But there was no answer.

Again asked the same question, but still there was no response. Mark should have seen it in his eyes. Hakim was furious.

"You left me down there to get eaten by that snake." he yelled.

"What snake?" asked Mark.

"A snake, that was in the tunnels. After you headed to the surface a giant snake came out of the tunnel and almost made a meal of me." Mark didn't believe it, he thought Hakim was playing a joke on him. Hakim assured him he was not lying and told Mark the story.

This was something Mark had to see with his own eyes. He climbed down the tunnel once again then a few moments later return to the surface, having taken a few pictures to document the ordeal. He couldn't believe a snake of that size was still in existence. Eventually, Mark wanted to return to camp but Hakim was insistent they were not staying the night if anymore snakes were in the immediate vicinity. They stayed perched upon the pyramid with a good vantage point until the sun rose the following day, and then returned to camp. They packed up their belongings and began to head towards the entrance of the city. Once they were amongst people again they made a call to Walter explaining everything that had happened; the map being correct yet challenging, the treasure chest and even the snake. Walter then made arrangements for them to travel back to Egypt and tipped of the Mexican authorities about the large serpent living in the catacombs of their park, agreeing not to take the ordeal public if they cleaned up the mess.

The following day Mark and Hakim were back in the air and on their way back to the Egyptian dig site, They'd found what they had been looking for in only three days.

CHAPTER 7.9

Christian and Bella got to Fiji midday two days earlier. They'd been spending their time taking in their surroundings and planning for their own treasure hunt. The island was beautiful, full of flowering trees and spectacular scenery. They'd been staying at a hotel the overlooked a fantastic bit of ocean with a beach that was practically their own. Bella found the whole thing rather romantic, every day they'd place fresh flowers in her room and the two of them spent most of their time watching the ocean. Sipping from tropical drinks, they'd watch the sunsets together, and, would even walk together along the beach.

Two days later they got a call from Walter who was in a rather surge of happiness finding out that Hakim and Mark had been successful in finding some treasure.

"In fact." he said. "Their findings coincided with the ring found in Egypt. The original ring was made of a material not found on Earth, according to a geologists study. That it could possess great power if used in the right manner. That the material was fluid like even though it was metal, it captured and projected light somehow."

They were astonished, but given everything that had happened she was still reluctant to believe that it was some sort of alien artifact. She figured Walter was a bit crazy and that what they'd found originated from Earth. But she was happy to hear that the maps Christian had found, the stone tablets, seemed to be accurate. That meant the second tablet pointed to somewhere of the coast of Fiji. It had taken a long while to figure that one out, that the numbers on the tablets corresponded to locations on Earth, as they were not quite as obvious as a modern day atlas.

Their research had shown that the island indicated in the map was the island of Tubou, about three hundred kilometers East of Fiji. Why there would be treasure there was a mystery. In fact the whole thing seemed rather mysterious, the ark empty except for a stone map. The two stone tablets that were in fact maps hidden in a cave not far from the original archeological sites. The only thing they could come up with was that whatever was in the Ark was buried a second time, hidden from the wrong people to find it, but why? It was just a hunk of metal, or perhaps an alien artifact. But, alien or not Mark might get the credit for finding this thing. It was Bella that had a hard time believing everything as she had not seen it with her own eyes.

Christian finished the conversation with Walter who'd become giddy with everything that had been happening. Fortunately the funding was going to cover the cost of the boat which even at a negotiated price was rather steep. The island was still 300 kilometers away and could only be reached by boat. They'd found a nice boat, about 75 feet in length but was going to cost 350 dollars a day. Even if they were at sea for months, would the costs still be covered; and that was why they hadn't left the hotel since they'd arrived; they were waiting for approval.

With the new information they went and purchased some dive gear at a local dive shop. Both Christian and Bella needed to take their refresher courses, diving courses because they were trained scuba divers, just not very experienced. Fortunately the captain was a divemaster in the world of scuba diving and would accompany them underwater; one of the perks of a 350 dollar a day venture. The captains' name was Howard and he and his wife owned the boat, fully and completely, the only problem was they had little money for anything else. He was even going into debt paying the fees to harbour the boat in the harbor.

They managed to finish the course in just a couple of hours and had been on the island for a grand total of six days. They knew Mark and Hakim were already heading back to Egypt or perhaps were already there. They set sail the morning of the seventh day from Fiji and were happy to be at sea.

It is a liberating feeling for a person that spends all their time on land to set sail on the ocean. Neither Christian nor Bella had ever been on a boat before, at least not one of this size. The way the boat rocks on the waves and currents of the ocean. The fresh breeze as it encompasses the boat, and generally a feeling of freedom not being landlocked as the boat sails the ocean blue.

Howard was a burly old man full of stories about the ocean, while his wife Gelinda did the cooking and cleaning upon the vessel. He had been in Vietnam and came home to a family that had tremendously changed. His mother and father had passed away while he was in service and Gelinda was the only thing he had left. They were married shortly after and he took the family's life savings and invested it on a boat. The two of them had been sailing the ocean ever since, but were running out of money.

Bella stood at the bow of the boat watching the waves dance upon the surface of the water; feeling the ocean breeze beat against her chest; she was loving and cherishing every moment. Christian took to chatting with Howard at the helm of the vessel. He was chalk full of interesting stories and there was never a dull moment around him. Howard learned about the treasure map, the purpose of their voyage, but Christian was careful to leave out as much information as he could. Howard didn't care, just as long as he was getting paid for the whole the thing. He was quite content not knowing.

The vessel spent the evening on an Eastward bearing and reached the island sometime in the middle of the night. They dropped the anchor and got some much needed rest.

The following morning Gelinda had prepared breakfast. There were eggs and bacon along with some fresh fruit and tropical drinks. Bella and Christian could see that they were moored a fair distance from shore. After breakfast they began to plan their dives. According to the map that had been drawn, they were looking for some sort of boat wreck beneath the waves and could only assume that whatever was on that boat was destined for a location other than were it was entombed by water. That somehow the cargo was scheduled to arrive somewhere else in the world.

That same day the sonar they were using to detect wrecks on the ocean floor broke. They would be diving blind, without the aid of the sonar.

Day after day they jumped into the water in search for any signs of a ship wreck, but day after day they found nothing. Well, not entirely nothing. The islands reefs were marvellous and spectacular on a majestic scale. They saw turtles, eels, all kinds of colourful fish and corals even the odd reef shark which Howard assured them were not at all dangerous.

The nights were spent starring at the stars from lounge chairs that sat in the aft section of the boat. Christian would name the constellations he could remember from an astrology class he took during his first year of studies. Bella found it fascinating, she almost took courses that would allow her to become an astronaut, but instead found archeology to be a little bit more practical. That night they both fell asleep under the stars.

The following day came early. They both woke about 5:30 in the morning. They had been at sea for roughly ten days doing about 3 dives per day, but still no signs of shipwreck. They were getting tired, as much as they loved being at sea and being in a tropical paradise, the redundancy of the days routines were making them tired. Plus scuba diving has a large amount of nitrogen in it and as such can make a diver feel more tired than they actually should be. Gelinda was just waking up and was about to prepare the morning feast. Both Christian and Bella were ready for some much needed food.

By 7:00, that morning they were preparing for another dive, about 90 feet of water. Each dive was carefully marked on a map that Howard had and every time they found nothing he'd mark an "x" on the map signifying they had already been there. Howard was hopeful this particular morning. They did their standard dive check then entered the water at about 7:45.

Both Bella and Christian were getting used to the habitual practices of scuba diving. They'd check for air, used the proper swim strokes underwater, buoyancy, things that a veteran scuba diver knows and does habitually. They created negative buoyancy then began ever so slowly to descend beneath the waves. They kept a constant vigil on each other while they were descending, then a black shape began appear, at first it was just an outline. Then it became clearer as they descended deeper. At about sixty feet it was easy to see the outline of a boat. A rather huge boat much bigger than the vessel they had been living aboard.

As they got closer to the bottom they became certain that this was the vessel that they had been looking for. They spent the dive swimming around the vessel taking a mental note of everything about the sunken ship. There was a gapping hole in the bow, the approximate length of the whole thing, even swimming around the cabin and ships helm. After about fifteen minutes they began to surface, did a safety stop at fifteen feet for ten minutes then surfaced. They swam back to their boat then exited the water as a group.

"I think that could be the vessel you guys were searching for." said Howard as removed both Christian's and Bella's dive gear from the water.

"It might just be." replied Christian as he exited the water.

They removed their wetsuits then sat down in the galley to talk about their previous dive.

"Wreck diving is dangerous." began Howard. "It takes a lot of skill and nerves of steel to dive a wreck. There are all kinds of thing that can go wrong on a wreck dive. I'm assuming that the next dive you two will want to investigate the boat further, looking for whatever it is you two are looking for."

"That's correct." said Christian.

"We shouldn't be too worried." said Bella "We have you to guide us." she finished.

"I've been diving for most of my life." said Howard. "But wreck diving is some of the most dangerous diving there is, especially when it is two rookies. People have been known to die on wreck dives. They get stuck or lost and can't find their way out of the boat, they drown." he continued.

Both Bella and Christian looked at each other. They wanted to find their treasure but didn't realize how dangerous finding it might be.

"We'll have to set up an air station, somewhere outside the vessel just in case someone runs out of air. Then we'll only go into the boat in pairs, the third party will have to wait outside the boat. That way no one will get lost or anything. Wreck dives can get pretty murky if too much silt is kicked up, it is very easy to get disoriented or lost."

Christian volunteered. "I'll enter the wreck, Bella you can stay at the surface or outside the boat if you wish. Howard and I will go on to investigate the wreck. It's safest this way."

Bella agreed. She would stay outside the boat for the time being.

"We'll enter the water at 11:30. That's exactly an hour and a half from now." said Howard. Then he got up and went to check on his wife.

"We are looking for some kind of chest, I would imagine. Walter said Mark and Hakim found whatever it was they were looking for inside a chest. Any ideas where they might hide something like that?" Asked Christian

"It's hard to say Christian. It could be in one of the cabins, the captains chambers it might even be in a storage facility somewhere on the boat. And we only have fifteen minutes at a time to look around the boat otherwise we take the chance of getting decompression sickness from staying underwater too long." replied Howard.

Christian agreed. "Maybe Bella should stay at the surface for now. It could take several dives to find what we are looking for." Bella agreed then went to her cabin to relax for a bit.

CHAPTER 7.10

Christian and Howard took a giant stride into the water at 11:35. They hit the water then began their decent beneath the waves. Howard's mask began to fog but he quickly filled his mask with water then purged it to clear the fog.

They descended down to 90 feet and approached the wreck. The water was warm but the shadows cast on the wreck looked almost ghostly. It had been sitting untouched for years and began to produce an artificial reef - the term for a sunken ship with corals and fish calling it home.

They had only been at 90 feet for two minutes and began to penetrate the wreck. It was dark, the belly of the vessel was in shadow. Howard turned on his torch and motioned to Christian to turn his on as well. The light illuminated the vessel for the first time in years. They swam in through a door that had been left wide open and began to look around;

it was the bridge, the part of the ship that drives the entire vessel. They found another door that entered into one of the hallways and carefully looked around in each room as best they could, sifting through anything that looked like what they might be looking for. The rooms were getting a bit cloudy because their fins were kicking up minute amounts of silt and debris. They swam down the hallway taking note of two stairways that descended to some lower decks, but swam past the stairways exploring every room on the first level.

The ship was a metal monster, at least 200 feet from stern to bow. It was a cargo ship which meant only the aft was built for people. The bow carried cargo and was easily eliminated as an area that might house the chest, but still needed to be explored to make certain.

Fifteen minutes came quickly and the pair exited the vessel and began to make their way back to the surface. Again the stopped at fifteen feet to do a safety stop then exited the water.

They were greeted by Bella, who in all honesty was glad she didn't have to dive inside the wreck. They explained what they had done during the dive and tried to map out the vessel with a pencil and paper. It wouldn't be until later in the afternoon that they would descend again and explore parts of the ship that they hadn't explored the first time.

At around four o'clock Howard and Christian took a giant stride into the water, again. Quickly they descended to 90 feet and quickly they entered the wreck. This time they swam down the hallway and into the stairwell that lead to the lower deck. The stairwell was tricky to navigate as it was designed for crew members aboard the vessel. It was tight and narrow, both Christian and Howard struggled to get through it. When they entered the lower deck, there was no light whatsoever. All the sunlight was blocked by the belly of the ship. They swam through the galley, then down into the engine room. It was dark and eerie.

It didn't take long but when Christian looked at his gauges and watch, he could see they had been down ten minutes already. It was time to start making their way towards the surface again. But Walter was too busy exploring the wreck. He swam ahead of Christian until eventually all Christian could see was the light from his dive lights. He couldn't tell exactly where Howard was.

Christian swam towards Howard and tapped him on the shoulder. Howard was busy looking at all the parts inside the engine room. Christian pointed towards his watch and motioned they had been inside the wreck for thirteen minutes and it was time to head back to the surface. Howard understood then they swam back towards the stairwell, through the stairwell and back to the first floor. They exited the wreck then began to surface. This time Howard motioned that they should do a safety for twenty minutes instead of fifteen because they had been at depth for longer than they were expecting. They surfaced again and were again greeted by Bella and Gelinda who were both happy to see they had survived the dive.

"Sorry about that." said Howard. "I got into looking around the engine room and lost track of time." Christian wasn't impressed but understood that it wouldn't happen again.

They passed their fins to Bella, and then climb the ladder back on to the boat.

"Next dive" began Howard. "We'll check out the crews' quarters." then he began to remove his wetsuit. Christian wasn't far behind him and began to remove his as well. He then went to a shower near the aft of the deck and began to rinse off the saltwater that he'd been swimming in.

Once he was dry, he sat down with Bella and began to further draw the wreck that they'd been diving, making an underwater map of the sunken ship. He hadn't been drawing for more than twenty minutes when Gelinda announced that supper was ready. She was a great cook; every meal aboard the ship was like dinning in paradise. Tonight she had made seafood jambalaya. Christian was starving, all that diving he'd done, and he'd worked up an appetite.

They sat down to a wonderful dinner. Howard told stories of his youth, and Bella and Christian talked about their studies in university, the trip to Egypt and disclosed the reasons they'd travelled to Fiji.

Howard and Gelinda were a bit shocked to hear the truth. "A bunch of young treasure hunters." Howard called them. Bella set up her camera and took a bunch of pictures. She'd been taking pictures since they got to Fiji and even while in Egypt. It was important, in her mind, to document as much of the trip as possible.

That evening they toasted champagne under the stars to the gentle rocking of the boat. They all slept soundly that evening.

***

The following morning Bella was the first to wake. She made some coffee and sat on the boat watching the sun rise. She decided dangerous or not that she should accompany Christian and Howard on the dive today. She figured it would be easier to scavenge through the sunken ship with three people instead of two.

One by one the rest of the individuals began to rise and shine. They ate breakfast and Bella insisted she'd accompany them on the dive today.

After breakfast Howard went about doing a dive briefing - an oral map of the things they would do and see while underwater. He wanted to push the limits today, being that air compresses under pressure and pressure is more prevalent at depth, in turn meaning you breathe more air quicker at greater depths. Today they would strive to be at depth for twenty two minutes. Ten minutes was not enough time to properly search the wreck. This meant they were at greater risk of getting decompression sickness, which is where tiny bubbles of nitrogen expand as the diver gets closer to the surface and can cause damage to blood vessels, the bends as it is known.

They began to put on their wetsuits. Bella was more nervous than the other two as she had not done any wreck dives prior, and was therefore more inexperienced. They suited up then jumped into the water from the back of the boat. The waves were bigger and stronger today which mean it was a little chaotic at the surface, but one they deflated their buoyancy compensators and ducked beneath the waves it was much calmer.

They began to descend towards the wreck. That's when Christian noticed a shark. It was a ferocious Great White shark, a man-eating shark. It was still 40 feet below them but they going to travel directly into its path. Howard had been in these situations before and just like in the dive briefing explained that he would go first. This time they swam towards the aft of the ship and would enter through a different door. They got to the aft of the wreck, but so did the shark. It swam within ten feet or so of both Bella and Christian and swam away, then circled back again towards them.

Howard signalled to enter the wreck, they would be safe in there, and that the shark would probably not follow them in there, probably.

They turned on their lights then found the aft staircase which as Howard assumed would lead them right down to third level where the crews' quarters were. It was a dangerous dive. The silt from two fins were bad enough but there was so much silt that the third person could barely even see their own hands.

Bella wanted to scream. She could see nothing and was in a dark stairwell. She waited for a minute and the silt began to fall back onto the rusting wreck. *'Finally'* she thought, she could see again. By the time she got to the third floor Christian and Howard were already exploring the hallways and rooms. Just like in the dive briefing she would explore the rooms on the right hand side and Christian the rooms on the left hand side.

She went into the first room and looked around. Wasn't anything too interesting. She went into the second room. Immediately she saw a skeleton, the poor fool had probably drowned when the ship sank. This unnerved her, her breathing increased, then she looked beside the bed and sitting on the floor were two chests. She tried to take one of them. It was heavy. The second treasure chest she could lift with her own weight. She got excited and began to breath even heavier than usual.

She swam out into the hallway and motioned with her hands that she had found something. The room was hardly big enough for two people so she carried the first chest out into the hallway. She motioned the second chest was too heavy and instructed Howard and Christian to carry the second one. Then she swam towards the stairwell. She'd had enough of being inside the wreck. Up she swam until she was nearly out of the wreck, then she remembered the shark. She glanced out from inside the wreck to see if in fact the shark was still around. She couldn't see anything then swam out from the wreck carrying the lighter of the two chests.

She began to swim towards the surface then remembered about the safety stop. Fifteen minutes to allow the nitrogen in the blood vessels to dilute. She inflated her buoyancy compensator struggling to hold on to the chest. Then she saw it, the shark. It was no longer swimming at the bottom of the ocean floor but rather had climbed up to 20 feet or so and was now beginning to circle her. Her breathing increased and so did her heart rate. She watched the shark as it swam just beneath her. She looked back at the wreck to see if Howard or Christian were around, but they were nowhere to be found.

She couldn't take it, and bolted towards the surface, then swam to the boat calling out for Gelinda to help her. Gelinda heard her screams then went to investigate. She passed Gelinda the chest then her fins and was out of the water quicker than a squirrel on peanut butter.

She had panicked and did two things scuba divers are not supposed to do, separate from the group and ignore the safety stop. She explained to Gelinda what had happened and Gelinda quickly got Bella a towel. Gelinda massaged her shoulders as if to say, it's all right, and don't worry.

She waited at the edge of the boat nervous about having left the other two behind. Seconds turned into minutes and minutes into several minutes, but there was no sign or either Howard or Christian. After what seemed like hours a balloon broke the surface of the water; it was Howard and Christian. Howard swam over to the balloon and began to drag it back towards his ship. They both passed their fins to Gelinda then exited the water.

They could see Bella was shaken as she was literally still shaking form her ordeal.

"We didn't know where you went, we thought maybe you stuck inside the wreck." said Christian. Howard was angry, they had discussed the do's and do not's during the dive briefing earlier that morning, but he never said anything to Bella.

Howard took off his buoyancy compensator then reached over the side of the boat and grabbed the balloon. "Give me a hand with this." motioning to Christian for some assistance.

"It took us a long while to get the chest up through the stairwell, and then Howard used a lift bag to get it to the surface." said Christian.

"I got the other chest to the surface but that goddamn shark was circling me and you guys weren't around. I even missed doing the safety stop." said Bella.

"You should be okay." said Howard. "They have a hyperbaric chamber in Fiji if we need to use it. But personally I'm eager to see what is in these chests." The chests were roughly the same size, but one of them was by far heavier than the other. Bella finally began to relax. She was safe and so were Christian and Howard. Howard went to the engine room and came back with a crow bar. He went to the heavy chest first and began to pry it open.

"Well would you look at that." exclaimed Howard as he opened the chest. It was full, full of gold and diamonds. Gold coins, hundreds or them, maybe even thousands. He dug his hand into the chest and lifted as many pieces as he could with his hand.

"Wow" said Christian "Talk about a payday."

"There's probably a million dollars worth of gold in there." said Howard. They were all still in shock because of what they'd found.

It was time to open the second chest. "Pass me the crowbar." said Christian. It had been a wild ride. They barely found the second cave in Egypt, the stone maps, and now a treasure chest. He began to pry it open, until the lid popped off. He lifted it ever so slowly. Inside were three bags, nylon bags. He emptied the first inside was a piece of paper and a watch. The ink had faded but it looked like a picture from somewhere in Cambodia, he could tell from the picture, he'd studied it in his classes, but the watch, the watch was still ticking. It too shone with a bright brilliance then dissipated. Inside the second bag was a pair shoe, different shoes something futuristic they shone with that same brilliance and then it disappeared. Inside the third bag was a head band it did the same thing when the light touched it, shone with a beautiful brilliance and then disappeared.

Bella was looking over his shoulder and managed to see everything. She finally believed. She took one of the bags and began to examine its contents. "Every bag has a map that corresponds to a location in the world. Each of these bags were supposed to be buried at these locations, a real treasure hunt." Christian agreed.

CHAPTER 7.11

The next step was to figure out what to do with everything. Christian got on the phone with Walter and explained everything he could to him. He must have been on the phone with him for at least twenty five minutes or so, when he finished he began to explain everything to the rest of the crew.

"Everything needs to go back to Egypt with us." he began.

"You mean we don't get to keep any of the gold?" asked Howard.

"No, because it was an archeological find it needs to return with us, however, you will be compensated for your loss. My boss has decided to give you an extra hundred thousand dollars for helping us find this wreck and the contents of the wreck."

Howard was shocked, he wanted the gold but he knew the money would help him. After all the first thing Christian told him was that "if" they found anything it would need to return to the people who were funding the expedition. But, somehow Howard knew if that wasn't the case Christian would have split it with him.

"If only I had found the gold on my own." Joked Howard.

The ship stayed moored to its location for another few hours, and then they picked up the anchor and were headed back towards Fiji. The ship steamed on until it reached the harbour late in the evening.

Bella and Christian slept aboard the vessel that evening, then in the morning started to make preparations to return to Egypt along with everything they'd found in Fiji. They said a fond farewell to Howard and Gelinda who in all honesty were very sad to see them go.

Three days later they returned to Egypt

In total they had found, the ark hidden from the world and its contents two rings, two watches some shoes and a headband all made from a material that was deemed not to be from our world.

CHAPTER 8

THE BEASTS SLAVE

Viktor Krusk lived in Russia his whole life. He remembered the Great War, how his father had gone to fight for Russia and his mother dying shortly after his father had left. He lived alone, stealing as means of survival. Some bread here, some meats there.

He remembered the day the war was won as he had stolen a paper that day. Then he left, he travelled to Yakutsk in western Russia and lived there all his life. He established some land for himself, built a home some 300 kilometers from the city. He lived a desolate lifestyle away from modern eyes.

In 1960 at the age of forty he was building a fire in the fire place near his home. He remembered the feeling of being watched. He glanced back at the forest but there was nothing there. Then he got the feeling again this time from a different location in the forest, but again there was nothing there. He walked towards the forest and began to look again. It was late in the evening and nearing winter, October, and the ground was already frozen. He looked carefully again then began to walk back to the fire he'd built. He hadn't slept in days and thought his brain was playing tricks on him.

He stood glancing into the fire then again got the feeling of being watched. He walked again to the edge of the forest and looked inside. He squinted to see if he could see anything moving. The forest was black, the forest seemed empty.

When he turned around there it was, a large wolf like monster with big giant teeth and large ears. It growled at Viktor and he fell over into the snow. It approached him. He tried to escape while on the ground digging his heads deep into the snow to move away from the beast.

Its large teeth and ferocious eyes then it spoke,

'You have been the first to see me in 400 years' Viktor was terrified. The only words he could muddle were screams of terror.

'Do not speak, think' the beast whispered.

It was using some sort of telepathy.

'I...I can hear you' thought Viktor.

'Good' whispered the beast.

'It used to be that people who gazed upon me died instantly with fear, I can see that you are brave' continued the beast.

'It has been a while since I have had a servant, most have lived long lives until their demise and most have gotten rich from the knowledge I have given them.' continued the beast. Viktor looked at the beast. It was only a few feet from him, saliva dangling from his huge teeth and his breath warming Viktor from the cold of the snow.

'But first you will bring me a horse, how I loved the taste perhaps it is more delicious than human flesh' Viktor thought he was going to be eaten right then and there, but instead did what the beast asked of him.

He walked to his stable still terrified form the ordeal, shaking, whimpering he took a horse by its reins and walked it out into the forest. He pulled a pistol from his pants and wanted to take his own life; instead he shot the horse and began to run back to his house.

'Good, in the morning you will take the contents of this chest and bury them as I have instructed, you see I have become accustomed to this place and climate and wish not to leave as I have in the past you shall do my bidding and be my slave until death' echoed a voice in his head.

Viktor ran back to house and shut the door. Weeping, sobbing, he lay down by his lantern clutching his pistol until the morning.

The next day when he returned to the horse, it was gone, he looked in the snow for footprints but there were none, sobbing, he open the chest and found diamonds and gold coins. He sobbed then dropped to his knees.

The first place he went to visit was in Mexico, he climbed into the pyramid and hid a chest behind a grotto then built a rock wall around it just as his map had instructed. There were several others and many places for him to hide the beasts' trinkets.

In his next task he was bound for Cambodia. His boat fell victim to a giant storm and just before he drowned, he used the pistol to take his own life. Now no one knows for sure but it is said the wolf heard his thoughts as he travelled from place to place. Viktor tried not to think as he did what the beast had asked of him, but no one understood exactly why he cried as he travelled from place to place.

CHAPTER 8.1

THE ELUSIVE MOUSE

Now I understand all of this might seem a little strange to you, but I assure you it does get even stranger. As I had mentioned my family had funded the project based on a map given to my grandmother years ago; I didn't understand the whole story until I found the box of dossiers and started to read them. A man by the name of Walter Burliss had been chosen to lead the archeological search and recruited several graduates to help him do so. As they continued to find things they were continually approved to receive more funding.

The original find what Walter refers to as the ark was built with such precision and beauty that it was assumed it had to have built by aliens, but was definitely built during biblical times. This then lead to the theory that they had taught us things like mathematics and science around the same time we started to become more intelligent. But there was no proof of that. The ark was made of early things, gold, silver, diamonds and gems and contained nothing that Walter described as an "alien artifacts".

After reading the dossier I felt angry and saddened by the claim that someone had stolen the artifacts they'd found from around the globe. Someone just walked into their camp and stole everything, even the ancient Chinese map that read "the well of life". And I guess that was why nobody around the world got to hear their story. Walter claimed they were just about to bring the whole thing to the press which he and his students felt would've made international headlines.

The ark never made it to a museum, instead was collected by the American government and studied, but many felt they would have tried to confiscate the items they'd found as well.

Walter concluded that whatever was in the ark originally was scattered by someone or something. The only conclusion he could come to was that whoever or whatever did the scattering was trying to keep its contents a secret, possibly from the Nazi's from when the map was written. In the end also concluded that it was a something because no man would go about relocating alien artifacts found in an ancient chest spoken of in early biblical times.

In the end the only evidence they had was as series of pictures used to document the trip and the items, some stone tablets, one thousand gold pieces, diamonds and of course the ark. But it made me wonder could the ring my father sent me all those years ago be one of those artifacts.

It turns out having a mouse in my house wasn't such a bad thing after It gave me some purpose as it lead me to some findings that otherwise would have gone unnoticed.

'Ahh, yes the mouse' I had almost completely forgot about the mouse I went to check my traps, now a total of fourteen, fourteen marvelous traps to catch a mouse that seemed impossible to catch. Time after time I could have swatted it with a broom or stick as it was becoming very used to me being in the same room with it and not trying to hurt it.

But still fourteen traps were not enough. To make matters worse the mouse had developed a little hobby of chewing through walls and wires all at the most of inconvenient times, in the middle of the night. For the past six nights now, as I lay almost asleep in my bed, heard the most malevolent of chewing noises that made it nearly impossible to sleep.

To get some sleep I decided to set up a tent, with my dog accompanying me, in the backyard to escape its malevolence and get the needed rest I deserved. So on it went readying and prepping traps by day and sleeping outside under the stars in the evenings. I began to wonder if I was dealing with just one mouse or several, surely a family of mice would find my home as entertaining as any, but, because of the lack of results from my previously, baited with peanut butter traps, came to the conclusion it was just one mouse. One horrific, possibly even evil mouse, who had made my days and nights a living hell.

It was a Saturday morning and I had had little sleep the night before, possibly dreaming of catching a small rodent mouse when the door bell rang. From outside the house I could hear the penetrating sharp noise of the doorbell. I ignored it at first thinking they would just go away and continued to dream about catching the mouse. But, again I could hear the doorbell chime from within the confines of my abode. I looked at my watch; it was 10:30 in the morning, Saturday morning, July 15th, 2015.

I quickly rolled over and attempted to go back to sleep. However, this person was persistent that was ten chimes already by my count surely they wouldn't continue much more than that. To add to the fact my dog was barking at the sound of the doorbell, a particular hobby it had developed over the years. In fact however, they did by the sixteenth chime I was up to my feet and moving towards the back door which would eventually lead me to the front door. Seventeen, eighteen, nineteen had this person no sense of dignity. I got to the door and opened it, shocked to see who was standing in front of me.

It was Peter Frontinac. I could have recognized that face from anywhere. Being that he'd been all over the covers of People magazine, McLean's magazine, just about every magazine ever written, but had aged. He had aged almost ten years maybe more, he was in his late thirties when he'd won that race around the world, now he looked almost fifty maybe even sixty.

"Aren't you Peter Frontinac?" I asked stupidly. I could've said anything better.

"Yes I am." he replied. "I am looking for Weland Gorbis is he around."

"That's my father's name, and no he is not around he hasn't been in years."

His face turned to sadness, he felt he had been beaten by fate.

"My name Jeremiah Gorbis, my father's name was Weland Gorbis, but like I said I haven't seen him in years. He was so upset about the last expedition he went his own way. I haven't talked to him in years."

"Expedition?" asked Peter, his mood suddenly changed

"Yes." I replied

"It turns out he had a real passion for history, but after his last expedition failed he'd spent most of his money and lived a life of solitude, but like I said I haven't talked to him in years." I continued.

"Expedition? Was it in Egypt?" he asked.

"Yes, it would appear so." I answered.

"Did your father ever tell you about what it was he was looking for?" asked Peter.

"Sort of, I found a bunch of documents in the last little while that explained he was looking for some sort of alien artifacts."

"A ring." he asked. "Did he ever mention anything about a ring?" he continued.

'How do you know about the ring?' I asked myself.

"Why don't you come in?" I said. "After all you are the great Peter Frontinac that circled the globe in a hovercraft." He agreed to come in, and then I began to make some coffee as he sat down at the kitchen table.

"What are all these weird things you have laying around?" He was asking about my mouse traps.

"They are mouse traps." I replied. "I've been trying to catch a mouse without killing it, but I haven't been having any luck." I continued.

"Please." he said. "If you have the ring I need it, the fate of the world depends on it."

'Fate of the world? This guy must have gone bananas.' I thought to myself. Then he went silent. He didn't say anything for at least a couple minutes. I continued to prepare our drinks, first boiling the coffee then pouring it into two cups. I even added sugar and cream but wasn't sure if that was the way he drank it.

"Alright mister." I said. "You have some explaining to do." he was still silent, but then looked at me right in the eyes. He knew I had it.

"My name is Peter Frontinac." he began. "Two years ago I circled the globe in a hovercraft and won a large amount of money. Shortly after that I was brought to the future chosen to participate in a great battle that could end life as we know it."

'Surely he'd gone bananas' I thought to myself.

"When I got there I was treated like a king. Women, the likes of which could drive a man crazy, food, scores of food, even a palace to call my own."

"Then I was told the reason I was there, to participate in a great battle against the forces of evil. One fight, to the winner the absolute power over what we know as the known universe. I trained in the arts of psychic warfare, was taught how to fight by futuristic standards, indeed they molded me into a futuristic warlord, to be the envy of what we call gods in this day and age."

"For seven years I trained, by a training manifesto that has yet to be discovered. It was me and forty others who were trained, until only the finest and bravest were left to battle against these evil forces. I was selected as one of the thirteen. Under the snow, in Antarctica lays and ancient alien outpost, in the distant future the rest of the human race lives there because the rest f the world is too hot, inhospitable."

'I thought about calling the police, but his eyes remained sincere.' I pondered to myself.

"These good aliens, future seeing seers, (not to be confused with the beasts of Sirius B) the builders of this outpost can travel great distances in a sort of sleep and have charted most of the futuristic universe, they've even mapped out which planets are hospitable to the human race. As long as we are good, they continue to serve us in secret, sort of like how we care for dogs and cats. This alien outpost was also the battlefield for this event. If we won, we were the rightful owners of these outposts and the planets they were built on; if we fail, the armies of darkness will approach in the near future and lay waste to these planets as they see fit, tormenting us, making us their slaves and worse."

He paused sipping from his coffee. "This is good coffee." he exclaimed as he sipped from it.

Then he began to speak again "As the day of the of the battle approached, time indicated it was time to battle, the ancient writings all depicted it, the Mayan calendar resets itself just as it did in the year 2012, everything since time was made pointed towards this battle. The ancient cities were maps showing where in the stars we could find our enemies and potential future colonisable planets; we could just never figure it out. At the exact time of the great battle, all of our ancient civilization ruins point directly to the corresponding stars and planets."

He continued. "I was a special exception, they never meant to take me, instead they wanted to take a man named Jesush to fight this battle, but his injuries in the end were too grave and his sacrifice too meaningful. If he had not done what he'd done, the people of this planet would not have evolved to what they now know as the modern day. In fact we'd still be 300 years behind in the general order of things. Still, his disciples were also chosen to fight, that thirteen of them would fight to save the world. Somehow they knew of this battle was to take place and that they could fight it. But over time their descendants began to die off, their lineage ending, eliminating them from helping in this final battle. My journey made suspect that I was strong enough to fight this battle."

'Interesting.' I thought. *'Either he was completely a wacko or perhaps there was some truth to what he was saying.'*

He continued still. "As the day of the great battle approached I began to doubt myself. I began to think that we would lose. That even after our training and battle we would lose, lose it all to the evil that we sought to rid ourselves of. I couldn't sleep, became restless in the final hours doubting the whole thing. Then a funny thing happened, my weapons were stolen in the hours leading up to the great battle. In a desperate attempt to find them I was thrown back to my time. I stole my weapons back from your father and used the other map to find "the well of life", the key ingredient to winning this battle. I have been walking this Earth for 30 years in search of the ring and believe you to be in possession of. I am a descendant of doubting Peter and if you have the ring I will show you how it works."

I was shocked; suddenly this all began to make sense to me.

"My father sent it to me when I was just a young child. I never knew much of what it was or how it worked, but I have it hidden here in the house, I will find it for you." Then I went to find the ring.

I walked up the stairs into the attic, then went to a small bunch of bricks and began to pull one of them from the wall. Once I removed it from the wall I reached in and found a small cotton sack and inside it was the ring my father had sent to me some thirty years earlier. It looked tarnished, like silver that hadn't been polished in one hundred years. I began to walk back towards the kitchen, first down the attic stairs then down the main set of stairs in the house. I could tell he knew I had it; his facial expression had already changed to one of delight and splendor.

"I am glad the Nazi's never found it." I tossed him the ring. He put it on his middle finger then it began to shine, shine like the purest of gold, like it was emitting light itself.

"I had arranged to bring my Melanie with me back to the minutes before the battle, but if I fail I cannot begin to imagine her grief. Instead I would like to bring you with me, you will return to this time if we win." he said.

I thought about it for a minute, there had been nothing exciting happening in my life for a long time. Perhaps this was my calling of sorts.

"Okay." I said. Then he stood up and walked over to me. Put his hand on my shoulder then pressed a button to a contraption from his pocket.

Everything faded to black then one by just like the colors of the rainbow we travelled, travelled through a sort of worm hole that gave way to color. From purple to blue, blue to green, green to yellow, yellow to orange and finally orange to red, the colors speeding up ever-so-slightly. Then I could see an image an image of the future and ever so gently landed in a market somewhere in Antarctica in the distant future.

Everywhere I looked people were holding signs, signs that read the end is near. There were markets selling food and people in rags, but it was all futuristic. I was in the future. I looked around but Peter was nowhere to be found. I was still in shock from the journey; my eyesight was blurry, hands trembling and weak. I could barely stand.

I looked up and the sky was full of spacecraft, some big, some small. I looked at my clothes; I was dressed in robes just like everyone else around me. It was almost as like I'd found the lost city of Atlantis.

Then a man I had never met before approached me asked me my name, then ushered me towards a giant building. Futuristic of sorts, I could only guess that it was the coliseum, the coliseum where this epic battle was to be underway.

CHAPTER 8.2

THE GREATEST OF BATTLES

Yougodid stood behind solid steal doors that were going to open at any second. A single tear began to form and fell from his eye. He had been training for this moment for many years and in that sense most of his life. A glimmer of light shone through the doors and with a hostile brow he could see his opponent for the first time. He looked back at his holding cell, then at his feet and kicked some sand towards the door.

Yougodid had been training for this moment for most of his life. He'd been selected from the thirteen to lead this battle. He was strong, mentally prepared for what was to come once the doors opened. But Yougodid was frustrated. The evil that he'd been trying to fight had got the best of him. In the moments earlier he knew Peter's weapons had been stolen and that might have taken him a long time to find them. *'No worries, for god is with me'* he thought to himself. He could defeat them all if he needed to, just one man. But he was fortunate; he had twelve of the best, finest warlords the world had ever seen, plus himself.

He was ready. He approached the solid steel doors, with just a crack open to look into the coliseum. He could see hoards of people, crowds by the thousands ready and waiting for their fate to be handed to them. He closed his eyes and then in his mind's eye could see his enemy. Two of them, he'd have to start by fighting two of them.

He wiped the sweat from his hands down the side of his clothes, counting down the seconds.

Then at last the doors opened, he had not yet drawn his weapons, he would wait to see how they would try to kill him. The crowd stood up as he walked from one of the coliseum fighters doorways. They cheered and roared as their hero moved towards the center.

At the same time two other fighters entered from the opposite end of the arena. They were holding their weapons made from that same metallic substance found in the ark.

These men-like creatures wore long black robes that covered their bones, bones that protruded from their skin like weapons. One held an axe that glowed blue and all that could be seen was the color of his skin pigmented red; and the other a sword glowing orange with a blue skin pigment. Although they were fast they were hardly moving from their doorway. They both stood almost ritually with their weapons held at chest level but their blades high above their heads

Yougodid continued to walk towards them to the sound of the crowd cheering then he powered up his weapons, and the crowd cheered even louder. First his shields, then his boots, then his helmet, he was ready to fight. His weapons were made from same trinkets Peter sought during his revisit to our time. Made of metallic substance, they glowed yellow; they could stop any bullet, even fire or water. Inside the shield he held two pistols equipped with poisonous shells, enough to down his enemies.

Yougodid got it; they wanted him to take the shot. He'd been trained in psychic warfare and was looking for their weak point as he plotted out his next few moves over the next few seconds. Taking the shot now would hit them if his aim was right, but he feared they'd have some other secrets ready for him in the future if he did.

These men-like creatures, called deviants, had been bred from our own DNA, hybrids of man and beast. People who were reported missing or abducted by UFO's ended up on these spaceships, in our future, to breed a god capable of killing a mortal man. It was the beasts of Sirius who did this in preparation for this battle; thought to instill fear before the great battle started.

CHAPTER 8.3

Continuously they pounded away at his shields, one of them striking, the other returning to his original position clutching its weapon close to the heart with the blade above its head.

Yougodid, in his minds' eye, knew that they would be changing their tactics soon and began to prepare for it. The deviants stopped hitting his shield then both returned to their archetypal position readying themselves to attack harder and more furiously. Yougodid crouched down with one shield in front of him the other sideways at his back.

The first deviant sprung forward and in an instant Yougodid jumped, kicking away its blade. He had also been trained in the Shaolin monk style of fighting. Repeatedly they'd strike and Yougodid would defend himself with a kick or his shield, because his boots were also made of the metallic substance, of light. One after another the deviants' offense was belittled by Yougodid's ability to stave off the danger from their weapons. At times, when the moment was right, he too would strike but it was constantly blocked by the one's sword or the others axe.

After a good few minutes it was clear to see that they were getting nowhere. That Yougodid was equally matched to fight both deviants. The crowd continued to roar as their hero battled against the deviants.

Yougodid would strike, using his shield as an extension of his fist. It was hard to hit them, they were moving very fast and able to counter any strike Yougodid would use against them.

The battle continued on growing more furious by the minute, the tempo had changed; now the three warriors were striking and blocking everything that was coming towards them. Yougodid changed his tactics and tried to get higher, he stepped upwards and the boots made of light fused tiny particles into matter, like invisible stairs he climbed higher; this time taking a shot from his pistols.

The bullet missed one of them, whizzing down from the upper sky, and was blocked by the deviant with the sword. Then the deviants disappeared, their robes festering into oblivion for a brief moment. Although Yougodid could not see them he could sense where they were and when they'd attack.

The first deviant appeared, practically out of thin air, striking Yougodid who blocked the attack. Then the second one would appear, causing a collision with their weapons. The deviants were taking turns disappearing then reappearing to throw Yougodid off.

His mind controlled his weapons. Fighting with shields made of light was very dangerous; many a trainee lost a limb or a finger while training with these weapons, because these weapons did not forgive. The shields could slice a tree clean in half or even a small car, but were programmed not to harm the user; meaning his boots did not burn his skin, nor did his helmet. Should a deviant stick its finger into the light it would disappear as if it never existed in the first place.

On and on the battle went. It was being broadcasted to what was left of the planet. Being that Antarctica was the last safe haven on Earth, only small colonies of people still lived at the ends South America, Africa and even small colonies at the North Pole as well.

People were unsure how to feel, being that their fate was in the hands of thirteen warriors.

Then up came a turret, four of them. These turrets looked like pine tree and could fire 100 bullets a second in every direction. Yougodid moved back away from the turrets to a distance that lessened the danger of being too close to one of these. He placed his shield right in line with his boots, crouching, knowing that not a single bullet could get to him. The deviants kept to an evasive vanish while the turrets laid siege to the inside of the coliseum.

Then the floor at the center of the coliseum began to give way in certain areas. Yougodid began to smile. Riding up on pedestals came the other twelve warriors. They sat back to back in pairs that made a full circle at the center of the arena. They sat motionless. Yougodid powered down his shields then walked into the center of the circle.

Seconds later, doorways opened around the arena. Human hybrids were released into the arena, twenty of them in total. There were four punishers, big ten foot tall behemoths, six guardians similar to deviants and ten pacifiers, small but with futuristic guns. They all began to charge the circle.

The men reached into their pockets for small vials of oxygen enriched water. They drank at the same time. Even Peter did, although he'd aged in time, searching for his weapons, the water made him stronger and feel younger again. But Peter was not the oldest; in fact there were three men that out aged him even though he did age during his search for his weapons. After drinking the water they all looked like they were in their thirties again and ready to battle.

They sprung to their feet and at the same time engaged their shields, boots and helmets. They ran forward and began fighting with their enemies. They fought as though they had rehearsed the whole thing prior to beginning the battle.

The fighters were of different ethnicities and cultural backgrounds by modern day standards, but all of them had great, great, great and many more great grandfathers who had pledge their lives and services to Jesush almost 5 millennia earlier. In the future they were united under one religion and one god, so by modern day standards they were diverse, but lived in a utopian society.

They fought with the power of twenty men, jumping, kicking, and fighting to lie to waste the intergalactic enemy who sought nothing more than to conquer the known universe while feasting on our flesh. They fought like warrior poets. Each move calculated before the next.

The crowd was on their feet cheering louder than ever for their heroes who had separated throughout the battlefield, striking, blocking the deviants and their allies. They moved with agility and speed, with courage and integrity, their weapons world renown as destroyers of evil. Each move more calculated than the next.

One by one the deviants and their armies began to fall. A final strike or kick often finished them off killing the hoards with ease. Their pistols found their mark and dropped these abominations with simplicity.

But also men were dying. The deviants and their kin were tougher then they let on and some of the men began to tire and some began to fall. The deviants were engineered to be stronger then Yougodid and his foot soldiers. So a punch to the ribs or gut would be almost enough to kill a man. Some men were better psychics than others and this meant some were weaker too.

One of Yougodid soldiers fell. He used his shield to take his life and the life force that allowed him to keep living quickly vanished from his body. They were still out numbered but fighting furiously jumping, assaulting and hammering the enemy.

The guardians were doing their jobs, confusing the soldier as best they could, leaving the pacifiers to attack without being noticed.

Yougodid continued to battle the deviants who would often disappear then reappear striking his fellow soldiers. The punishers used their war hammers pounding away at the twelve. Yet the twelve still managed to fire off their shots as needed. Although the bullets would hit the punishers, their huge bodies and advanced metabolic systems prevented them from dying.

On and on the battle continued.

Then in the center of the ring beamed down the leader of the beasts. It had been occupying one of the ships in orbit around the arena.

His armour was made of blue gold, a mineral rich on its planet. He began to assault the soldiers of light causing them to cower at malevolence. His name was Vexx and he began to address the crowd using an amplified psychic medium stating this planet now belonged to him and his minions.

CHAPTER 8.4

The beast had been seeing this day for a long time. He'd spent many years living in the Russian frontier free from peering eyes and sorrow. Since the humans had begun to migrate towards the poles he'd lived a relatively solitary existence. No home to call his own, just wondering the frontier that his people wanted to claim.

As the battle drew nearer, he began travelling to the South Pole during the last moon of autumn, knowing that he would need to face his advisory; the same person that he cut off from using the stargate to prevent the beasts of Sirius from ever taking over Earth.

He travelled south through Asia then across the Polynesian islands to Australia. From there swam south to Antarctica, running by night and sleeping by day. He avoided human colonies as best he could by staying clear of their camps.

He travelled for weeks until finally he had the coliseum in his sights. He stole some robes and covered his face as he travelled through the center of town. Some people would see him for what he was and try to attack, or back away with fear. He just kept moving until now; he was only feet from the coliseum.

The city was in chaos. Mothers were weeping for their children, and, children were weeping for their mothers. Some people had even fled the cities in fear, setting up refugee camps where water and food was available. In all the excitement the everyday chores of farming and sanitation became less important so the city was indeed a mess. The times of apocalyptical revelations had come.

The beast got close enough to the coliseum, and then began to scale the outer wall, drinking the last of his oxygen enriched water as he climbed.

'Ah yes my old friend you have come to apologize' thought Vexx.

'No apologies this time Vexx, this time you meet your maker.' replied the beast as he scaled the outer wall.

The beast got to the top of the coliseum and could see the battlefield from an elevated perch. He leaped forward almost a thousand feet in the air then landed graciously in the center of the arena.

'This time.' began the beast *'I am your ruler'* continued the beast.

Vexx began to remove some his armour letting it fall to the sand at the center of the arena.

The turrets came up temporarily halting their conversation and battle. Everyone took defensive positions as the turrets fired bullets into the outskirts of the arena. One pacifier was hit by the bullet and quickly dropped dead from its intensity.

The beast leapt onto the walls of the arena to avoid getting hit by any bullets, but Vexx remained in the center, his armour stopping any bullets that came his way. Then the beast leapt into the air striking Vexx with a hit in the face. This only angered Vexx and they began to scuffle in the center of the arena. They were rolling around in the sand hitting each other furiously, using elbows and teeth to inflict damage on the other.

The beast had a hard time getting past Vexx's armour and so used every move to make contact with Vexx's face. Vexx kicked him off and he flew twenty feet in the air, only to land on his feet and come rushing back at full force to hit Vexx in the chest.

Both Yougodid and Peter could see this new scuffle out of the corners of their eyes. Then they noticed a ship moving into position above the arena. "Its center is a teleportation device to beam down additional members of Vexx's army." Shouted Yougodid

Yougodid called out to Peter, "Can you take out the ascension relay on that ship so that no others can beam to our surface."

Peter looked at him and said "Yes."

He clipped his shields to mounting magnets on his shoulders then engaged some rear thrusters on his suit. He took flight in seconds and flew upwards towards the craft. He disengaged one of his shields and struck the craft as it was powering up to bring down more beasts. The craft sputtered then a small explosion could be seen and the ship moved out of position from overtop of the coliseum, falling in the distance.

Peter gently returned to the coliseum floor to continue the fight.

Peter looked back at the beast and Vexx, Vexx was winning the battle, striking him furiously in the face. He was bloodied and barely moving.

The beast could hear Yougodid who was continuously asking the beast his name.

'My name is Luscious.' Answered the beast.

Luscious was tired, beaten and fell mostly dead in front of Vexx who cheered outrageously at his victory. Then Vexx turned and was met by Yougodid's gaze. Yougodid was shocked that a beast was there to defend him and his people. Had he found this beast himself, years ago, especially on Earth, Yougodid would have destroyed the beast. Most of what the planet learned about these aggressors was that they were heartless, warlords, hell-bent on ruling the entire galaxy.

Yougodid began to strike at Vexx but his armor seemed to be protecting him. *'Only one shot.'* thought Yougodid but Vexx heard it clearly. Vexx's armor contained traces of the metal used to make the shields Yougodid and his men were wielding, his weapons of light were useless against this powerhouse. Yougodid used a spinning series of kicks but Vexx blocked the attacks with his forearms.

Yougodid wanted to retreat. His weapons were useless against Vexx and further more Vexx had plenty more soldiers ready at his disposal, luckily Peter had disarmed the transporting system just minutes earlier preventing a total obliteration.

Yougodid needed to regroup with his soldiers, psychically he asked them to regroup, but, Vexx could hear him. He walked backwards towards the center of the arena and his soldiers followed, leaving behind the demon fiends they were battling. The soldiers had yet to drop a single punisher, who wielded their war hammers with tremendous force. In fact their shields were useless against the punishers because their weapons were made of the same material. In essence, breaking a limb to counter the speed and ferocity of the war hammer weapon; instead the soldiers had been ducking and rolling when a punisher was in the near vicinity.

It looked like a quick huddle, but was over in mere seconds. The soldiers ran to opposite ends of the arena, and then two at a time flew just like Peter did, to the opposite end of the arena. One punisher swung so violently and mercilessly at the flying soldiers that it connected with another punisher, hitting him square in the jaw, killing it instantly. The second belittled and embarrassed stood in shock for several seconds before another soldier flew in slicing through its neck with its shield, decapitating the punisher leviathan. It fell to the ground with a tremendous clatter, followed by the roar of the crowd.

Seconds later, the deviants downed another soldier. He could no longer use his shields as protection as the deviants were attacking too strong, too fast. He fell face first into the sand kicking up dust as he fell.

Yougodid continued to battle on, but was being taunted by Vexx and his wicked ways. He continued to belittle the soldier and describe in detail Vexx's victory.

'There is no way you can win' Echoed Vexx's voice in Yougodid's mind.

This only enraged Yougodid more; however his tactics seemed to be working. Yougodid's psychic aura no longer allowed him to be in control; in fact he began to envision his own demise. Yougodid used every split second decision to counter the fate he was now envisioning. Originally, he had been in control of the battle and used his psychic abilities to his advantage, now he was using it to stay alive.

Vexx was now walking towards him, challenging Yougodid at every possible level. Yougodid reached into his pouch and drank the oxygen enriched water. His muscles were weak from the fight but as he drank, the water began to heal his aching muscles. He finished the vial, and then turned to face Vexx.

Vexx was laughing, still taunting the warrior. Suddenly Yougodid received a horrible telepathic image. His army would be losing *'unless'*. He was like a computing genius, envisioning every move before it happened. Now he needed to right a wrong in his visions so his army would not fall. Instead of acting on his psychic visions he needed to try to correct them.

Yougodid turned to Vexx then leapt into the air. He landed just feet away from Vexx and began striking at Vexx furiously. Although his hits were not penetrating his armor he wanted to tire Vexx as best he could. Vexx would leap into the air and land in other parts of the arena, met by Yougodid's soldiers, who would try to attack the beast. Everywhere the beast would leap pacifiers would follow, engaging the soldiers in battle. The pacifiers would stay far enough away that they could not be struck by the boots or the shields.

Yougodid finally realized that he was afraid to fight Vexx. Perhaps that is what his plan was the whole time. Yougodid looked at Luscious; he was dead, pummelled to death by his advisory Vexx. He chased down Vexx and challenged him to fight.

'You need not worry about these other men, just fight me.' thought Yougodid.

Vexx heard this and took his attention away from the other soldiers. He growled at Yougodid then leapt into the air with an aerial bombardment that took every last bit of strength to block. Vexx punched with his armored fists trying desperately to connect with Yougodid's body.

The time was right, Yougodid used his boots and stepped into the air, and then did a back flip over the top of Vexx. With immense precision he fired a single bullet once he was over top of Vexx. The bullet rushed out of his weapon and travelled six feet or so before striking Vexx in the left eye. A single shot.

Vexx tried to scream with outrage, but it was too late, the bullet had already left its mark. Vexx dropped to his knees and with his last breath released a muffled scream then fell dead in the coliseum sand.

CHAPTER 8.5

Peter and a few soldiers had been trying to defeat the deviants, who were quite skilled at disappearing in time for pacifiers to unleash a siege of bullets on the men.

Peter was never a truly gifted psychic at least not compared to Yougodid and some of the other men. But he was reading a pattern in their battle plan. He began striking at open areas just as the deviants would appear. Some of the other men were following his example all the while defending themselves from the pacifiers.

In the blink of an eye one deviant appeared right behind him and Peter could sense him there. He spun around with his shield positioned horizontally slicing right through it. The upper torso fell away from its body and its hands dropped the sword it was carrying. The other men swarmed the last remaining deviant leaving it nowhere to turn eventually killing it.

It was time to clean up the arena, metaphorically speaking. The remaining soldiers hunted down and destroyed what was left of the demon hoards, until every last one of them lay dead on the coliseum floor.

The crowd cheered as the men regrouped in the center of the arena and congratulated one another on a job well done. They hoisted Yougodid into the air for his valance and courage. The ships surrounding the coliseum dispersed as their leader had been defeated and for the first time in ten thousand years there was no beast calling Earth its home.

Up from the center of the arena, the same place the soldiers were standing stood a holographic image producer. It was the aliens, the builders of worlds. They congratulated the soldiers for their victory and announced to the crowd the outposts in the outlying star systems. Strangely enough they spoke English. They began to explain that they were form Earth but most left millions of years ago to explore the galaxy. Hard to believe, but, that they were descendents of the dinosaurs, mostly reptile. Through no fault of their own they began to go extinct and had been mostly dead since mankind began to evolve, leaving behind maps, taught us mathematics and pledge an allegiance to this planet, there home world. By the time we started building, structures like the pyramids, the Mayan temples and Stonehenge, there were only a handful of these creatures left on Earth. In a way, they always wanted us to win. They even let us in on a little secret that on the other side of the sun existed a planet known as Heaven, in the same orbit as our planet Earth, full of animals, oceans, plant life, an exact replica of our Earth, just human free. This was our chance to start over.

Each of the soldiers were awarded lands there and technology to get us there and back had already been developed by these peaceful star travellers. They hoped that mankind would win this battle and foresaw a victory, in our favor, although it was a complete gamble right up until the end. The outposts they'd built existed on 13 planets in the Milky Way, all habitable to what was left of the human race.

The crowd roared and cheered as they heard the good news. It was the best thing to happen to this planet since sliced bread, metaphorically speaking. Many people cried as they heard the news, others full of humbling laughter. Mankind got the opportunity to start again.

CHAPTER 8.6

In the hours after the battle I sought to find Peter. I was full of despair and anxiety about whether or not I would return home. In one hand I could travel the galaxy in the name of heroes who'd fought for the planet all in the name of good. On the other, my family would miss me, not knowing where, (or when I was), and ultimately miss me.

I found him shortly afterwards. He was talking with Yougodid when I interrupted them. He reached out and shook my hand; I was honored to meet him. Peter then took me aside and asked me if I was ready to return home, I wasn't sure how to feel. Part of me wanted to stay the other wanted to see my family again.

It was with a heavy heart that I said yes. He took me aside then gave me a contraption from his pocket and said. "When you press this button you will return to your own time. You will be the last to travel through time as we have decided it too dangerous to let just anyone be a time traveller." then handed me a letter to give to his mother. "Oh." he continued "Let the people know there future is waiting for them." Words to live by I guess. I shook his hand then went to find a quiet spot to push the button.

I walked through the city, it was in jubilation. For the first time in a long time it seemed like people were happy to be alive.

I got somewhere outside the city then pressed the button. For the second time in my life I was a time traveller. I went through the same colorful wormhole and could clearly see where I was going to land, in my backyard.

But something was different, my dog was barking furiously. I arrived just feet from where my house once stood but all that was left was a burning pile of smothered wood. I was puzzled, perplexed. *'My house, it's gone.'* In the time I had been gone, roughly 26 minutes from the time Peter and I left, my house had caught fire and burned to the ground. I was standing there baffled at how this could happen. *'Did I leave the stove on, perhaps something in the microwave?'* I was however just in time to see the fire department show up, even though they were at least ten minutes too late.

Then wouldn't you know, up on top of the burned tinder's climbed a mouse. A mouse just standing there looking at me.

The fire department would later tell me that a small bunch of old frayed wires started the fire. It wasn't long after that that my mother phoned, and my father to see if I was okay. I was sad to tell them about the house but they insisted it was better that I was okay. My dog was fine too, she was tied to a tree near her dog house in the backyard. The neighbors said she was barking before the fire engulfed the house. The problem was I had lost everything that was in the house, the dossiers, and old antiques. This story is all that is left. The only proof I have that any of this ever happened.

The mouse to this day I believe was trying to warn me about the wires, had I been in the house something awful would have happened, so I guess both the mouse and Peter saved my life that day. I was 24 years old when that happened.

Printed in the United States
By Bookmasters